# ACCLAMATION FOR JUDAS THE APOSTLE

"A thriller with theological underpinnings, set both in steamy south Louisiana and the Old City of Jerusalem... a fascinating fictional exploration of the least understood and most maligned figure in the salvation story... this is the most original work of fiction I have edited."

—Catherine L. Kadair, freelance editor.

"Most Christians and many religious scholars accept the story that Judas betrayed Jesus for money. But did he? The author offers the reader a religious mystery every bit as gripping as The Da Vinci Code. Set in South Louisiana and covering three continents, this crisply written debut novel is a page turner full of suspense, with a fascinating look at the motives of one of history's most loathed villains. Judas the Apostle presents the possibility of alternative groundbreaking biblical history that is also a compelling read."

—Jim Brown, Author and Syndicated Talk Show Host
(Produced by Clear Channel Communications and syndicated by Genesis Communications, Minneapolis, Minnesota).

"An edge of the chair thriller, a stunning history and geography lesson, and an unparalleled glimpse into the past of one of history's most maligned figures...Judas the Apostle tells a great, and truly plausible story, against  the rich and often diverse tapestry of Louisiana, America's most colorful and mysterious region."

—Bill Profita, Radio Talk Show Host, 107.3 FM,
Baton Rouge, La.

"This is a page-turner with both mind and muscle.  Its thrills and intrigue are offered up with an equal dose of historic heft.  It carries you along as it makes you reconsider the well worn stories you thought you understood."

—Anne Dubuisson Anderson,
Writing and Publishing Consultant.

# JUDAS
# the apostle

# JUDAS
# the apostle

Van R. Mayhall Jr.

iUniverse, Inc.
Bloomington

# Judas the Apostle

*iUniverse books may be ordered through booksellers or by contacting:*

*iUniverse
1663 Liberty Drive
Bloomington, IN 47403
www.iuniverse.com
1-800-Authors (1-800-288-4677)*

*Because of the dynamic nature of the Internet, any web addresses or links contained in this
book may have changed since publication and may no longer be valid. The views expressed
in this work are solely those of the author and do not necessarily reflect the views of the
publisher, and the publisher hereby disclaims any responsibility for them.*

*Any people depicted in stock imagery provided by Thinkstock are models,
and such images are being used for illustrative purposes only.*

*Certain stock imagery © Thinkstock.*

*ISBN: 978-1-4759-3155-6 (sc)
ISBN: 978-1-4759-3153-2 (e)
ISBN: 978-1-4759-3154-9 (dj)*

*Library of Congress Control Number: 2012911310*

*Printed in the United States of America*

*iUniverse rev. date: 7/27/2012*

# ACKNOWLEDGMENTS

This book would not be a reality without the tireless support of my wife, Lorri, which is gratefully acknowledged. Hearts!

I have also greatly appreciated the support of my family. Particularly appreciated is the support of my ninety-two-year-young father who read every page of every version and always asked for more.

A special word of thanks is due to my editors, Anne Dubuisson Anderson and Catherine Kadair, both of whom were great and did not give up on a novice writer. Thanks, also, to all the great people at iUniverse.

To my friends, colleagues, and fellow Louisianans, although this book is purely fiction, I hope you will find familiar places and profiles from our beloved common heritage. God bless.

This book is dedicated to Mama Lo, now and forever.

# PROLOGUE

# AD 73

Now on his knees, Elazar ben Yair hung upon the point of his own sword as he stared out from the western wall of the impregnable fortress, Masada. The sun was setting, blood-red, as his vision clouded. He had wedged the hilt of his sword in a small crevasse in the top of the wall to prevent it from slipping. Elazar had then crouched over the upright blade, placing it against his abdomen, and collapsed upon it. The pain had been unbearable at first, but now he felt little except the inexorable march of the razor-sharp point toward his heart as his body weakened from loss of blood. Soon enough, it would pierce his heart and his life, and the great revolution would be finished.

His people, the Sicarii, had been in revolt against the authorities, chiefly the Romans, as long as Elazar could remember and longer—some sixty years. They had been branded assassins because they used short knives to dispatch their political enemies. When the Romans sacked Jerusalem in AD 70, Elazar had led the remaining Sicarii in their flight to Masada.

The invincible Masada redoubt had been created by a Roman, Herod the Great, one hundred years before as a refuge for himself in the event of a revolt in the new Jewish territories. A twelve-foot-thick wall, with multiple fighting towers rimming the one-thousand-foot

Masada plateau, had been built as well as an abundance of residences, baths, and of course, the palace for Herod.

When the Sicarii arrived at Masada, it was garrisoned by only a small Roman force encamped at its base, which the Sicarii had quickly overrun. Now, Elazar ben Yair and his followers had committed the ultimate insult of claiming Masada for themselves.

The Sicarii had storehouses of grain and herds of animals. An internal cistern system built by the Romans guaranteed water. The 960 men, women, and children on top of the Masada mountain could remain there for years.

Numerous sorties by the Romans up the paths to the fortress had all ended in failure and death for the attacking soldiers. Elazar had thought that once the Romans realized the futility of assaulting the stronghold, they would lay siege to it. Given the superior position and supplies of the Sicarii, this battle could last years, and the Romans might eventually give up. But to Elazar's shock, rather than wait them out, the Romans had changed tactics. Elazar now reflected that his people had been defeated not by Roman soldiers but by Roman engineers.

The Romans had brought fifteen thousand slaves, including many Jews, to Masada. Unceasingly, the Romans had driven them to build an enormous ramp of thousands of tons of rock and dirt on the shortest side of the plateau. Slowly, relentlessly, the ramp had taken shape and moved up toward the lowest and weakest wall of the fortress. With their simple bows and arrows, the Sicarii initially could slow the progress but not stop it. Eventually, the Romans had built large wooden shields so that the arrows of the Sicarii were useless. Finally, the ramp lay adjacent to the outer wall of Masada, and the Romans brought up their battering engines to breach the wall. Soon they would be inside.

Elazar had called his people together and pressed them in the face of the final Roman assault. He had told them of the fate awaiting them and their wives and children at the hands of the Romans. Each would be tortured, and those who survived would be sold into slavery. Better, he told them, to die as free men.

Every warrior knew the dirty business that was at hand, and none had shrunk from it. No soldier wanted to be thought last among equals even though his love for his relations, his wife and children, was unquestioned. Knowing Elazar's plea to be just, with tears in their eyes they had put to death their families as if they were strangers. Elazar had looked into the eyes of his own wife and seen equal parts love and acceptance. To ease his suffering, she had laid his dagger against her throat and entreated him to finish it.

When only the warriors were left, they had drawn lots, and of the hundreds, ten had been chosen to continue the bloody work to its conclusion. Willingly, all the rest had knelt by their kin and submitted gladly to the swords of the ten. When this was done, those left had drawn lots again, and Elazar had been chosen to complete the killing, which he did, afterward studying what had been wrought. Now sure he was the last of the last, Elazar had set fire to everything but some of the food stocks. The Romans would know that the Sicarii had not been driven by hunger but had died as free men.

As the Romans breached the wall and approached like ghostly specters with weapons drawn through the smoke and fire, Elazar's sword neared his heart, and he was glad. Although he was dying along with the others with him, he knew the Sicarii would survive to fight again.

# PART 1

# MADISONVILLE

Going home must be like going to render an account.
> —Joseph Conrad, English novelist (1857–1924)

# CHAPTER 1
# MADISONVILLE, LOUISIANA

# PRESENT DAY

He was angry. His plan had been to get to the old man's house at least an hour earlier. But at 2:30 a.m. on the small-town streets, only two cars had been moving, his rental and the village's only cop on duty. To avoid suspicion he'd had to drive on through and out of the town. Even so, the cop had followed him to the city limits before turning back. This had forced him to find a secure place to park and to hike back to the target. He was now an hour and a half behind his carefully planned schedule.

"Damn," he muttered under his breath. Like German trains, he always ran on time.

But from the beginning, when he had gotten the call, this job had seemed alternately rushed, delayed, or out of kilter. Since this assignment was in the United States, he had flown commercial from his home base in the Cayman Islands to Canada. There he had simply walked across the border and, through a series of untraceable transportation legs, arrived here and now.

Standing across the way from the old man's Water Street house, he smoked a cigarette, with the glowing end hidden in his gloved fist. The black water of the river was at his back, visible now only as a

3

deeper shade of dark against the bank. He was dressed in his usual work clothes: black trousers, black synthetic sweatshirt, and black soft-soled shoes with no identifiable tread. He wore a black backpack containing the tools of his trade. Since the light was dim, the moon having set, he could not be seen from more than a few feet away unless, of course, someone had on night-vision goggles, as he did.

He stubbed out the cigarette carefully, capturing the butt and putting it in a small bottle he carried for the purpose. His DNA would not be found at this job. From the same bottle he took two partially smoked cigarettes he had picked up in the Canadian airport and laid them on the ground where he had been standing.

Excited by the prospects of his work, he removed from his backpack a small crowbar and a silenced .38-caliber revolver, manufactured to police specifications, and headed toward the old man's house. Others in his line of work favored automatic weapons, Glocks and the like. This dark specter knew that automatics sometimes jammed, and although they carried more rounds, the five shots in the jam-proof .38 were all a skilled person needed. And skilled he was. He was the best in his field. His employers required no less.

He carefully worked his way around the side of the house. It was one of a number of small homes overlooking the river lining this side of the street. Everything was completely quiet at this hour, now after 4:00 a.m. Not even a dog barked. A small stoop led up to the back door. The door itself was wooden with an ancient lock, and a glass pane covered the top half of the door. He saw this would be easy. He wedged the crowbar between the lock and the door jam. Many of his ilk used lock picks, but in his experience the crowbar got him in faster and made the entry look like a burglary or a home invasion. The cops would waste time looking at local thugs and DNA from the Canadian smokers.

As he started to lever the crowbar against the door jam, he had a thought. *Could it be?* He withdrew the crowbar, grabbed the door knob, and gently turned it. The door swung silently open. He had heard there were still places like this, but he'd never expected to find one.

He entered the kitchen, knowing the old man's bedroom was in the front of the house opposite the living room. The item he had come for was supposed to be in the living room. He would have to be very quiet. He gently closed the back door, and with the night-vision goggles in place, he carefully picked his way around the kitchen table and moved into the combination dining/living room.

Standing in the middle of the living room, he scanned the mantelpiece where he had been told the object would be. Why such a precious thing would be kept in such a place was beyond his need to know. But there was nothing there. With growing anxiety, he surveyed the entire room carefully, but the item was not there.

*Shit! Now what?* As he turned, he heard an alarm clock in the next room go off and saw a crack of light from under the bedroom door. He quickly ripped off the night-vision goggles and waited. The thief liked to kill, but this was not supposed to be a killing mission. Adrenaline spiked within his body as he crouched, partially hidden behind a recliner, in wait for whatever was coming. The door opened, light from the bedroom flooded in, and the old man walked stiffly into the living room.

"Wha—" He was able to get out only part of the word before the shadowy figure fired his weapon, silently spitting a .38 hollow point slug into the old man's chest. He staggered, took a step, and then stumbled once. He went down hard and didn't move. A pool of blood began to spread around his body.

Satisfied the old man no longer posed any threat, the interloper tore through the front bedroom and then the rest of the house, searching for the item. After twenty fruitless minutes, he had rummaged through the bath, the rear bedroom, and the kitchen. The thief returned to the living room, lighting a cigarette as he walked, and there found a surprise. Where the old man should be lying dead, there was nothing but the pool of blood. He put the cigarette to his lips and drew in a long satisfying pull before bottling the stub and readying himself to hunt his quarry. He had not found the article, but at least he would have the satisfaction of putting the old man in his grave.

Drawing the .38, he headed toward the front bedroom where the bloody trail led and where he knew the old man must have somehow dragged himself. He entered the bedroom looking left, and clearing that direction, he swung right. The old man, bleeding profusely, sat in an overstuffed chair next to the bed, holding a 12 gauge pointed

5

directly at the thief's chest. The intruder's reflexes were like lightning as he sought to trigger the .38, but they were no match for the single-0 buckshot that poured with smoke and fire out of both barrels of the shotgun, tearing the thief's chest and life away.

# CHAPTER 2

Clotile Lejeune leaned back in the seat as the big Boeing 777 lifted off the runway in the direction of the sea-driven prevailing winds. Early fall mornings in Seattle were cool, and she had opted for a lightweight, gray wool travel suit. Her long-sleeved pink blouse picked up the faint reddish highlights in her dark hair.

Cloe, as she had come to be known in her transplanted home, felt like she had turned her face from the future and that she and her son, J.E., were headed toward the past at five hundred miles per hour. All that Seattle and the Northwest were, Louisiana was not. Seattle was new, young, and progressive. On the forefront of the computer age, it crackled with energy. The possibilities were endless. Indeed, she had managed, through hard work and perseverance, to work her way up to the number two position in the Ancient Languages Department at the University of Washington. Louisiana, on the other hand, was mired in the past, still partly an agrarian society whose cities had been bypassed by the likes of Dallas and Atlanta. New Orleans itself was the poster child for "old world" in the United States. In about three hours the plane would deliver her directly to that other world, one in which she was almost certain she no longer belonged. Almost certain.

She thought about the urgent and confused phone call she had gotten from her uncle Sonny the day before, the call that had launched this unexpected trip. Uncle Sonny was brother to her father, Thibodeaux Lejeune. Although the small Louisiana village of Madisonville was her place of birth, she'd had very little to do with her hometown or her family there for at least twenty-five years. She had talked to Uncle Sonny, but never during that time had she

7

spoken to her father. Thib had never met J.E., his only grandchild. But something terrible had happened to Thib, and Uncle Sonny would not or could not talk about it on the phone. He had broken down completely during their conversation. Cloe knew only that the father she had run away from more than two decades ago for painful, unforgivable reasons was now dead under unspecified circumstances. She wondered whether there had been some grisly accident. She would know soon enough.

Whatever had happened, and regardless of how she felt about him, she had told J.E. that duty required her to return to Madisonville to bury her father. J.E., born Julian Evan Lejeune, now a twenty-four-year-old Special Forces officer, a first lieutenant, certainly knew about duty; he had completed a full tour in Iraq and currently was back in the States awaiting reassignment. J.E. was a highly trained and experienced intelligence officer. His ability to learn about people and events on his laptop and through his other intel resources was extraordinary.

When she had told her son about the phone call, J.E. had said, "Mom, if it's your duty to go back, then *we* are going to Madisonville together."

On the huge airplane, lost in her thoughts and becoming drowsy, Cloe nodded off. Sometime later, as she slept, she suddenly felt her long-dead mother at her side, whispering something in her ear, something that she could not quite grasp but was certain was urgent. She knew it was a matter of life or death. Her mother's words seemed to be becoming clearer. Cloe almost had them.

"Mom … Mom … wake up, we're preparing to land." J.E. was gently tugging at her arm.

Cloe was groggy and at first unsure of where she was. As the dream disintegrated, Cloe felt her mother had been trying to warn her about something, something very important. Well, she thought, dreams could be just plain strange. But she still had trouble shaking off an ominous chill.

As they looked out the small, hard window, they could see that the plane was approaching New Orleans. Two two-lane raised concrete highways stretched across the water as far as they could see. There was heavy traffic on the long bridges. The sight of Lake Pontchartrain brought back to Cloe memories of many a happy summer.

"That's the Lake Pontchartrain Causeway," she explained to J.E. "I remember joyful times when my mom and dad would pack up for the day, and we would cross the causeway to New Orleans. Sometimes we would spend the day at Pontchartrain Beach with its rides and concessions. Once in a while, we would go to the French Quarter, Jackson Square, and the museums and, on those trips, the Cafe Du Monde for café au lait and beignets. The Causeway, that's the way we'll take home."

"Home?" J.E. asked.

"I mean to your grandfather's house," she quickly replied.

"You can continue to kid yourself if you want to, Mom," responded J.E., "but I know better. Aren't you the one who orders Louisiana's Community Coffee online? Aren't you the only person in Seattle who has both Tony Chachere's seasoning and Crystal Hot Sauce on the breakfast table?"

She laughed and wondered whether her son was not wiser than she was in many ways. Still, there were many things of which he was not aware. Life was complicated. To start with, there had been the terrible row with her father all those years ago. At age seventeen, she had fallen madly in love with a young man in Madisonville, Evan. His family had worked on the water for as long as anyone could remember, and he was a hand on one of the shell dredges on Lake Pontchartrain. Thib, when he found out about the romance, had forbidden her to see Evan. As far as Thib was concerned, that was that. But of course, there was much more.

As the big plane swooped down toward the Band-Aid–sized runway, the airport and environs grew in size and detail. The plane gently reunited with the earth and coasted slowly to the end of the runway. It then turned onto the tarmac, powered up to the gate, and mated with the docking station. In a matter of moments, J.E. and Cloe were off the plane and headed down to the ground level to pick up their luggage and look for transportation; they would talk a cabbie into taking them across the Lake to Madisonville.

While J.E. went to look for the baggage, Cloe stood in a little out-of-the-way area, watching the passengers flow by on their way to the airport's exits. She was still thinking about her mother; the dream weighed heavily on her. Cloe and her mother had been so close all those years ago. If she had lived, Cloe might have reunited with her family. Marie Louise was never really well in the last year or so of her life and died a couple of months after Cloe had left Madisonville, pregnant and in disgrace.

Even now, she vividly remembered the last unforgivable scene with her father. She had gone to the dredge-crew landing that night to meet Evan to tell him she was pregnant. They had known each other in school for years and had been dating secretly for months. She and Evan had talked previously of marriage and had even picked out a plain wedding band. In spite of the trouble she would be in with her father, she was happy thinking of the future with Evan and their child. When she got to the landing, the place was lit up with emergency lights, police, and an ambulance. They told her that a terrible accident had taken place on the dredge. Evan had been killed.

Cloe was in shock and did not want to go home to face her father. So she went to the only person she could trust with her secret: Uncle Sonny. That night she shared everything with him.

He kindly listened as she poured everything out to him and then said in his whispery voice, "Clotile, your dad's gonna be furious, but you've no choice but to go home. You can stay here, but Thib'll come looking for you. He'll hear about the accident. Your dad loves you very much, but you got to give him some time on this."

She knew Uncle Sonny was right, so she went home.

These decades later, she could remember like yesterday the horrible scene that had come later with her father.

"I told you not to see that boy, that he was no good for you!" her father shouted at the family table in the kitchen.

"Dad, I couldn't help myself. I loved Evan," she said, sobbing. Her mother was in bed, terribly ill and weak, and could not come to her aid.

"You're not much better than a common whore lying with a dredge-boat hand, getting yourself knocked up. What will people say?"

"Oh, Daddy," she said.

"I'm so disappointed in you," he screeched back. "You're supposed to go to college, to LSU. You're supposed to make something of yourself, to become somebody. Now you've ruined your reputation and our family's good name."

On and on it went until he was exhausted with rage, and she was sick with shame.

Her mother had passed away a short while after Cloe left home. Thib was devastated, and by the time Uncle Sonny had tracked her down through the bus company and innumerable calls to apartment buildings, boarding houses, and real estate firms in Seattle, her mother had been gone for weeks. She had missed the opportunity for a last good-bye and lost her last bridge to home.

She was still thinking about her mother, her father, and Evan when one of the approaching passengers caught her eye. Most of the travelers were dressed casually, some like tourists. This man was clad all in black, including a black jacket. Cloe studied him more closely, noting that he was clean-shaven and had a dark, swarthy complexion. Although she abhorred profiling, she had to admit he looked foreign and, somehow, vaguely dangerous.

As he neared her, the man glanced briefly in her direction. For the merest moment, their eyes locked, and then he looked quickly away. Cloe wondered for a splitsecond whether it was a flash of recognition she had seen in his eyes. A sharply ill-at-ease feeling descended on her.

As she studied his face, she was drawn again to his eyes. His eyes! There was something very odd about them. Then she realized they looked dead, almost like shark eyes. She thought of a killer shark circling its prey. Cloe shivered with a sudden chill and looked for J.E. What was happening to her? The man kept coming closer, drawn along with the crowd. And then he swept on past her with the outflow of passengers. Cloe last saw him entering a Mercedes limo.

Shaking off her odd reaction to this total stranger, Cloe saw J.E. approaching with the baggage.

J.E. took one look at her and said, "What's wrong? You look like you've seen a ghost."

"Nothing, let's get out of here," she replied, glancing over her shoulder. "Just some creepy-looking guy in the crowd."

As they left the airport, the heat struck Cloe like a physical force. According to the airport clock, the temperature was 96 degrees and the humidity 94 percent—"Feels like 104 degrees," the clock marquis cheerfully reported. Cloe had forgotten that fall in Louisiana can remain tropical in both temperature and humidity. She began to perspire under her wool clothing.

Above the cacophony of loading and unloading, J.E. yelled, "I've been cooler in Iraq in the middle of summer! I'll grab us a cab."

Cloe replied mechanically, "It'll be cooler on the water." She recognized this was something her mother had always said. In her healthy years, Marie Louise had had a homespun wisdom for every occasion.

As they turned to look for a taxi, an old crew-cab pickup truck pulled up in front of them. It seemed to be about a mile long, and with its off-white color, it gave the impression of Moby Dick on Firestones. The truck had a dent or two, but the engine sounded strong. The driver reached over, rolled down the window on the passenger side, and waved to them.

Cloe blinked, realizing that after all these years, there sat ninety-year-old Sonny Lejeune—Uncle Sonny. With one look at her uncle, Cloe forgot about her mother and the incident in the baggage area—the old man was clearly troubled by something, terribly troubled.

# CHAPTER 3

"There is something we need to talk about," said Uncle Sonny as he piloted the barge-like truck back across the causeway.

Cloe was in awe that Uncle Sonny was still driving at his age, but from her occasional phone conversations with him, she knew that he was still very active and his mind remained sharp.

"Mr. Lejeune ..." began J.E.

"Just Sonny is good, or Uncle Sonny if you like, J.E. Time we got to know each other. We're all just about the only family any of us has left."

Although there was a roomy backseat in the four-door crew cab, they had stowed the luggage there and now sat three abreast in the front. Cloe studied Uncle Sonny out of the corner of her eye, marveling at how little he had changed from what she remembered. Because he had lost an eye in a fishing accident in his youth, Uncle Sonny moved his head in short, bird-like bursts to aid his remaining good eye. Unlike his barrel-chested brother, Thib, he was built like a string bean. He wore a clean white T-shirt and khaki pants. He might have had the same thing on the day before Cloe left.

"Listen, Clotile, we've a lot to catch up on, and we'll do that over the next little while," said Uncle Sonny gently. "But you need to know that your dad's death wasn't just an awful accident."

"What? ... But you implied it was," Cloe responded softly.

"I couldn't tell you what happened on the phone," said Uncle Sonny, his shoulders slumping. "I almost can't believe it as I sit here today."

"What happened?" asked J.E. bluntly.

"Thib was shot to death in the Water Street house."

13

Cloe sat back, the breath knocked out of her. "How? Why?"

"Early in the morning the night before last, someone broke into the house and shot him. Thib may've walked in on the guy because it happened about the time he would've been getting up to make coffee. Thib and I had coffee at his house every morning at five o'clock."

"Has the guy been caught? Was it a robbery?" asked J.E.

"Thib got him before he died—both barrels of Thib's old 12-gauge square in the chest," said Uncle Sonny. "He was dead before he hit the floor. Thib died in the old chair in the bedroom."

"Oh, Mom ... I'm so sorry," whispered J.E.

"I can't take this in at all. I mean ... murdered," said Cloe, her voice rising with shock. "Why ... why would anyone kill my father? I don't remember him having any enemies, and God knows he didn't have much to steal."

"Nobody has any idea," said Uncle Sonny. "The police're looking into it. We may know something in a few days."

Cloe doubled over in the cab of the truck and gasped for air. Who would kill her father? Why? "Uncle Sonny, I need you to stop. I can't breathe."

J.E. put his arm around her as Sonny slowed the truck, turned into a crossover between the twin bridges, and stopped. Cloe grabbed the door handle, threw open the door, and jumped over J.E. to get out. She ran to the railing overlooking the lake and deeply breathed the moist air. After a minute or so, she turned to Uncle Sonny and J.E., who were now standing right with her. She sat down on the curb of the crossover and wrapped her arms around her knees.

*What am I doing here?* she asked herself. Odd, she thought—yesterday, she had been in Seattle enjoying the upward arc of her career and her son on leave. Today, within one hour of touching down in Louisiana, she'd had a vivid dream of her mother apparently trying to warn her about something, had felt vaguely threatened at the airport by someone she had never met, and now had learned her father's death was the result of a grisly homicide. True, she had not seen or talked to her dad in more than two decades, but murder? "My God," said Cloe. "Who was it?"

"Well, that's the thing, Clotile," responded Uncle Sonny. "The killer wasn't local. Nobody here knew him. We pretty much know the criminal element in the town. The cops're checking it out. The guy had no identification and was decked out like a pro. Cops think somebody might have put him up to this, but they aren't saying much right now."

# CHAPTER 4

Except for Cloe telling J.E. and Uncle Sonny about the dream of her mom and the peculiar man at the airport, they passed much of the rest of the trip in shocked silence.

As they drove, Cloe's thoughts turned to happier memories of her life in Madisonville before the break, while growing up in the small town. Her mother had been up every morning to fry bacon or sausage and then eggs in the drippings. She could almost smell the aroma of rich, dark-roast coffee that had hung densely in the kitchen. There were always biscuits with butter and tree syrup. In the mornings the family planned the day at the breakfast table, and in the evenings they discussed the events of the day. It was at that very table, Cloe realized, that it had all come to an end with the terrible fight with her father twenty-five years ago. The pain of losing both her parents and of regret—aching, hurting regret—threatened to overwhelm her. She began to breathe faster again and knew she had to calm herself.

Time and distance flew by as Cloe daydreamed. Looking up, she saw Uncle Sonny maneuvering the old truck across the swing bridge over the Tchefuncte River and then turning onto Water Street, the street on which she had grown up.

Cloe saw that although some things were new, the core of the little town remained largely unchanged from her youth. The riverfront was lined with several ancient oak trees whose canopies stood gnarled and bent as the land's affront to the prevailing winds off the lake. Numerous smaller oaks planted in her youth were now coming into their own. Memories flooded back of fun on the "wall"—what the residents had always called the waterfront. As they drove by, she could see the children—the "river rats"—jumping off it into the river. The Tchefuncte was still so lovely.

They drove slowly by the Water Street house where she had been raised, now roped off with yellow police tape. The house could be described as a shotgun-style structure, but a wide porch across the front and running down one side gave it a more elegant bungalow look. Her mom had been proud of that porch and had often sat in the swing in the front. Cloe had spent the first seventeen years of her life in this house. Now, once again, Cloe was shaken by the thought of the events that must have transpired in the little house. She began to feel nauseous and dizzy. "Uncle, please hurry on," Cloe pleaded.

They picked up speed and continued on to Uncle Sonny's house a few blocks away. "We have about twenty minutes before the service," said Uncle Sonny as he parked the big truck.

*Barely enough time to freshen up*, Cloe thought, but the travel arrangements had been the best she could manage at the last minute.

A few minutes later, they met in the living room. J.E. had donned his dress uniform complete with rank, insignia, and campaign ribbons. At six-foot-one and about 190 pounds, he looked splendid. He had the same build and dark—almost black—hair and large brown eyes as his grandfather. Uncle Sonny had told them there would be a military funeral of some sort.

"The funeral's gonna be old school, just like Thib," Sonny said.

"I gotta think that the circumstances of Thib's death may bring out the curious and maybe even the press," said J.E.

Cloe worried that J.E. might be right.

"We'll see," the old man said.

Cloe still wore her travel suit but had freshened her makeup and changed to a darker blouse. She had the same almost black hair as her son and her father, but crystalline blue eyes from her mother's side of the family. For better or worse, she was as ready as she would be for her father's funeral.

Uncle Sonny had put on his one tie and had an old plaid coat over his arm. Sonny's obvious discomfort would have been comical on any other occasion. His short-sleeved dress shirt revealed strong, muscular arms that men half his age would have envied. The made-to-order, permanently knotted black tie graced his collar. His large hands, although somewhat gnarled with age, showed the strength and roughness of a lifetime of hard work.

The three generations of Lejeunes piled silently into the old crew cab and drove the few blocks to St. Anselm Catholic Church. St. Anselm was a Benedictine priest and scholar a thousand years ago who, although Italian-born, had risen to the level of Archbishop of Canterbury and Primate of England. For some unknown reason, the "Father of Scholastic Theology" had been chosen as the patron saint of the tiny church in the rural, river berg of Madisonville.

"Uncle Sonny, I appreciate you making all the arrangements for Dad's funeral and burial," Cloe said. "I just couldn't get here any earlier. I don't know what I would have done without you."

"Nice of you to say that, Clotile, but I didn't do a lick of work on the arrangements."

"But there's really no one else," said Cloe with surprise. "Who did it?"

Sonny gave her a tight grin. "Clotile, your dad—my brother—learned just about everything he cared about learning in the military. You may not remember, but he was a very methodical man. Thib long ago wrote up what he wanted in the way of last rites. Not only did he leave written instructions, but he also met with Father Aloysius, the pastor, to give him directions—some would say orders—as to what he wanted. He also paid for everything in advance."

"My God," said Cloe, but as she thought about it, she realized this was the way of the Greatest Generation. She could remember times early on when her mother and father didn't have two nickels to rub together but would rather be beaten than have someone do for them or be dependent on others.

As they approached the church, the sky began to darken, and the clouds brought some small, but welcome relief from the heat. Still, she could see the anvil-shaped tops of the afternoon heat-driven thunderheads rising and forming. Soon they would race across the sky, spilling their contents, probably on Madisonville.

As if reading her mind, Sonny said, "Yep, what we've had this summer and fall is a new kind of hot. But today, of all days, we're gonna get wet."

They parked and hurried up the two steps into the church. St. Anselm was one of those gymnasium-like Catholic churches commonly built in the 1960s. Cloe had not been in a church, much less a Catholic church, in years. When she broke from her father, she had left her faith behind as well. She had forgotten about the calming feeling that now passed through her as she entered the door—leaving the noise, smells, cares, and troubles of the outside world for the quiet, tranquil atmosphere of the interior. The fragrance of incense lingered faintly in the air, triggering recollections of her youth. She had attended mass in this church so many times with her mother and father.

"It hasn't changed a bit," she murmured. She saw that J.E. had a look of respect and reverence on his face.

"Mom, who are all these people? The place is full."

Cloe looked and saw that all four sections of the old church were filled with people. Mourners—some young, but most older—also lined the side aisles. She could see their respectfulness and tear-filled eyes. They were not the curious or the prurient as J.E. had worried; these were Thib's friends. A number of uniformed police officers flanked the exits. The thought passed through her mind that they might be there to note any strangers or to look for anything unusual. "J.E., it looks like the whole town is here," she said.

The caisson on which the casket was situated was draped with a brand-new American flag. Its vivid colors offered a striking contrast to the muted tones of the church.

St. Anselm's parishioners were a devout people. They wore their faith close to the surface. It was a community where the men were often in physical danger in their employment on or around the water. Sometimes even their families were under threat from frequent squalls and hurricanes. Other than St. Anselm, Our Lady of Prompt Succor was the town's most revered icon.

An usher escorted them, with great respect and dignity, to the first pew. Still slightly nauseous, Cloe felt unsettled as she scanned the crowd. Her eyes focused on her father's coffin, which jolted her. She wondered if one of these people could have had something to do with her father's death. Hadn't her mother always said that every barrel has its rotten apple?

Immediately, mourners began to queue up and pass by them, each with a loving hand or hug and a murmured message of sympathy. Cloe recognized a few of the old faces, but many were complete strangers. She tried hard to read the faces, but eventually they became a blur. The line continued around the coffin, where scores gently touched it, said a brief prayer, or made the sign of the cross.

"Mom, who *was* this man, my grandfather?" asked J.E. softly between mourners.

Cloe saw a look of pain and confusion in her son's face over a grandfather he was meeting for the first time at this funeral. Cloe had no answer for him or for herself and could only quietly hug and hold him as the mourners paused in respect.

Cloe could hear distant thunder. The storm was coming, relentless as death itself. The ushers began to shepherd what were obviously Thib's friends and colleagues back into their places so the funeral mass could begin.

All turned back toward the priests and a gaggle of servers gathered in the vestibule. Although considerably older and grayer, Cloe recognized Father Aloysius from her youth. With him was a second priest, a stranger to her. He was arrayed in very fine vestments, leaving Father Aloysius looking a little frayed beside him. The man's eyes seemed riveted on Cloe.

"Mom, is that Father Aloysius?" whispered J.E., his eyes on the older man.

"Yes," she said in a low voice. She had mentioned the pastor to J.E. along the way. "But I don't know the other priest," she said, becoming somewhat uneasy under this stranger's gaze.

"Well, he certainly appears to know you," murmured J.E.

Cloe thought about that and wondered whether Thib or Father Aloysius had spoken to this newcomer about her. Was his gaze one of interest, or was it condemnation for her past sins that might include, in his eyes, her abandonment of her deceased father? She could feel vestiges of Catholic guilt begin to churn in her gut as she had not felt in years.

Cloe shivered and said, "Yes, I think he does."

# CHAPTER 5

The organist hit a note, and the two priests and the attendants began to move down the center aisle as the church choir led the congregation in the singing of "America the Beautiful." The new priest forgotten for the time being, Cloe smiled to think of Thib selecting this music. It was so like the father she remembered from the old days. Somehow the weight of the burden she had carried all these years seemed to lighten a bit. She glanced at J.E. and could see that he was at attention.

Father Aloysius paused at the casket and, with the assistance of his retainers, sprinkled holy water on the polished wooden shell holding the earthly remains of her father. Cloe, almost automatically, bowed her head, falling back into the ritual she had learned as a child. The priests then ascended the raised dais on which the altar was situated and turned to the assembly.

"We are here in the name of the Father, and of the Son, and of the Holy Spirit, to celebrate the life and the salvation of our brother, Thibodeaux Lejeune," Father Aloysius and the new priest intoned in unison.

Cloe's eyes began to tear, and she could hear the muffled sobs of some within the congregation. The funeral mass commenced, and the lightning, thunder, and rain began violently pounding the little church. As the service proceeded, Cloe felt her spirits rise in spite of the weather and the circumstances. The majesty and mystery of the Christian rite of the Eucharist began to come back to Cloe. She sat transfixed by the proceedings. The thunder grew louder, and Indian summer lightning strikes turned the church walls flash-bulb white every few seconds, as if the angels and the saints had created a symphony of glorious music and theater to welcome Thib home.

Several people went to the lectern to speak of her father, of those he had helped, of his sense of community, and of the senselessness of his death. Funny, she thought, how compassion to a total stranger was sometimes easier than a kind word to a family member, even though that family member might crave that sweet contact but be unable to initiate it. Sometimes we are joined only by our separateness.

The depth of the feelings expressed for her lost father was so evident and sincere that she ached inside. Conflicting emotions assaulted her. After a while, it came to her who she was, and Cloe could no longer hold her last, ugly contact with her father in the cold smallness of her heart. At some point during the service, love began to flow back into her much like the rain pouring insistently on the roof of the small church. Somehow a circle was being closed, and a wholeness and wellness were enveloping her.

"Cloe, Cloe ... the mass is over," she heard Uncle Sonny saying in his low, whispery voice.

She looked up, half-dazed, and saw that everyone was standing, waiting patiently for her. The organ and the choir were performing the refrain to the beautiful parting hymn chosen by Thib: "And He will raise you up on eagles' wings / Bear you on the breath of dawn ..."

Father Aloysius and the new priest were standing respectfully with the altar servers and attendants in front of the casket. The outsider looked at her with piercing eyes of recognition. He knew her, but who was he?

Eight young National Guard soldiers had taken their places around the coffin. They looked even younger than J.E., perhaps nineteen or twenty years old. Father Aloysius nodded and then led the procession toward the foyer of the church. The honor guard moved the caisson and its mortal burden in the direction of the vestibule.

The rain still pounded on the church roof, but the lightning strikes had begun to move off to the north. As the priests stepped through the entrance to the church, members of the laity, the Knights of Columbus, moved forward and provided slickers and umbrellas.

When the casket reached the door, Cloe saw the young men bend and hoist it onto their strong, broad shoulders. Their motion was flawless and fluid, as if the heavy coffin had somehow been rendered weightless. Perhaps in the extremity of the moment, it had shed its binding, earthly weight.

The solemn procession moved out of the church into the heavy rain. Cloe thought that the church crowd would certainly disperse and run for their vehicles. Perhaps a few would drive down to the town cemetery. The police, returning to their more mundane duties, had blocked off Main Street, which ran in front of the church, allowing only foot traffic.

The cemetery where Marie Louise was buried was only two blocks north of the church, and it quickly became apparent that the funeral-goers intended to proceed on foot to Thib's last resting place. The new priest was there in the lead with Father Aloysius.

Cloe could see J.E. just ahead of her, striding strong and straight, having fallen into the cadence of the honor guard, and her heart almost burst with love and pride. As she looked back into the torrent, she saw the entire church congregation walking along behind them to escort Thib. Many had on parts of military uniforms. Some had hats, coats, or just ribbons on a dress shirt. It was apparent that most of the men and not a few of the women were veterans of the armed services. They had come to escort a comrade and a friend to his final post at that last bugle call.

Cloe fell back for a moment and studied the mourners—the set of their jaws, the angle of their chins—as they forged through the calamitous rain, looking like the prows of a thousand ships relentlessly plowing on, cleaving gale winds and seas. What kind of people were these? These were the people of her youth, of Madisonville, and on a broader level, of Louisiana. The pride of her origins came to her now. How had she allowed herself to be separated from her roots, from her church, and most of all, from her father and mother? Stubborn pride was all she could come up with at that moment, but it seemed to fit.

Cloe heard something akin to a murmur from the hundreds in line. No, she thought, it was not a murmur, but more like a chant, one of fervor and reverence.

"Uncle Sonny, what is that sound?" she asked, rejoining him in the procession.

"Cloe, has it been that long? They are saying the rosary as they march along."

Sure enough, Cloe could now hear the new priest call out the opening part of the "Our Father" or the "Hail Mary" and the recited response of the congregation. The faces of the people reflected the flint-like solidness and sureness of their faith.

At the grave site an enormous canopy had thankfully been erected. Several hundred people were either under or around the cover. The honor guard gently, and with great dignity, set the coffin on the funeral bier. Father Aloysius said a few last words, which were so warm and delivered with such intimate knowledge of her father that Cloe knew they would stay with her. The other priest hung back, assisting Father Aloysius when needed.

Upon conclusion of the graveside ritual, Cloe could hear the quiet commands of the young officer conducting the honor guard. They had maintained their station around the coffin but now moved out.

"Ten hut, left face, hut, hut, hut …" he called softly as they filed out and lined up for a final salute. The two ranking noncommissioned officers approached the coffin and tenderly began the process of properly folding the now-drenched flag. All became quiet, and Cloe noticed that the rain had finally ceased.

When the riveting ceremony was complete, the young officer approached Cloe directly, bowed, and presented the flag to her. She was stunned at first but then realized that she was the next of kin. As she looked up to accept the flag, her eyes were drawn to the crowd, and as she swept the mourners, her gaze froze on dead, shark-like eyes in the assembly.

*Oh my God—that man again!* she thought, fumbling the flag onto the wet soggy ground.

Cloe blinked and gaped wildly but could not find the man who had passed by her at the airport. Had she actually seen him? Had she imagined it? The ranking officer retrieved the flag, knocked the dirt off, and presented it again to Cloe. Taking it, she shook herself, concluding that the day's events must have left her seeing things.

Just then the guard came to full attention, snapped, and held a tight salute. There was a pause for several counts—no sound other than the late fall rain dripping from the canopy and the nearby trees—and then a lone bugler straightened, raised the simple horn to his lips, and began the mournful notes of taps. The long notes peeled out into the mist much like fingers of fog as the first signs of the gathering evening began to show.

Thibodeaux Lejeune had rejoined his beloved Marie Louise.

# CHAPTER 6

In Louisiana, it is customary after a funeral to hold a reception for the mourners. As with everything else, Thib had planned for this and had arranged for one of the restaurants on the riverfront to bring in food.

Uncle Sonny opened his home, and for several hours people visited and shared stories about Thib, after first going home to change into dry clothing. Cloe had likewise changed and J.E. had hung his uniform to dry, donning casual, civilian clothes.

Oysters on the half shell, boiled and fried seafood of all types, and rounds of beef with all the trimmings had flowed like cornucopias from several stations in and around the small house. Truly, the seafood on which the mourners feasted had slept in either the river or the lake the night before.

Thib had made arrangements for several kegs of beer to be brought in from a regional brewery located a few miles north in Abita Springs. A bartender mixed cocktails and offered wine. Even in death, life was good; such was the Louisiana philosophy.

Cloe met the Madisonville chief of police, who asked that she and J.E. come by his office the next day to give a statement.

"Chief, I know nothing about the crime and haven't seen or talked to my father for twenty-five years," Cloe told him. "As to J.E., he's never even met his grandfather."

"I see," observed the chief.

"My uncle said Thib's death was a homicide and that the killer was some sort of professional criminal," Cloe said changing the subject and wondering if she might learn something from the chief.

"Right now it looks that way," replied the chief.

"You know, Chief, I studied the faces of the people at the funeral and, afterward, at the reception. I saw and heard nothing but respect and love for my father and sorrow over his death. I would find it hard to believe that anyone from here was behind this."

"You never know about people," the chief said. "We'll have to see where the evidence leads. Judging from the way the house was torn up, the killer was looking for something. It may have been a burglary that went bad. Whatever it was, the killer didn't find it because he had nothing on him except what he brought. Please do stop by tomorrow."

Upon rejoining J.E. and Uncle Sonny at the reception, she told them of the brief conversation with the chief and of his request that they go by his office the next day.

"I'm not sure we can add anything to the investigation, but if there is any chance, we've gotta go," responded J.E.

"Yes, I told him we would come," said Cloe. "The man seems very thorough. I wouldn't be surprised to learn that Madisonville has a pretty good top cop in the chief."

As the conversation waned, the voices around them seemed to grow louder and she heard J.E. remark to Uncle Sonny, "I don't get why these people are here partying and laughing like nothing much has happened."

"J.E., they're celebrating your grandfather's life in the best way they know how. Talk to some of them, and you might learn something."

True enough, when J.E. and Cloe had discussed the day's events later that night at Uncle Sonny's house, they'd found they had learned a lot about Thib. Some things Cloe knew from her youth, but a lot of the gaps had been filled in for her before the night was over. She now knew that Thib and Sonny had gotten involved in boat building after the war. Some of their crafts had been commercial skiffs built of cypress from nearby swamps.

After she left home, Thib apparently had realized the area's potential for recreational boating and with Uncle Sonny had begun a line of fast, sea-kindly fiberglass fishing boats. Inboard- or outboard-powered, it didn't matter. The boats were economical, fast, and terrific for reaching the far-flung fishing destinations in the

Lake Pontchartrain basin desired by many area anglers. Some were custom-built for professional fishermen from all over the state. Thib and Sonny sold a lot of boats.

Sonny had never married, and after Marie Louise's death, the brothers had become inseparable. They had continued to live simply and invested their earnings in real estate. Although they took some lumps, Thib and Sonny did pretty well. J.E. had found out from some of the mourners, confirmed by Internet sources, that his grandfather and great-uncle had continued on this path for a number of years and then had sold everything except the old houses. They had both purchased lifetime annuities from a large insurance company, assuring a constant and comfortable income for life for each. The brothers had then, literally, gone fishing, just like when they were kids.

Thus, it appeared the sum and substance of Thib's estate was probably the old Water Street house, since his lifetime annuity had died with him. Thib had gotten the full measure of his bargain with the insurance company by the time of his death at age eighty-nine. The only issue would be whether Thib had left debts that Cloe would have to clear up.

***

Cloe awakened early the next morning in the guest bedroom at Uncle Sonny's house as she had so often risen in her own bedroom on Water Street when she was young. There was something about the light and the birds in the neighborhood that made it impossible to sleep late. It was a wonderful something. She could immediately see that it would be a typical late fall Louisiana day, balmy and humid.

Soon it would be time to go to the lawyer's office with J.E. and Uncle Sonny. As requested by the police chief, they stopped briefly at the police station on their way to the lawyer's office, but as Cloe had expected, there was nothing they could directly contribute to the investigation. The chief insisted that Cloe fill him in on some of the details of her background, saying one could never tell what piece of information might lead to something.

Cloe told him of the break with her father and of her odyssey to Seattle, where she ultimately had settled in student housing, where no one would notice her. She lived in a rooming house and made fast friends with the lady, Mama Flo, who owned the place. When J.E. came, Mama Flo was a surrogate grandma, keeping him while Cloe worked and went to school. Cloe received her GED, went through Seattle Community College, and eventually attended the University of Washington. There she was attracted to ancient languages, including Greek, Aramaic, and the like.

She found she had a gift for the old languages and did groundbreaking work as she obtained her master's degree and, in due course, her doctorate. Now back at the University of Washington, she was the number two person in the ancient languages department. She wrote and lectured widely and believed she would be elevated to the chair's position upon the retirement, in a few months, of the current chair. Cloe noted, with some irony, that she had become somebody—that educated career woman her father had wanted her to become.

After hearing her story, the chief grunted and thanked her, saying he would keep her apprised.

***

All the events and information from the past day were still going through Cloe's mind as she, Uncle Sonny, and J.E. entered the attorney's office. They were offered coffee and shown into a meeting room paneled with deep, well-oiled hardwoods from the area. A large conference table occupied the center of the room.

At the end of the table sat the attorney, J. Nichols David. To his left was Father Aloysius. *What in the world is he doing here?* Cloe wondered. Even more surprising was the presence at the table of a third man, the priest with the riveting stare who had said the funeral mass alongside Father Aloysius.

The three men rose to their feet as Cloe, J.E., and Uncle Sonny entered the room. David introduced the outsider as Monsignor Albert Roques. The monsignor smiled and bowed deeply from the waist. Cloe and J.E. looked at each other in confusion.

Uncle Sonny said gently, "Clotile, J.E., sit down. You've a lot to hear, and some of it you may not believe or like."

Nichols David glanced down at what seemed to be some sort of agenda in front of him. But it was the monsignor who spoke.

"Signorina Lejeune, did your father ever speak of the Atlas Mountains in Tunisia?"

"No," she said, perhaps more sharply than she had intended. "I have come to hear my father's will, and I have no idea why you and Father Aloysius are here."

"Signorina, you are correct. Please pardon my impertinence. We should proceed to the will. Explanations can follow. Signor David, if you please."

The lawyer picked up a two-page document, cleared his throat, and opened his mouth to begin.

But J.E. interrupted. "Wait a minute—this is a private matter. We should hear this with family only."

Uncle Sonny replied, "J.E., they each have an interest in Thib's estate. This is all according to Thib's instructions. Nick, please skip the formalities and get to the point."

Cloe could see the lawyer was now off-message and unsure of how to proceed. He glanced down at the document and, after a moment's hesitation, summarized it quickly.

"Your father," he said, looking at Cloe, "left all his personal effects to the Society of St. Vincent DePaul for the poor. This includes the contents of the Water Street house except to the extent that you want anything. He bequeathed the Water Street house itself to St. Anselm Church in the name of Private Robert 'Bobby' Morrow. Proceeds from the sale of the house are to be used for the purpose of establishing and funding scholarships to the church school for children of deceased servicemen and women in this area."

Cloe was thunderstruck. She had neither needed nor particularly wanted anything from her father's estate, but to be so callously left out in favor of people whom she had never heard of or known seemed a terribly hurtful message from the grave. Was this Thib having some last revenge on her? Well, what had she expected anyway? But what of J.E., his grandson and only rightful heir beyond her? The warm feelings of the funeral were beginning to fade.

She began to lean over the table and thought, for a moment, that she would simply lay her head down until the pain passed. But she would not let these people—especially this total stranger,

30

this monsignor—see her distress. She straightened up and reminded herself that Thib had never even met J.E.

"That's not quite all," the lawyer noted, and this time he read directly from the will. "I leave my most precious possession, the old oil jar, to the most precious person in life to me, my daughter Clotile."

"Oil jar?" Cloe blurted out. Then she blinked as she absorbed the meaning of the rest of Thib's words. Her eyes now filled with tears and began to brim over. The monsignor rose and offered a clean white handkerchief. The man, whoever he was, was nothing if not gallant.

"Clotile … Cloe, Thib loved you beyond his life, and he followed you closely," said Uncle Sonny.

He pushed a large scrapbook toward her; he had taken it from the Water Street house, he said, with the chief's permission. She began to look through it. It was filled with articles on her and, lately, on J.E. Every event in their lives that had garnered some press or Internet mention had been included. A few dealt with J.E.'s high school athletic career, and one chronicled his return from Iraq. Some were stained and yellowed with age. The more recent ones were crisp and new. The last entry, only a few weeks old, was an article from an online Seattle newspaper speculating on her possibilities as the next department chair.

"If only one of you two stubborn, knuckleheaded sapsuckers had reached out," said Uncle Sonny, shaking his head. "Thib would have, once he finally got over the razor-edged hurt of the loss of Marie Louise, but he saw you had your life, and he didn't want to intrude."

Cloe dabbed her eyes.

J.E. asked, "What's the old oil jar?"

She had to think for a moment. "It's just something that your grandfather picked up in Africa during the war. It's about eighteen inches tall and, maybe, eight to ten inches in diameter, but it bulges in the middle. The jar's been on the mantelpiece at the Water Street house for as long as I can remember. My dad never really said much about it except it reminded him of the only Louisiana soldier that he had lost during the war."

The monsignor said, "Yes, and that Louisiana soldier was Private Robert 'Bobby' Morrow."

As Cloe tried in vain to figure out the significance of all this, she studied the monsignor more carefully. He was about J.E.'s height but a little thinner. He could be in his mid- to late forties and would be considered handsome by most standards. He was beginning to gray at the temples, and his features had a somewhat sharp look to them, as with a person who might have recently lost a good deal of weight. She did not believe this to be the case, though, and favored the conclusion that he was very active in the gym, as was Cloe herself. The monsignor wore a full-length cassock, eggplant black with deep crimson piping. He spoke with a faintly European accent, one that was hard to pinpoint.

"So in my father's mind there was an emotional connection between the tragic loss of a young soldier's life in the war over sixty years ago and an old jar that they found. The jar was merely a keepsake," Cloe continued. Turning to the monsignor, she said, "But I still don't understand—why are you here?"

There was a pause, and Cloe sensed a feeling of expectation growing among those in the room. As the feeling intensified, she noted that J.E., David, and Father Aloysius had their eyes riveted on the curious cleric.

"Well?" asked J.E. finally.

"Your oil jar may be the most important relic discovered since the birth of Christ," the monsignor stated quietly.

# CHAPTER 7

It took everyone a moment to process what the monsignor had just said. The most important relic since the birth of Christ?

"Cloe," Nichols David said with kindness, "Thib left a letter for you. It's to be read only by you. It's in the sitting room next to my personal office."

She was still reeling from the news that her father had been murdered in his own home. Now this. Things around her felt alien and odd, but she allowed herself to be led into an intimate space next to the lawyer's inner office.

Once she was alone, Cloe opened the letter, which had begun to slightly yellow with time. She looked at the well-crafted script of her father's hand.

> Dear Clotile,
>
> By now, as you read this, I imagine I'll be resting next to Marie Louise in the town cemetery on Main Street. Please understand that I long for this very thing … to be with Marie Louise again. The first thing I want to tell you is how much I love you and J.E. I'm so proud of you and I wish we could have fixed things up between us. But it was a very hurtful time with your situation, your mother's passing, and all. I don't think I was really myself for years after you left and she died. I started to call a hundred times, but I was afraid you wouldn't want to hear from me. I have missed you so much and my heart hurts for the loss of you and Marie Louise.
>
> You will have heard the contents of the will, such as they are, from Nick. This is the way I want things. But to know

why, I must tell you the story of Bobby Morrow, which, in many ways, is also my story and, perhaps, your story too.

It began in early 1943 as I stood next to a new replacement in my unit, Private Robert Morrow, in the belly of a Dakota waiting for the pilot to finish his preflight checklist. The airplane was a modified version of the Douglas C-47 Sky Train. It was stripped to the bare ribs and metal but fitted out to transport thirty paratroopers and gear along with the crew of three. This was an extremely important mission. No expense or effort had been spared to make it happen. There were nine other Dakotas just like it warming their engines in formation for takeoff at the Algiers landing strip.

Aboard were twenty-eight military souls of varying experience, me and a brand-shiny-new private from our home state of Louisiana. Morrow and me had become friends as much as a sergeant and a private could. You could say that Private Robert Morrow and me were from the same state, but we were from different worlds. For me, and maybe for you, everything changed that night in Africa when the Dakotas flew on that fateful mission.

We had been thoroughly briefed and trained for the mission but had not been told, for security reasons, exactly where it would take place. We knew it involved a night drop, mountainous territory, and a small-fortification assault. We had received special training with mountain gear, grappling hooks, ropes, and special boots. Rucks had been lightened and it was expected that the mission would take no longer than twenty-four hours. The mission was to assault and knock out one or more small fortifications.

The job was to take out Italian positions in the hills on the north side of the Gafsa Pass, which runs through the Atlas Mountains. Once we knocked out the Italians and took those positions, our tanks and infantry could storm through the pass, flanking the Germans on the southern coastal plains of Tunisia.

The British Eighth Army had taken Tripoli, and the combined German and Italian forces were concentrating on the defense of Tunisia and its jewel of a Mediterranean deepwater port, Tunis. If Tunis could be defended, Hitler believed that the battle for Tunisia might last many months, perhaps years, delaying Allied plans for the invasion of Europe.

In a coordinated fashion, the British Eighth Army was attacking from the north, and the handwriting was on the wall for the Afrika Korps if our mission was successful. The German army would be trapped on the north and south by Allied forces and hemmed in on the west by the mountains and east by the sea. The beginning of the end of the North Africa Campaign would be upon them.

Cloe sat back and reflected on the stress and responsibility that her father must have felt at that time. Thib had been just about J.E.'s age as he flew toward his destiny in the Dakota. And her father had had a double duty. Not only was he literally jumping into a life-threatening situation, but he also had made friends with this young, cherry private from Louisiana and probably felt responsible for him. Her respect for her father grew, and she began to see how formative this experience must have been for him. Once again she fell back into 1943, the distant past, but right next to her father.

The Dakotas were now airborne and heading almost due south from Algiers. Although the drop zone was southeast as the crow flies, it was necessary to stay away from the arc that marked the outer limit of the range of the German and Italian fighters based in Axis airfields in Sicily and Sardinia. We flew south and then east to reach the drop zone near Gafsa in Tunisia.

I looked at my watch and stood up and yelled, "Heads up, we're about ten minutes out. Police up your gear and get ready to hook 'em up."

Private Bobby Morrow was one of the army's ninety-day warriors. Some said ninety-day wonders. Either way, he had been rushed through basic training and had no experience. This was his first mission. That's the reason I kept him close to me, that and the fact we were both from Louisiana.

Bobby Morrow was from the town of Alexandria, located in the dead center of Louisiana. His father was a banker in a small bank that had, somehow, survived the Depression. Bobby had graduated from high school and was in his senior year at LSU, except that Uncle Sam had other plans for him. He was Baptist, had never had a beer or a cigarette before entering the army, and in civilian life had a steady girlfriend with marriage and kids on her mind. The future was very bright for Bobby Morrow, and I was committed to seeing he got back to his future.

Clotile, the important part is we all jumped out of that Dakota and just about everyone made it safely down. We had a couple of bumps and bruises but nobody out of action. We rendezvoused with our CO—commanding officer—and pretty soon we were headed for the Italian positions. The company was spread out to the right and left. Bobby was with me and we went right down the middle. Bobby was scared but he had steadied out some.

Morrow and me felt our way through the stygian blackness of the hills overlooking Gafsa and El Guettar. The Battle of El Guettar had begun. We clamored up a short rise and topped a crusty berm. I thought I heard something or someone off to my right, so we hit the dirt and I considered for a moment we might have been flanked by the Italians. But we listened for a bit and could not confirm anything. It looked like everyone including me had a case of nerves.

Bobby was worried we had lost contact with the company but I told him we were good. They were just ahead with the company spread out to the left and right.

Bobby and I slid down the back side of the berm and suddenly the ground gave way, and we plunged into an inky black hole. Over time the wind must have eroded the top of an underground cavern. We fell some ten to fifteen feet. Neither of us yelled, and both of us made use of our training, rolling to soften the impact where we landed.

Dazed briefly, I lay still for a few seconds trying to get my senses and figure out what had happened. I knew I was all right, and I called to Bobby. He said he was not hurt and, although he had bumped his head, he wasn't seeing stars and did not think he was bleeding.

I flicked on the muted flashlight I had been issued and looked around. The first thing I saw was Morrow's face, white as the tail of the proverbial deer in the headlight. As I spread the light out somewhat, I saw the outlines of a cavern and the drifting, settling debris of a long-silent and undisturbed space.

The place had an almost sacred atmosphere. Strange, that, there in the middle of the desert.

I knew we needed to get out of there and join the men. We could hear the thumping of mortars and the racking, rolling sound of machine-gun fire as the surprised Italians fired wildly in response to the attack. From the volume of the weapons fire, I could tell we were downrange of the fire fight and, if we did not join the battle, the battle would soon join us.

I unveiled the night vision lens from the flashlight and the beam shot out powerfully for several yards. It was a large cave filled with what looked like cinder blocks. How could that be? When I approached the objects I could see they weren't cinder blocks at all but some type of pitchers or vases.

Clotile, the strangest thing was that while at first glance everything appeared random, as I studied the cave or catacomb, whatever it was, I began to see some type of order.

Bobby saw it right away and said that it looked like something he had read about in school in an archeology class he had taken. He said it might be an ancient cache of documents and manuscripts, sort of an old underground library.

Bobby looked at them closely and confirmed they were vases or jars, some kind of containers. He said they looked old and that he did not think anyone had been in the cave for a very long time. I thought at that time that Bobby seemed to know a lot about this.

I told Bobby it could be anything from rancid old oil to very well aged wine but he was awfully persistent that this was something.

The jars were about eighteen inches high, about ten inches in diameter at their midsection, and were sealed with some substance at the neck. They appeared to be made of clay or a ceramic material. Some had letters of a strange language on them.

We fanned out to explore the area. My light revealed the near wall of the cave. Bobby said it did look more like a catacomb with hollowed out chambers or shelves in the walls. Instead of bodies on these shelves, there were more jars.

Bobby got real excited and said they might be organized like books on the same subject. He began to focus on the nearest section.

I thought to myself, "College boy," but Bobby was studying the scratches on the wall over this particular rock ledge.

Bobby said he had had to take a couple of courses in the classic languages which were then required for college students, and he thought the scratches were in ancient Greek and were some sort of inscription. Finally, he turned and looked directly at me with something like amazement in his face and told me he thought the inscription over this particularly ledge might mean the jars in this alcove had something to do with the biblical figure of Judas Iscariot. He just stood there looking at me with wide eyes and then he got this great big smile on his face.

Clotile, I can remember the look of wonder on Bobby's face as if it was yesterday. It was like he had been looking for shells on a beach and had suddenly kicked over the Holy Grail and he knew it right away.

He said that this was something, something big. He wanted to know what I thought we should do. He said we had to have evidence.

I told him we could do nothing because we had orders and a battle to fight. There was nothing for us to do but to try to get out of there and to catch up with our unit. I could see we could climb out near where we had fallen in, and I began to move in that direction.

Clotile, if we had left then when I wanted to, everything might have been different. But Bobby wouldn't let it go and said this might be important. It might be more important than the battle.

I told him to grab a vase, or wine jar, or whatever the hell they were, and let's get out of here. The mortar fire had increased and the machine-gun fire had intensified exponentially. The battle would be won or lost in the next few minutes.

Over the noise of the fight he yelled to grab a jar out of the Judas niche. There were eight to ten jars on this shelf itself.

I grabbed the nearest Judas jar and fastened it inside my ruck sack. I saw Morrow do likewise and we both scrambled up and out of the hole. I was trained not to stay in one place and ran for the top of the next berm just as I heard a mortar shell whistle overhead. I fell behind the small ridge and turned in time to see Bobby emerge from the cave entrance.

I screamed for him to get down but it was too late. The mortar landed about five feet in front of Bobby and exploded, vaporizing the soldier, his equipment, and his jar. As the smoke cleared, I could see there was nothing left and the cave entrance had been sealed.

Cloe inhaled and exhaled deeply. She thought about her father in these circumstances, a leader who had lost a young soldier he had dedicated himself to seeing safely home. There was nothing he could have done, but it must have eaten at him the rest of his life. She wished she could have somehow changed things. She returned her eyes to the letter.

Well, Clotile, that's the story as best I can recall it and set it down. There was nothing I could do except rejoin my unit. After I got there, we reorganized and knocked out the Italian positions as we had been detailed to do. I went through that battle and, indeed, the rest of the war without a scratch. How do you figure something like that? Bobby Morrow was killed by virtually the first shell aimed and fired in his direction. There were not even any remains to send back to his family to bury. Not even a dogtag. All they could do was hold a memorial service with an empty box. Yet after five years of fighting I came home completely unmarked, physically.

So now you know why the jar is my most precious possession and why I want you to have it. It was Bobby's idea to bring it out. He must have known something or had some insight about it. I know you have the education, interest, and background to see that it is properly studied. While there were a lot of jars in that cave, this jar was purchased with a precious currency—the lifeblood of Private Robert Morrow of Alexandria, Louisiana. My faith tells me this jar is special. Find out why, Clotile.

Love,
Dad


Cloe bowed her head and sat for a long time, thinking about her father, her heritage, and the charge Thib had given her. She thought about his death. Finally, she straightened in the chair. She *would* find out why—about a lot of things.

# CHAPTER 8

"Perhaps I should begin with my background," said the monsignor.

"Yes, perhaps you should," said Cloe stiffly.

The monsignor, Father Aloysius, and J.E. had joined her in the attorney's sitting room. She sat with J.E. on an overstuffed couch, and the monsignor and Father Aloysius sat opposite in deep-blue leather armchairs. Seeing no reason not to, Cloe had given them the gist of Thib's letter. The lawyer had made his apologies and left for an urgent appointment.

The monsignor continued smoothly. "I am posted to the Vatican and have served in this position for several years."

"What position?" asked J.E.

"Ah, the young signore goes to the heart of the matter. I am a special assistant to His Holiness, Benedict, the direct successor of St. Peter," he replied. "Quite a thing for a peasant boy from the Acceglio region along the French-Italian border. But I did well at seminary and was sent to Rome for what you would call college and advanced studies. My field is forensic theology. A rare and highly specialized field, it focuses on the physical, demonstrated proofs of theological hypotheses or beliefs."

The monsignor looked at them and smiled. Apparently, he felt that what he had said was the answer to all their questions.

Cloe, a scientist herself, considered his statement. "Forensic theology ... some might consider that a contradiction in terms. Plainly, there's only one reason a practitioner of such an exotic discipline might come to Madisonville, Louisiana."

Although this man was obviously thoroughly educated and well spoken, Cloe wondered whether he was the academician he was

41

making himself out to be. Whatever he was, she thought, there was something odd about him. He had the edgy look of a person who had seen many things, not all of them good.

"Yes, you are correct," he said. "The jar has brought us here. This is not our first trip. Let me begin with the Atlas Mountains."

"Who the hell is 'us'?" asked J.E.

"The 'we or us' I refer to is the Vatican ... my predecessor and, of course, lately myself."

"Proceed, Monsignor," said Cloe.

"Shortly after Thib returned from the war, the Vatican received correspondence from the pastor at St. Anselm's—Father Aloysius's predecessor—relating some of the extraordinary events of which you learned today from your father's letter. Some details my predecessor secured from contemporaneous battle reports. At the pope's direction, the priest who preceded me in this role came to Madisonville and interviewed Thib in detail. That report forms much of what I will now relate to you.

"In summary, as your father's letter says, something happened to Thib and Bobby Morrow. They were separated for a time from the main force of their company after they were dropped close to the Italian positions. He and Morrow fell into some sort of cave, which was full of vessels like the old oil jar. Thinking they might be important, each of the men grabbed the nearest container from a niche Bobby had identified and headed back to rejoin their unit. Unfortunately, Private Morrow was killed by an Italian mortar round exiting the cave."

"Whoa," said J.E., leaning back on the couch and visualizing the scene. "Poor unlucky bastard. Wrong time, wrong place."

"Certainly true," said the monsignor. "Thib must have felt responsible, although there was nothing he could have done to change the result. From our reports, he managed to join the battle, and his actions were crucial in reorganizing his men, who had been repelled initially by Italian mortar and machine-gun fire. He led a final charge that took the fortification and allowed, the next day, the Allies to power through the pass, sealing the fate of the Axis forces in Tunisia. Hundreds of thousands of prisoners were taken, along with untold amounts of war materiel. Both Thib individually and the unit as a whole were decorated for their actions that horrific night."

"My grandfather was a hero?" asked J.E. with awe.

"Yes, certainly at the Battle of El Guettar, but not just there. My file indicates he distinguished himself a number of times in the invasion of Italy and then in the war in France and Germany. He never accepted a field promotion, although many were offered.

"After the war, he came back to Louisiana and took up residence in Madisonville. He brought the oil jar back and put it on the mantelpiece, where it remained all the following years. This is where my predecessor found it when he interviewed Thib long ago. Polaroid photos of it were sent back to the Vatican with the report. It has been of keen interest to the Vatican since that time."

"Yes, I remember it to some degree. My father never said much about it except that it reminded him of a friend he had lost in the war. It was earthen and sealed with wax, tar, or some other substance. It was quite plain and completely unremarkable. It could have been a clay pot from the local nursery."

"Yes," the monsignor responded softly. "Can you remember anything else about it?" He leaned closer.

She tried to think back and picture it. "It had something written on it. I can remember running my fingers over the slightly raised letters on the jar. No, not just something—two words. It was nonsense to me at that time. I couldn't read it, but it made an impression on me. Now that I have read my father's letter, it all makes more sense to me … Can I have a piece of paper and pencil?"

The monsignor stepped to the attorney's desk and returned with pencil and paper.

Cloe turned to J.E. and squeezed his hand. She had a look of intense focus.

J.E. looked first at the monsignor and then at Father Aloysius. "Gentlemen … get ready, the doctor is about to operate."

Cloe stepped into her zone of concentration, mentally recalling the long-ago images of the writing on the jar. No one was more serious about her work than Clotile Lejeune. She began to sketch the ancient letters that she remembered tracing with her finger so many times at the Water Street house. There appeared to be two words in a strange, almost alien script.

"No," she said. "That's not quite right." She thought for a moment, and her focus intensified. She erased a portion of the lettering and tried again. "Yes, I believe this is very close to what I remember," she concluded. "It must have been written in ancient Greek. I haven't thought about it since I lived in the Water Street house, but I'm sure this is it."

They all looked at the incomprehensible phrase, and J.E., turning to his mother, asked, "What does it mean?"

She thought for a moment and then looked J.E. in the eye. "In ancient Greek, it says 'Ioudas Iskarioth.' That's what Bobby Morrow must have seen on the niche in the cave!"

# CHAPTER 9

The room was silent for a long moment.

"But what does *that* mean?" J.E. finally barked, breaking the spell that had fallen over the little group.

"Well, it seems pretty clear," said Cloe. "But let's be careful. What we have is an old jar that was apparently found by your grandfather in Tunisia over sixty years ago that has an ancient Greek inscription on it. Those are the only facts we know for sure." The scientist in her had taken over. She looked down at the paper and began to doodle a bit as her mind examined the possibilities.

The monsignor sat forward and said, "I believe the signorina would agree that the ancient Greek inscription most likely translates into the English phrase 'Judas Iscariot.'"

"Judas Iscariot … yes, yes, certainly … but Monsignor, I don't think you have finished what you have traveled all these miles to say."

The monsignor smiled. "The rest of the story is both history and speculation. The historical side is that we know just a bit about Judas Iscariot from the Gospels. We all know of the biblical figure of Judas cast as the arch villain and betrayer of our Lord Jesus Christ. However, most of what we know of Judas is incomplete or ambiguous."

"Well," said Cloe, "one thing I can add to the discussion is that the name 'Judas' is nothing terribly exotic; it's simply the English spelling of the Greek form of the Hebrew name Judah, which is the root of words such as Judeans, Judas, and even the term 'Jew' itself. Its literal meaning is 'praised.' But I have no idea about Iscariot."

The monsignor responded, "The precise derivation of what we call the last name 'Iscariot' is unclear. One theory says that the proper translation of 'Iscariot' is 'man of Kerioth,' which is a Judean town or, more properly, a collection of small towns in a certain region in Judea. This could suggest a more rural or suburban origin for Judas. Some have advocated a literal meaning of 'Judas Iscariot' in modern parlance as being 'Jew from the suburbs.'

"However, the Gospel of John refers to Judas as the son of Simon Iscariot. This could imply that it was not Judas but his father who was from Kerioth. Incomplete and misleading information about Judas abounds."

The monsignor had warmed to his story and once again leaned forward to emphasize his points. He steepled his fingers and made to continue.

But J.E. interceded. "Can anyone actually believe that the jar in my grandfather's home has something to do with the biblical figure who betrayed Jesus Christ?"

Plainly, this whole thing was beyond J.E.'s sphere of experience or knowledge. Nevertheless, Cloe could see that he was fascinated. They all were.

"No one can know for sure, as we speak, if the two are connected, but the circumstances are certainly interesting," commented the monsignor. "As I was saying, this is just one theory of the derivation of the last name of Judas, although it is probably the majority view of the scholars on the subject. The other theory is much more intriguing and perhaps sinister. This school of thought holds that Iscariot identifies Judas as a member of a group of alleged assassins, the Sicarii, who were Judean rebels intent on driving the Romans out of Judea. Did you know that Judas was the only Judean among the twelve Apostles? All the rest were Galileans. Another thing that is almost too astounding to credit: do you know who the only other Judean in the group was?"

"You just said he was the only Judean among the Twelve," said J.E. bluntly, riveted.

"There was one other ... Jesus Christ," said the monsignor simply.

"No, no," asserted Cloe. "He was a Galilean like the others. Monsignor, you're wrong about this. Jesus is referred to many times in the bible as the 'Nazarene,' which is derived from 'Nazareth,' which is located in Galilee."

"All true, but I ask you, where was Jesus born? In Nazareth?"

The group became quiet again. Finally, J.E. said, "Jesus was born in Bethlehem because of the census. Bethlehem is in Judea. Technically, the way we think about it, Jesus was a Judean."

"Yes, along with Judas, the only other Judean in the inner circle," concluded the monsignor. "Which gets us back to Judas's last name ... Some say Iscariot translates to something like 'knife or dagger man.' However, certain historians assert that the Sicarii did not emerge until about halfway through the first century."

"If that is true, then Judas could not have been a member of this Sicarii," observed Cloe. "He would have been long gone by then."

"On the other hand," said the monsignor, "fifty years, when looked back upon from two thousand years in the future, might not be significant. If the historians are off only a few tenths of a point in their calculations, Judas might well have been a member. Moreover, there were some reports of the Sicarii as early as AD 6. If Judas had fallen in with the Sicarii, this could entirely explain his joining with the early Jesus movement, which was viewed in orthodox Jewish circles as a band of revolutionaries."

"Wait a minute ... I remember now," said Father Aloysius. "Wasn't there some sort of showdown between the Romans and the Sicarii?"

"Right you are," replied the monsignor. "After the Romans sacked Jerusalem in about AD 70, the leader of the Sicarii took his band of revolutionaries, numbering some nine hundred men, women, and children, to a mountaintop fortress called Masada. The Romans caught up with them there and, according to most history books, wiped them out."

"Tragic," J.E. said. "The battle was covered in my military tactics books. I'm amazed to learn that Judas may have been an early member of the sect."

"Judas's supposed actions as the betrayer of Christ are well known," the monsignor continued. "All four of the traditional Gospels chronicle Judas's betrayal in some detail, although from somewhat different perspectives.

"The Gospel according to Mark, which was one of the earliest Gospels written, contains no explanation as to why Judas acted in the manner he did, saying only that he went to the Jewish leaders of the time, offering to betray Jesus, and they agreed to pay him for this. Although it's not clear there was a quid pro quo, one could conclude he was motivated by the money.

"The Gospel of Matthew, which is believed by some scholars to have been written a bit before Mark's, is more specific and adds detail. In Matthew's account, Judas goes to the Jewish high priests to negotiate the betrayal and the amount of money that it would be worth. They settle on thirty pieces of silver. Unlike in Mark's account, Judas initiates the exchange, and there is no question that a bargain has been made. The obvious message here is that Judas's motive is greed."

Cloe blinked and struggled to remember some scripture from her days of study at the church school. She had returned to her hometown to bury her father and was now engaged with two priests in a discussion of Judas Iscariot, learning more detailed information than she even knew existed. Why? she wondered. Where was this going?

The monsignor continued. "Luke's Gospel, which was written at about the same time as Mark's, adds a new wrinkle. Luke says that Satan entered into Judas and led him to betray his leader. Indeed, in the last accepted orthodox Gospel to be written, John states that Jesus knew all along that one of his disciples was a devil."

"To be sure," remarked Father Aloysius, "Christ Himself at the Last Supper marked the villain as the one who dipped bread with Him: Judas! Toward the end of the Passover meal, Jesus tells Judas to do what he must do and to do it quickly. Rather enigmatic when you note that none of the other Apostles seems to have been in on the conversation, which was carried on openly at the table among them all. They appear to have been more focused on declaring themselves not to be the traitor than on noting who Jesus said was the traitor.

"Yes, plainly Jesus knew what Judas was up to, that it could lead to his being turned over to the high priests and, possibly, to the

Romans. Yet he did nothing to stop Judas or to avoid the apparent treachery," the old priest concluded.

"One could almost suppose that Jesus and Judas desired the same result," commented the monsignor.

"So much for the biblical and historical views of Judas, but what does the oil jar represent in this mystery?" asked Cloe. She was growing a little impatient with the roundabout history lesson and wanted to understand the connection of all this to her and the jar.

"We have reason to believe that the oil jar may contain, or reference, the direct writings of or about Judas Iscariot," said the monsignor. "And if so, it could be one of the most monumental finds ever." The monsignor rose and started to pace in his excitement at the possibilities.

Cloe's scientific interest was piqued as she began to process the enormity of what she was hearing and the possible implications for her career. "We've got to go to the Water Street house immediately and get the jar," she said. "Arrangements must be made for it to be properly opened and studied. I know from my work that LSU has a very good facility for unsealing and opening the jar under the required, controlled conditions."

"That may be true, but we can't retrieve the jar from Thib's house," said Father Aloysius.

"Why is that?" asked J.E.

"Because it's not there." The priest continued, "Cloe, at Thib's request, we took custody of the oil jar and removed it to the sanctuary of St. Anselm's. Thib was sure it was important, and as his health got worse, he began to worry that something might happen to the jar. He told me that a person had appeared at his house one day wanting to buy the jar. The man was very insistent. Thib said no, but the event spooked him. Nor would Thib tell me who the man was. It was all very mysterious. After that, he became frantic about its security."

Cloe nodded. "I understand, Father. I'm just glad it's safe and that my dad's efforts have not been in vain." Her mind was buzzing with the information about Thib and the jar and the apparent fact that someone else knew something about it! Why else would Thib be frantic to preserve it? Did that someone want it enough to kill for it? What did the stranger know about it? If Thib knew who the man was, why wouldn't he say? She could see the dots, but how to connect them?

Father Aloysius continued, "He called me and asked that I come and take possession of it. I called the Church, and in due course, the appropriate vessel was sent to me to care for it."

"Yes," said the monsignor, "the jar had been exposed to the heat and humidity of Louisiana from the time Thib had returned from the war. We sent Father Aloysius a windowed chamber that could house the jar but also keep it at a constant temperature and moderate humidity so as to dry it out and continue to preserve it," said the monsignor.

"All good," Cloe said, but the little voice of doubt in the back of her mind wondered why these exceptionally well-informed priests were so keen on helping her with the jar. "Now that I'm here, it's time I take the jar, get it properly opened, and find out what secrets it holds, and perhaps we will learn who exactly Judas Iscariot was."

# CHAPTER 10
# JEWISH QUARTER, JERUSALEM

He had pored over the ancient manuscript for hours. With sensitive fingertips he caressed the handwritten text, and his delicate nostrils inhaled the smell of the aged ink and papyrus. The relic was magnificent and valuable beyond imagination.

The man had acquired it in the usual way. When his efforts to purchase the relic had failed, his servants had murdered its owners and stolen it for him. He smiled with satisfaction at yet another addition to his vast collection.

He knew it was late, but he still burned with energy. Here in his bunker deep under Jerusalem, he had all the time in the world to spend with his newest prize. The roomy area that served as his inner office was lit with candles, giving off a soft glow. Never could he get enough of their intoxicating aroma. Truly, this was the only way to study old manuscripts, with the very light by which they had been written.

He sat back at the ornate table, stretched, and rubbed his eyes. When he heard the door open, he looked up to see his manservant enter the room.

"Good evening, Master. You must be hungry." The servant presented a small silver tray with his master's favorite caviar, toast points, and a very cold, dry chardonnay. The servant might have chosen a different wine served at a more appropriate temperature, but the man knew wines were not the servant's strong point. The servant had other assets, not the least of which was his unquestioned loyalty to his master.

"I have news from our people in the United States," the servant said. "The old soldier is dead."

"Is that confirmed?" asked the man evenly, though excitement had begun to well up in him.

"There can be no doubt. The man is dead."

"What of the jar? Did we recover the Judas relic?"

"There is no word on the location of the jar," responded the servant. "Indeed, our man sent to fetch it has not checked in with our intermediaries and may not have succeeded in his assignment."

"Goddamn his cursed soul for his failure," responded the man, his voice rising. "Between the soldier's stubbornness and the meddling of the infernal Catholic Church, the jar continues to elude me ... but that will change."

"But Master, the jar may have no value beyond that of a nineteen-hundred-year-old piece of pottery. It might not be what you think it is," observed the servant, risking impertinence with his master.

"Why, then, is the Vatican so interested in it? We know the Holy See itself sent an emissary years ago to talk to the soldier," the man said. "Apparently nothing came of that. But shortly thereafter, an expedition was commissioned to Tunisia, where the old soldier had fought in the war ... No, there is much more to this than meets the eye. I am convinced the jar is highly important, perhaps revolutionary, and I believe the Vatican also thinks so."

"If we know the old soldier is dead, the Vatican knows," the servant said. "They will send their people. Getting the relic will not be easy." He knew his Socratic efforts to assist his master were useless, but he felt obliged to try. Such was his nature. He braced himself for what was certain to come.

The man seemed to grow in size, darkness, and malevolence as he absorbed the servant's words. The servant sensed a gathering of his master's will. The candlelight flickered over the man's face, creating deep though fleeting shadows here and there, revealing an almost bestial look of hunger.

With a scowl that turned the servant's blood cold, in a voice like the slamming of the door to eternity, the man uttered what the servant knew was a terrible, unspeakable blasphemy. "God can send Benedict himself and all His legions, but none shall stand against me ... I will have that jar!"

# PART 2

# BATON ROUGE

When he found that Jesus had been condemned, Judas his betrayer was filled with remorse and took the thirty silver pieces back to the chief priests and elders. "I have sinned;" he said. "I have betrayed innocent blood." "What is that to us?" they replied. "That is your concern." And flinging down the silver pieces in the sanctuary he made off, and went out and hanged himself. The chief priests picked up the silver pieces and said, "It is against the Law to put this into the treasury; it is blood money." So they discussed the matter and bought a potter's field with it as a graveyard for foreigners, and this is why the field is called the Field of Blood today.

Matthew 27:3–9 (The Jerusalem Bible, 1966)

# CHAPTER 11

Cloe thought that the monsignor and the Vatican had been ever so helpful. But to what end, she wondered?

Although she'd had reservations, Cloe had accepted the monsignor's offer of his car and driver for the trip to Baton Rouge. The Catholic Church carried enormous weight and sway among the predominantly Catholic population as well as with the political class. Thus, making the necessary arrangements, particularly with the vice-chair of the ancient languages department of a prestigious university in attendance, was not difficult. The scientists at LSU were eagerly awaiting their arrival. The precious jar was safely nestled in its portable climate-controlled vessel in the trunk of the monsignor's car.

As they wound their way through Madisonville, Cloe spotted the old library building and thought about the first books she had read from the town's small collection—the Bobbsey Twins books, stories of prepubescent detectives for whom no mystery was too formidable. She wondered whether she would want to invite the good offices of Bert and Nan to help her in her quest to find her father's murderer and unlock the secrets of the jar before all was finished.

They were heading up Highway 1021, leading to the interstate highway, when J.E. spoke up. "Father Al, didn't you feel a little funny that a vessel labeled with the name of the betrayer of Jesus Christ was given sanctuary in your church?" he asked.

"That irony certainly occurred to me, J.E., but we can't be sure of what's inside the jar. Further, Christ himself was the first to reach out to sinners, tax collectors, and others reviled by the Jews and Romans of his time. Indeed, some scholars have speculated that even knowing what Judas would do, by identifying Judas as his betrayer at the Last Supper, Jesus was actually reaching out to him … maybe even offering him the opportunity to repent," concluded the priest, smiling.

Cloe thought about that for a moment, decided that the priest was probably right, and considered her own family's missed opportunities for forgiveness and reconciliation. She longed for a second chance.

Cloe, sitting in the passenger seat, turned to face the two priests, who were sitting with J.E. in the backseat. "You said that Thib resisted efforts to have the jar properly analyzed. How long have you known about the jar and suspected its contents might be important?"

"Perhaps I can answer that," said Father Aloysius as the monsignor's driver pulled onto the highway and headed west toward Baton Rouge. "When Thib returned from the war, long before you were born, Cloe, he tried to integrate himself back into the community. This included inviting the parish priest—my predecessor, Father Gillespie—to his home for supper. He and Marie Louise put on quite a meal, but talk soon turned to the singular item that now graced his mantelpiece. Thib told Father Gillespie how he had come to own the jar and what it meant to him.

"Father Gillespie, or 'the Big G,' as we called him in seminary when he came 'round as a guest lecturer, was a giant of a man and had been a chaplain in World War I. He had seen some of the worst of the worst. He was both fierce and gentle, if you can understand the contradiction."

Cloe's thoughts immediately jumped to J.E., knowing this description could also be applied to her son.

"He and Thib became fast friends, and the Big G was Thib's personal confessor. If anyone other than Marie Louise knew Thib's heart, it was Father Gillespie," said the priest.

Cloe briefly wondered whether her father had said anything to the priest about her.

"Did Thib tell Father Gillespie anything about the location of the cave where the jar was found?" asked Cloe, putting her personal thought aside. She wondered about the other jars Thib and Morrow had seen.

The monsignor spoke up. "All Thib knew was that the cave was in the drop zone in the Atlas Mountains near the Italian fortifications. He wasn't able to go back there during the war because the US Army was at that time on a sprint into Sicily and then into Italy. Thib did believe his jar had something to do with Judas. Bobby Morrow had told him that. However, once we became aware of the situation, the Vatican commissioned a team of experts to look for the cave. Nothing was ever found. Perhaps it would have been different if we could have persuaded Thib to go back with us, but this was not to be. Thib could not be swayed to try to find the site since that was where Bobby Morrow had died. The search was abandoned after several fruitless months in the field."

"So this may be it," J.E. said. "Whatever, if anything, is in the oil jar may be all that's left."

"Regrettably so," the monsignor said, "unless there are clues inside the jar that can help us locate the cave. Thib said there were scores, if not hundreds, of jars there. Some were organized into the shelves or niches, but many were merely loosely grouped on the floor of the cavern. There is simply no knowing what might be found there. It could rival or exceed the Dead Sea Scrolls and similar discoveries."

Cloe considered the possibility of hundreds of unopened jars containing God-only-knew-what information from millennia past. She felt she was on the edge of a great chasm of information and being sucked toward the rim.

"My predecessor met with Thib and Father Gillespie several times over the years, but Thib was insistent that the oil jar not be disturbed," said the monsignor. "It was the memory of Bobby Morrow that kept the oil jar on the mantelpiece. That did not keep us from searching for the cave, but it most assuredly kept the jar on the mantelpiece."

Cloe chuckled. That was the Thib and, indeed, the father she had known—stubborn, sometimes beyond reason, and steadfast in the belief of his correctness. But she considered it very odd that her father would, without very good reason, break this lifelong pattern shortly before he was killed, asking the Church to take possession. The explanation that he had become more anxious about it as he aged just didn't quite fit. No, he must have known someone else wanted the jar very badly. But who? She shivered in spite of the warmth of the day.

The stretch of highway from Madisonville to Baton Rouge revealed a gradual yet striking change in topography—from the bayous, swamps, and ponds of the North Shore of Lake Pontchartrain to the pine forests of Livingston Parish and ultimately the live oaks of Baton Rouge. Cloe knew that a broad spectrum of native Louisianans lived along the same highway: from cradle Catholics in the south and east to faith-filled Protestants in the midstate communities.

As Cloe gazed out the window at the changing landscape, she wondered about the person or persons behind her father's murder. Right now the potential suspects were as diverse as the geography she passed. Someone seriously wanted something Thib had, possibly the jar. Someone in Madisonville? Maybe someone in this very car! Maybe none of the above. Every time she thought she felt some insight pulling her in a direction, something would happen to create doubt or confusion.

Father Aloysius brought them back to the subject. "Well, the contents of the cave may all be lost. We won't know that for a while, but the good Lord has a way of working within us. I wouldn't be surprised if Thib's humble jar proves to be the most important thing in the cave—or, for that matter, the most important thing found in any cave to date."

Cloe admired the old priest's optimism and his ability to tap into a needed resource of strength and emotion seemingly at will. Still, there was the scientific method to be respected. "We need to manage our hopes and expectations," she said. "We are spinning a little out of control here; we have an old jar with a Greek inscription, possibly with the name Judas Iscariot on it. The jar may be empty, or if not, its contents may long have been reduced to sludge by time and the elements."

"Possibly," said the monsignor, "but the jar is in good condition from external observation, and of all the relics found over the years, there has been only one other that purports to be of or about Judas, if not by Judas, and it is of recent origin, coming to the direct knowledge of scholars by means of a very preliminary translation only in 2006."

"And what document is that?" Cloe asked. This monsignor was ever the fount of mystery.

He turned to her with bright eyes blazing. "The Gospel of Judas Iscariot."

# CHAPTER 12

Cloe took a moment to absorb the monsignor's words: a Gospel of Judas Iscariot. Could this bear on her jar or its contents? How amazing to think of a Gospel by or pertaining to the man reviled as the villain in the Jesus story. Could it be that there was more to the story than had been presented? Every door opened in this mystery revealed two more.

Cloe was eager to hear more of this new Gospel, but they were now entering the campus of LSU. The buildings, she noted, were predominantly of an Italian Renaissance design, marked by red pantile roofs, overhanging eves, and honey-colored stucco. Live oaks with huge draping limbs seemed to be everywhere. Cloe had never actually been here, and she was struck by the sprawling, lovely campus.

"Father Al, this is absolutely beautiful," she said. Cloe saw the priest smile at the familiar abbreviation of his name.

"The research facilities at LSU are excellent," noted the monsignor. "I spoke personally to the dean of the College of Basic Sciences. Since our little project crosses over several disciplines, he promised to have the correct personnel at our initial meeting. He has a conference room reserved for us."

Cloe noted that the monsignor went directly to the business at hand. The rest of their troupe had chatted amiably on the way to Baton Rouge, but the monsignor had spoken only to the purpose of the trip. The old adage that her mother often used about still water running deep came to her.

A few minutes later, they were comfortably seated in a large conference room that could easily accommodate sixteen people. The room spoke of scholarship, age, and great care. The big hardwood table looked handmade of native cypress or oak. There was an ornate serving piece opposite the table that held coffee, food, and various condiments and serving utensils.

Two people Cloe took to be lab technicians had brought the vessel holding the jar into the room, and it now sat at one end of the long table. A group of young scientists was clustered around the container, examining it and talking in muted tones.

An interconnecting door between the conference room and what was obviously someone's personal office opened, and two older, distinguished gentlemen entered. Standing at the head of the table, one of the men who looked to be in his late fifties began to speak. "Welcome to LSU and to Baton Rouge. My name is Michael Broussard. I have the honor of being dean of the College of Basic Sciences here at LSU." The dean had a deep voice and an air about him that instilled confidence.

"Allow me to introduce my colleague, Dr. Ransome Harrell. Dr. Harrell is the dean of the College of Arts and Sciences. Between the two of us, we have command of most of the labs and machine and equipment shops, not to mention the university's electronic facilities. We are also blessed to have our very own supercomputer, which we affectionately refer to as 'Mike' after Mike the Tiger, the mascot of our national-championship athletics programs. Our history, language, and antiquities experts are also here."

Cloe reflected on the way Dean Broussard had said the university was "blessed" to have such a mighty computer. Certainly, such an expression would not be repeated in the secular halls of her university. Yet it seemed perfectly normal and natural in Louisiana even among these scientific elite.

"Good morning and welcome," said Dr. Harrell. "We do appreciate you coming to us with your mystery." Dr. Harrell was short and balding and appeared to be older than his colleague. But he too had a clear-eyed intensity about him.

"Please help yourselves to the pastries and coffee on the sideboard," he said with a smile. "As you can see, the rest of the team is already engaged in the project. We could barely contain them until your arrival. You will meet them as they go through their specific tasks," said Dean Broussard.

Cloe stood up, strode to the end of the table, and shook hands warmly with both scholars, who then took their seats. "We are in your debt for welcoming us to your great facility and making available your research capabilities." She made the necessary introductions and opened the business end of the meeting, much as she was accustomed to doing in Seattle.

"The monsignor has already briefed you on what we know of the source and history of the oil jar. In summary, the oil jar was picked up in Tunisia in 1943 near the Atlas Mountains. It was buried in a hidden cave with many others of its type. The inscription suggests a Greek influence or origin. The translation of the Greek inscription yields, indubitably, the name of the arch traitor of Jesus Christ: Judas Iscariot. As we know, Judas not only betrayed Christ according to the Gospels, but he and his actions became the justification for the persecution of the Jews in many cultures. Why his name would be inscribed in Greek on the exterior of such a vessel is a tantalizing mystery. But there are many other questions to be answered, not the least of which is the age and, certainly, the nature of the jar's contents, if any."

As she spoke, Cloe studied her audience and noted a closed look on Dr. Harrell's face. Glancing around, she saw she was the only woman in the room and wondered briefly if he was unused to female colleagues taking charge of the proceedings.

She continued, "The vessel inscribed in ancient Greek with the name of the betrayer of Christ, found in a cave of this sort and, apparently, being of great age, certainly alerts any scholar to the possibilities. The task of our science will distinguish between what is merely possible and what is true."

"Yes, but we are only concerned with the scientific inquiry," responded Dr. Harrell. "We have absolutely no interest whatsoever in any religious overtones or implications." His manner was stiff and defensive.

Cloe found it interesting that he would make such a bald statement out of the clear blue, particularly after Dean Broussard's comment about the university's "blessings." Perhaps Dr. Harrell was intimidated by Cloe or by the monsignor and his background. First impressions being what they are, Cloe was not entirely sure that she would like working with Dr. Harrell.

"Fine," said Cloe, determined not to let her initial impression and a perhaps random remark interfere with the working relationship between her and an important colleague on the project. "There is also the bizarre circumstance that the only reason I'm here with the jar is that my father was murdered a few days ago, bringing me back to Louisiana for his funeral. Thus the jar has come to me, and I have come to you."

"My goodness," said Dr. Harrell, clearly stunned. "We are so sorry to hear of your loss. We will do everything we can to help."

Cloe noted that Dr. Harrell's concern seemed genuine, but that Dean Broussard said nothing, perhaps believing that Dr. Harrell had spoken for both of them. When she mentioned her father's death, she had seen the monsignor and J.E. both looked closely at her, J.E. with concern and the monsignor with renewed interest.

"What can we do to move the examination of the jar along?" the Vatican's man asked.

"Nothing," responded Dr. Harrell. "We just need your permission to break it open."

# CHAPTER 13

"Break the jar!" exclaimed J.E. "What the hell are you talking about? I thought you people were supposed to be scientists. I could break the jar all by myself." J.E.'s mind had wandered during the introductions, but this had jerked him back to the present.

"J.E., they don't mean to literally break the jar, although sometimes that's the by-product of the first step in such an examination," responded Cloe, who had returned to her seat. She smiled at J.E., her gentle and fierce warrior.

"Quite right, Dr. Lejeune," stated Dr. Harrell. "I have started badly here. What I mean is, I need permission to break the seal on the jar."

Cloe thought about his misstep and wondered whether the good doctor had really bad people skills, as brilliant minds sometimes do, or he was just plain insensitive. Time would tell, she thought. Cloe also noted the acknowledgement of her PhD and realized these gentlemen had thoroughly checked into her background and credentials. She turned to her son and her new friends and saw all were anxious to move forward.

"You have my permission," she responded. "How do you propose to proceed?"

"What we would like to do first," replied Dean Broussard, "is move to the photography lab and carefully photograph the jar. We will outfit you in more appropriate garb for this exercise." He stood up and began to shepherd the various scientists out of the conference room. The technicians carefully lifted the vessel to move it to the photography lab.

He next turned back to Cloe. "Dr. Lejeune, we want you and your colleagues to move through every step with us and to approve everything we do before we do it. Agreed?"

"Absolutely!" she responded.

***

All in all, Cloe thought this initial meeting had gone pretty well. She smiled at the pleasant weather as she and the others left the building for the walk across the LSU quadrangle toward the photo lab. When the Indian summer sunshine bathed her face, she felt like she had almost traveled back to her college days. The quadrangle area was a large courtyard at the intersection of numerous walks and paths from the many college buildings surrounding it. Students walked briskly between classes, chatting and laughing.

For a brief moment Cloe wished she could throw off the weight of the mystery of her father's death and the responsibilities of the day and join the students. Their energy and excitement were contagious, and the canopies of the ancient oaks lining the quad provided a cooling shade. Too soon, they reached the photo lab. There, they donned white lab coats and protective eyewear and were instructed in rudimentary emergency lab procedures.

Cloe thought "photo lab" was a completely inadequate term for this place. The size of the room was difficult to estimate because of the manifold and huge pieces of equipment it contained, along with the computer consoles and monitors located at several stations throughout.

The ceiling was extra high, probably nearing eighteen to twenty feet. Cloe's eyes were immediately drawn to the center of the large room, where a stout table was permanently fixed to the floor. It was constructed of some material which was unusual in her experience as it appeared to be neither wood nor metal. Attached to it were various locking and mounting devices apparently made of the same material as the table. She hadn't seen this setup before and wondered about the purpose and construction. While they had walked over, the vessel containing the jar had been rushed to the lab by the technicians and was now firmly mounted on the table.

"That is our central optical field table," said one of Dr. Harrell's assistants. "It is made of a carbon composite, with a transparent top,

65

that has proved to be almost completely neutral in our photographic analyses. We don't want the table or the mounts interfering with our photographic projects. Also, we want to be able to photograph the bottom of the subject without moving it."

Although the table configuration was new to her, Cloe knew a good bit about this type of photography through her participation in the cataloging of numerous ancient manuscripts in Seattle. However, even her alma mater did not have the range or sophistication of reproduction equipment she was seeing here. She thought that, in the future, she might send her work to LSU for photography and related analysis.

"The cameras and other pieces of analytical equipment are configured to move to the subject rather than vice versa," interjected Dr. Harrell, seeming to read her mind. "In this way we can perform a variety of optical examinations without having to change the position of the subject, whose physical condition can sometimes be quite delicate.

"What we are going to do first, with your permission, is thoroughly photograph the jar through the windows in the container vessel. We will use extremely high-speed, high-quality thirty-five-millimeter film. We will then photograph the jar digitally using an exceedingly high-resolution digital camera that interfaces directly with Mike, our supercomputer.

"The entire episode will be programmed into Mike, and the computer will then conduct the analysis. Of course, this process entails no risk to the subject. Our goal is first to make a record of what we have and then to take a look at the exterior of the jar at a computer resolution beyond the human eye. This process is so detailed, it can even capture fingerprints on some types of surfaces, though the non-glazed, rough exterior of the jar will be a challenge even for Mike. Mike then interprets the images and translates them into something graphic for us. It's really quite amazing."

"Wow," interjected J.E., "as an intelligence officer, I have trained in countries that don't have this level of sophistication."

The visitors gawked at the equipment and awaited the go-ahead signal from Cloe.

"Please proceed, Dr. Harrell," she said. She watched as one of the scientists manipulated a computer terminal, sending the robotically controlled cameras swarming over the jar and its container like football players in a scrum. The equipment snapped, whined, and reeled on top of and around the jar. Lights flashed, and coordinated strobes ignited the scene. The jar was photographed from every angle, including the bottom.

When the commotion ended, there was a silence in the room that seemed to permit only muted conversation. The absence of activity now was as riveting as the whirl of effort had been a moment before. Cloe heard the air conditioner humming faintly.

Finally, Dean Broussard said, "What comes next is extremely interesting. We not only have regular and digital photography here; we also have X-ray, infrared, and ultrasound capabilities, among others. However, we must have your permission to remove the jar from its protective vessel. We cannot get maximum results from these operations unless the jar itself is exposed to the equipment."

J.E., obviously enthralled in the proceedings, piped up. "Let's go!"

Cloe just smiled and asked, "Dr. Harrell, is there any risk to the jar during this segment? My father maintained the jar intact for sixty years. I'd hate to lose it my first week."

"Almost no risk, Dr. Lejeune," responded the doctor. "Believe me, we all have the same interest here."

*Do we?* Cloe could not help but think. But she just nodded to proceed.

The jar was painstakingly freed from its container and secured to the table. Because of the radiation, the group witnessed the process this time from behind a lead-lined partition replete with thick observation windows. Once again, machinery pulsed, hummed, and crisscrossed over the table. X-rays, infrared radiation, and ultrasound were robotically applied and calibrated, and the results collected. The jar glowed with lights that seemed to span the entire spectrum of color and beyond. Finally, that profound silence seized the room again. Once more, the equipment ticked metallically as it cooled. This time there was a distinct smell of ozone in the room. Cloe smiled, half-expecting someone to scream, "It's alive!" However, the modern

HVAC system quickly evacuated the air in the area, and the antiseptic aroma returned.

"Well, that's it for today," said Dean Broussard. "Even the supercomputer will need some time to process the billions of bytes of information that have been collected, and it's been a long day for Mike's human colleagues. The jar and its vessel will be securely stored in our walk-in safe. Best we retire and reconvene tomorrow when we will have a complete report on what's been found."

Cloe saw that J.E. had still been brimming with enthusiasm and now looked disappointed, but she accepted that there was little left to be done today.

"That makes a lot of sense," remarked Cloe. "It has been a long day but, I might add, a very exciting one." It suddenly occurred to her that they had not even talked about overnight accommodations. The day's activities had been so riveting that she had forgotten this detail.

"Goodness, in the excitement, I have completely forgotten to find a place for us to stay. Is there anything near campus?" asked Cloe.

"No need to go off campus," said Dean Broussard, smiling. "We have taken the liberty of booking you into our on-campus facility, the Cook Hotel. I think you will find the accommodations very comfortable. Further, we have booked a private room at the Faculty Club for dinner. I'm sure it's been a while since you've enjoyed a south Louisiana Creole dinner."

"Marvelous," replied Cloe, enormously relieved. "I certainly have the energy for that." Cloe knew that, if nothing else, her home state was justly famous for its hospitality and its magnificent food.

***

The party had agreed to meet at the club at seven o'clock. It was still light, but a stunning sunset was in the making as Cloe, J.E., and the two priests walked the pleasant three or four blocks from the Cook Hotel to the Faculty Club. The air was filled with the scent of fall pine boughs, and the lightning bugs had begun to fire off their visual symphony of cool light flashes. It was a moment that Cloe would soon look back on as the calm before the storm.

The monsignor, Cloe, J.E., and Father Al were just being seated when Dean Broussard and Dr. Harrell entered the private room set aside for them. The room was almost completely candlelit, with the exception of some discreet indirect lighting. A heavy table covered in a white linen tablecloth dominated the intimate room. Portraits of what Cloe took to be past icons of the university tastefully decorated the walls.

Dr. Harrell acknowledged them warmly, a break from his earlier demeanor, and Cloe noted he had a wry smile on his face. Cloe's pulse quickened a bit as she studied the scholar. Something was up. Was it good news or not?

J.E. must have sensed this too. He said, "Dr. Harrell, you look like the cat who has swallowed the canary."

"Indeed," responded the academic with a dramatic pause of which any Shakespearean actor would be justly proud.

"What is it? Have you gotten any of the test results back?" asked J.E. All turned to Dr. Harrell.

"Yes, but what information I have is of only the most preliminary sort, and certainly, what I have been told is by no means conclusive. You will remember that when we left, our supercomputer Mike had just finished the X-ray, infrared, and ultrasound examinations of the jar. Mike had already done the computer-driven photographic study in both film and digital versions. Mike has come up with a couple of very preliminary conclusions. Much more remains, of course, to be done to confirm these findings."

Cloe, half-amused, noted that the scientists imbued the supercomputer with human-like characteristics. Well, they rightfully thought of Mike as a colleague.

"Oh, for goodness sake, Dr. Harrell, what is it? Out with it!" exclaimed Father Al, giving voice to what everyone else was thinking.

Cloe held her breath without realizing she was doing it. She edged to the front of her chair.

"Well, Mike has apparently picked up additional writing on the jar, some of which is so faint it is difficult for the unaided human eye to see. The supercomputer has also concluded that there is something solid in the jar. It's not wine, oil, or any other liquid. Right now it's just an infrared, ultrasound-generated shadow. But X-ray confirms something is there. We don't know if it's just hard sludge or if it's something that has been preserved for these many, many years. Obviously, we have no idea what it is or how old it is."

Cloe exhaled, surprising herself, and briefly gasped for air. "What about the writing?" she asked. "What does the new writing say, and where is it located on the jar?"

"The writing is in two places. There are at least two faint marks on the bottom of the jar, but even Mike is having great difficulty figuring out what these may be. While we may never know what they are, you should look at them—human examination can be more intuitive than Mike's computer logic of ones and zeros. The other is decipherable and is written in ancient Greek, just like the name 'Judas Iscariot,' and is located immediately before that name. Mike thinks it is all one phrase."

"What does it say?" asked Cloe. She had a premonition and felt the small hairs on the back of her neck rise, but she wanted to hear it from the scientist.

"We want you to look at it before we can be sure. You are, after all, the expert."

"Dr. Harrell, what does Mike think it says?" asked Cloe, pointedly. She looked steadily at Dr. Harrell.

"It says 'The Gospel of Judas Iscariot,'" answered the academician.

# CHAPTER 14

With this revelation all eyes turned to the priests.

"What have we tumbled onto?" queried Dr. Harrell.

The monsignor pushed his chair back and looked around and then settled his gaze on Dr. Harrell. "If I understood your report correctly, the only thing we know now that we did not know this morning is that the jar has an ancient inscription *possibly* announcing the 'Gospel of Judas Iscariot.' Isn't that correct?"

"Good heavens, Father ... can't you see the significance of this?" asked the doctor.

"This may advance the scientific inquest, but it is far from proof of anything," responded the cleric.

Cloe's spirits slumped a little. The monsignor certainly had a way of throwing cold water on things. Still, she thought, he was tempering his own excitement.

"Quite right," responded Dr. Harrell. "We also have said this was purely a scientific inquiry with no interest in any religious themes or overtones. But I must say this investigation has turned in an unexpected direction. Should this jar truly contain a written Gospel, possibly authored by or even featuring Judas Iscariot, it would turn the Christian world upside down, would it not?"

"Possibly, although that would depend on its authenticity and its content. As a matter of fact, one version of a Gospel allegedly written by or about Judas Iscariot already exists," replied the monsignor. "Let us begin our meal, and I will tell you what we know."

The monsignor bowed his head and waited. The others did likewise as the monsignor blessed the food and their mission. Even

71

Dr. Harrell assumed a respectful posture, although it was plain that he was unused to such practices.

When the prayer was over, Dean Broussard nodded at the head waiter. A smoking hot chanterelle mushroom bisque was served, together with a Ferrari chardonnay. Warm loaves of crispy French bread were brought in next, and Cloe broke off a chunk, in the Louisiana manner, and slathered it with butter.

Dean Broussard noticed Cloe's enjoyment of the buttered bread and pointed out, "The butter comes straight from the cow, here at our Agricultural Center."

J.E., meanwhile, was trying desperately to rein in the scattered bits of stray bread on the tablecloth and his lap. "Dean Broussard," he said "this is wonderful, but I'm making a terrible mess with all these crumbs."

"Not to worry. Every good south Louisiana host judges the satisfaction of his guests by the amount of bread crumbs left at table. I can see that you are pleased," said the dean.

"Monsignor Roques, pray continue with your story," said Cloe.

Recapping his earlier conversation with Father Al and Cloe, the monsignor explained to the scientists the probable meaning and origin of Judas's name as well as Judas's role in the betrayal of Christ as chronicled in the orthodox Gospels.

"But the Gospels are ambivalent and perhaps in conflict about what happened to Judas after the betrayal at Gethsemane. The Gospel of Matthew says that after Jesus was condemned, Judas was filled with remorse and took the thirty pieces of silver back to the chief priests and elders. Judas told them that he had betrayed innocent blood and that he, Judas, had sinned."

Even though Cloe had heard this in the previous conversation, she continued to be amazed at these details that were laid out plainly in the text of the New Testament.

"This seems to have occurred after Jesus's condemnation but before his crucifixion," continued the monsignor. "Note that Judas reportedly repented the betrayal *not* after Jesus's execution but after the sentence was imposed and before it was carried out. The timing is very important here as it suggests that the death of Jesus Christ was not Judas's intended outcome. As you might imagine, the Jewish officials were completely uninterested in Judas or his remorse at that time since he had served their purpose."

"Fascinating, isn't it?" said Father Al. "If you focus on just the language in Matthew, you could conclude that Jesus's condemnation might not have been the end result that Judas was expecting or had sought." The priest laid down his soup spoon and dabbed his lips with the crisp, snow-white napkin.

"Yes," said the monsignor. "We will return to that theme after we finish with Judas's demise as told in the synoptic Gospels. Matthew says the priests and elders rebuffed Judas, and he flung the pieces of silver down in the sanctuary and went out and hanged himself. The priests were in a quandary as to what to do with the money since in their view it had become 'blood money.' According to Matthew, eventually they used it to buy a potter's field as a place to bury foreigners."

Father Al took up the story now. "Luke's version of the events at Gethsemane and Jesus's arrest is very similar to Matthew's, but the Gospel of Luke contains nothing about Judas's death. The same is true of the Gospel of Mark. There is no mention of the circumstances of Judas's death at all. This has always struck me as odd since Judas's betrayal is so pivotal in the Jesus story."

The monsignor nodded. "The perfidy of Judas is actually the fulfillment of the scriptures that foretold the betrayal of the Lamb. The Gospel of John adds additional details of Jesus's last hours but does not mention the apparent suicide of Judas."

The group paused to absorb the idea that only one of the orthodox Gospels mentions the demise of Judas. Cloe's scientific juices were once again churning. "That seems an absolutely astonishing omission," she said. "If I were a conspiracy theorist instead of ancient languages devotee, I might make something of that. Surely, there must be more."

"There is at least one additional reference to Judas's passing in the accepted books of the Bible," noted the monsignor. "In the Acts of the Apostles it is written by St. Luke that Judas himself used the blood money he received from betraying Christ to purchase a 'field' and that he, Judas, fell headlong and burst open, and all his entrails poured out. When the people of Jerusalem learned of this, they called the field the 'Bloody Acre.'"

"So which is it?" asked Father Al. "Did Judas fling the money back at the priests and elders in a fit of remorse and go out and hang himself, as Matthew writes, leaving the priests to buy the potter's field? Or, as is maintained in the Acts of the Apostles, did Judas survive only to use the blood money to buy the field himself and somehow suffer an ignominious death of disembowelment?"

"Certainly a significant difference in endings for one of the most important figures in the orthodox Gospels," commented the monsignor.

J.E. seemed troubled by something and turned to face the monsignor. "The Acts version makes no sense. How do you fall down in a field and bust open like that? It must be false."

"One has to understand the location of the Bloody Acre, or Hakeldama, as it is called by the Jews. It's on the edge of the Hinnom Valley. Jerusalem itself is located in mountainous terrain. The entirety of Hakeldama was not the flat open space we now think of as a field. Remember, too, people of that era were often buried in caves as opposed to interment in open fields as is more the norm today. This very place exists in the present day, and it is as vertical as it is horizontal. Thus, Judas's death could very well have happened just as Acts says."

The waiters had now laid down a simple endive lettuce salad with an impossibly light oil and vinegar dressing. The dean stated that the vegetables too came from the Ag Center.

"How can we know what really happened?" asked J.E. after a little while. "While we didn't go to church much, I can tell you, while in Iraq, I did some serious scripture reading. There was also a Catholic chaplain who helped me a lot. This seems like such a crucial part of the passion of Christ. Why don't scholars know clearly what happened and, frankly, why it happened? You're casting doubt on the motivations of and, maybe, the actions of the traitor. What's the real truth?"

Cloe blinked at this and said, "J.E., I didn't know you were interested in all this." She silently chastised herself for not doing more to see that J.E. received a better foundation in their faith.

74

"Mom, as they say, there are no atheists in a foxhole," responded J.E. Turning to the monsignor, he repeated, "What's the truth?"

The monsignor paused in thought for a moment and then said, "For that, young sir, circumstances suggest we should immediately turn our attention to the existing Gospel of Judas Iscariot."

# CHAPTER 15

While coffee was served, Cloe thought of her failure to teach much religion to J.E. Yet it seemed his experiences had brought him to the very faith she had been taught. Now she and J.E. were coming to, or maybe back to, the same religious place.

She reflected on all the ideas that had been exchanged and the information she had obtained in just this one day. She imagined the pragmatic Thib saying, "Progress had been made." There was no way she could avoid seeing how they were alike in that respect. Once again her emotions swirled in a painful internal maelstrom. Now at virtually every turn in this quest, she could feel his presence through their similarities. These things, Cloe held in her heart.

She remembered the promise she had made to Thib two days earlier in the lawyer's office: She would find out why the jar was special. And more importantly, she would find out how it was connected to his murder. Someone wanted that jar. Why? With a scientist's patience, she accepted the mystery would unfold at its own speed. She would wait and be there when it did. Although they had just begun the journey, she was optimistic that in time the jar would yield its secrets.

"Tell us then," she said to the clerics. "What's in this Gospel of Judas you're talking about?"

Father Al replied, "Well, since the jar came to us, I have been reading up on the topic of Judas. From what I've learned, the existing version of this so-called Gospel was discovered in the 1970s in Egypt by a tomb robber turned amateur archaeologist. The man was not interested in the discovery except for the possibility of some profit."

"Sounds like a regular Indiana Jones," quipped J.E.

"Yes, yes … to be precise," said the monsignor, "it was discovered near Beni Masah, Egypt, as part of a leather-bound papyrus set of documents known as the Codex Tchacos. Written in an ancient Egyptian language, Coptic, it has been reliably carbon-dated as originating in the third to fourth century AD."

Once again Cloe noted that both priests, particularly the monsignor, were very knowledgeable about these rather obscure places and esoteric details. Perhaps all priests were. She wondered.

"So there already is a Gospel of Judas Iscariot," said J.E.

"Yes, there is," responded Father Al. "It only became known and was made available to scholars some twenty years after its discovery because its owners tried to maximize the codex's value on the black market. Numerous efforts were made to sell all or part of the codex, but at the asking price there were no buyers. Suffice it to say the codex's travels and history are the stuff of a novel. It suffered a rather shabby, harrowing journey during which it deteriorated badly."

The monsignor continued, "No one knows what might have been learned if the codex and the Judas Gospel it contained had been delivered into competent hands when found. As it is, some parts of the Gospel are largely intact, but many are in fragments. Scholars have made heroic efforts to assemble as many of the fragments as possible, but there remain pieces that may never be made part of the whole."

"I wonder what the existing Judas Gospel can tell us about our vessel," remarked Cloe. She hadn't heard anything yet that might establish a link.

"Because of the poor condition of the text, it has taken years since the Judas Gospel was put in the hands of scholars to reach the point where we have a reasonable working translation. That occurred in about 2006," said the monsignor. "But there is a formidable difference of opinion as to what exactly it does say because it has numerous gaps, and the translation of some of the old Coptic words is uncertain for linguistic and technical reasons."

"I'm anxious to hear something about its content," said Cloe. "Perhaps knowing something about it will help us better understand what we may find in the jar."

"Possibly. There may be a connection between our jar and the available Judas Gospel, or maybe none at all. We won't know until we see what's in the jar," concluded the monsignor.

"This is all a bit confusing," said Dr. Harrell. "We need some way to distinguish this existing Gospel from whatever we may find in the jar. After all, we now know the legend on the jar reads 'The Gospel of Judas Iscariot.'"

"Quite so. Why not simply refer to the existing Judas Gospel as the 'Coptic' version?" suggested Father Al.

"Good, that will keep things straight," agreed Cloe, glancing at Dean Broussard to gauge his reaction to the conversation. She noted his eyes seemed hooded—guarded, she thought—and he was scanning the room with disinterest, as if he had moved on from the discussions.

Odd, she thought, but when his eyes met hers, the dean quickly interjected. "Why don't we all have some bread pudding with bourbon sauce?"

Laughing, J.E. said, "Don't tell me. The bourbon was distilled right here on the premises."

There was laughter all around, and Dean Broussard replied, "Well, that is one thing I hope is not homegrown here at the university."

Cloe was still pondering the dean's response and mood when she heard J.E. ask, "What's next for tomorrow, Dr. Harrell?"

"We have finished phase 1. Phase 2 will include an attempt to open the jar. This is the most dangerous phase because it is always possible the jar or whatever is in it could be damaged or even destroyed in the process. Certainly, every effort will be taken to avoid that."

Although she wanted to hear more about the Coptic Judas Gospel, Cloe recognized that the evening was drawing to a close. She began to inch her chair back, preparing to leave, and said, "Monsignor, I'd like more on the Coptic Gospel as we move forward."

"Absolutely," he replied. "We have plenty of time."

Father Al moved to stand too. "Perhaps it's best that we call it a night and start fresh tomorrow morning. Good night all, and thanks for the hospitality and the wonderful evening." Once again, he had expressed what everyone was feeling.

Cloe and her group left by the rear exit, out through the veranda at the back of the Club and into the parking lot. In the now-darkening evening, the waning moon above was still nearly full, clearly displaying the man in the moon. Her mother would always point out the "man" to her, claiming his expression was one of surprise or, perhaps, horror at what he could see on the earth. As a child, Cloe had been amazed and delighted by this sight on the river and her mother's story. At the end of this tale, her mother would always wonder aloud what kind of God could think of a detail like that.

The academicians had departed through the front entrance and turned toward their respective offices.

The two priests chatted like old friends and trailed behind J.E. and Cloe as the group struck out in the direction of the Cook Hotel. The sidewalks here were broad, and a few students hurried along, probably headed to the numerous dorms in the area. Cloe noticed the glow of the LSU stadium lights against the sky in the distance. The air was warm and moist and smelled wonderfully of sweet shrub, one of the Indian summer essences that she had nearly forgotten. She and J.E. walked along the road down a bit of a grade and onto a small bridge that crossed a drainage canal. Along with the priests behind them, they seemed to be the only people about in this area.

"A couple of days ago, we were in Seattle going about our daily routine, me working on my writings and you awaiting orders. It's funny how life changes in a heartbeat," Cloe mused. "Today we are enmeshed in a two-thousand-year-old mystery, literally one of biblical proportions. Dad is gone and buried, and we're busy trying to find out about an ancient relic he brought back from Africa more than sixty years ago. Then there is the mystery of how Thib died … and why. It makes you wonder what might happen tomorrow."

"Weird, all right … but tonight's not even over yet," quipped J.E. with a sardonic grin.

Just then a great roar of voices arose somewhere behind them, swelling, and as they both turned back to look for the source, they noticed a dark vehicle headed swiftly down the short grade directly toward them.

"What the hell?" shouted J.E., who moved immediately to his mother.

At the same time, one of the priests screamed, "Watch out—the car is out of control!"

Time slowed down to a matter of heartbeats, and Cloe saw the long vehicle hurtling directly toward her as its lights grew almost impossibly large and bright. Adrenaline spiked, and her stomach dropped, but she was frozen in the dazzling insect-like headlight beams. Her legs were encased in concrete. She could barely breathe, much less move. Cloe began to pray.

The car's engine roared as its rpm spooled up, and the killer vehicle accelerated, relentlessly pursuing its lethal course toward them. There was no stopping it, and in a matter of seconds, it would crush her and J.E. against the stout metal railing wrapping around the bridge. Cloe prayed harder and prepared herself for the worst. She cried out for J.E.

The hot oil smell of the engine and the heat wave the car pushed ahead of it rolled over them. The car itself was just behind. Cloe felt as if she were in a dream where she could not move to save herself. But this was not a dream.

The car was now so close that for a fraction of a second, her senses heightened by impending doom, she glimpsed the driver's face over the steering wheel, and the sight sent shudders of revulsion through her—it was a face with lifeless, dead eyes. Shark eyes.

"Oh my God!" she screamed.

Just before impact she felt a strong arm around her waist, and the next thing she knew, she was weightless for a moment in midair. Then she and J.E. were dropping like rocks. J.E. had grabbed her, and they had both flown over the rail and off the bridge away from the car. She and J.E. hit the slanting surface of the canal's dirt bank just as the black car struck the bridge railing where they had stood only a moment before. The impact was thunderous. The bridge itself shook as if it were coming down.

Just before they hit the ground, J.E. yelled, "Roll!"

As they rolled and tumbled down the bank, Cloe saw alternately the moon and the dirt, the moon and the dirt, and then just the dirt wall of the bank. At the bottom they splashed into the ankle-deep water and came to rest.

They lay there for a moment, collecting their wits, and heard the powerful car back up and roar off to the south. Tires burned in the death-dealing vehicle's mad attempt to escape, and the smell of scorched rubber filled the air. As the sound of the fleeing car diminished, they heard the priests shouting and, apparently, running toward them.

Father Al appeared on the bridge, looked over the railing, and yelled, "Cloe? J.E.?"

The monsignor never stopped; he vaulted over the railing and landed like a cat on the sloping surface of the bank. The second priest shimmied down the bank also to come to their aid. Despite his age, Cloe saw that Father Al could move quickly when he needed to. The pair helped Cloe and J.E. to their feet and back up to the bridge. Cloe was trembling despite herself.

"Mom, are you all right?" said J.E., holding her.

"Yes, I think so," replied Cloe. "What was that?"

Father Al, out of breath by this time, gasped in between phrases as he said, "Cloe, J.E. saved your life. If he had not grabbed you and leaped into the canal, that darned fool in the car certainly would have run you down. Obviously, someone had way too much to drink at the pep rally."

"Was that the roar we heard?" asked J.E. "That's the only reason we looked back and saw the car."

"Yes, the LSU/Ole Miss game is tomorrow in Tiger Stadium. The pep rally the night before is a longstanding tradition, but I'm afraid some students go overboard."

"So," J.E. said reflectively, "you think the driver was just some drunken student ..." It was a statement rather than a question.

"Certainly," said Father Al. "What else could it be?"

Cloe faced them all, her fear turning to anger as she said, "That was no student! I saw him for only a split second this time, but I have seen that driver before."

# CHAPTER 16

After the incident on the bridge, they had called Dean Broussard. He had jumped into his car and arrived as they were still trying to clean up and settle themselves. He urged them to go immediately to the campus police and report what had happened. Cloe and J.E. agreed, but the monsignor was of another opinion.

"Perhaps it was nothing more than an accident. You will only spend valuable time at police headquarters, and in the end it will come to nothing."

"Monsignor, I certainly don't want to make my second trip to a police department since coming back to Louisiana to bury my father, but I tell you, I think I've seen the driver before, maybe twice," asserted Cloe. She related to them the events at the airport and the grave site.

"Well, you should certainly tell the police about this, but you are not even sure it was the same man," the monsignor responded.

Cloe thought this an odd response from someone in such an authoritarian system as the Catholic Church. Maybe this was just indicative of his own experiences with police authorities. But once again she had cause to question the monsignor and his reactions to events. She remained unsure about him.

"That's not showing much confidence in our fine campus establishment," responded Dean Broussard. "If nothing else, it was a hit-and-run, and in the United States we are required by law to report it. Besides, it's possible that someone in the car may be injured and need help."

"Perhaps so," agreed the monsignor finally, reluctantly.

J.E. concurred. "It's our duty. We have to go to the authorities." He thereby closed the door on further discussion.

But when they began to load into the car to drive to the campus police office, the monsignor demurred. "Sorry, I was engaged in conversation with Father Al, and I did not see what led up to the actual collision, so I do not think I can be of any assistance," he said. "Besides, I must call and report the events of the day to my superiors. With your permission, I will also check with the authorities in Madisonville to see if there is any further information on your father's death. I will say good night and continue on to the hotel."

"Well, certainly, Monsignor, if you think that's best," Cloe responded, thinking the monsignor a bit presumptuous. "We will meet you at the lab in the morning ... say nine o'clock. Would that work, Dean Broussard?" asked Cloe.

"Absolutely," responded the dean.

"So be it," said the monsignor, waving as he headed off on foot toward the hotel.

The drive took only five minutes in spite of the stragglers from the now-completed pep rally who seemed to be everywhere.

Soon they were sitting in the concrete block, pillbox-like structure that served as the headquarters of the LSU Campus Police as the friendly young officer took their statements. Desks and chairs were of the hard wooden variety of indeterminable age. Definitely bureaucrat chic.

The predominant color in the office was something with way too much yellow to be considered an earth tone. Lighting in the building was supplied by harsh overhead fluorescent fixtures. A faint hum and an odor of ozone persisted in the background. Cloe wondered whether the atmosphere was the result of some misguided study on the most uncomfortable, unfriendly environment that could be created short of a medieval torture chamber. Certainly this must be intimidating to miscreants, but what of the poor officers and employees themselves? However, as she glanced around, Cloe saw that they all seemed oblivious to the surroundings. Proof, she ruminated, that human beings can get used to almost anything.

After introductions by Dean Broussard, the chief of police listened carefully to what had happened at the bridge. Father Al, Cloe, and J.E. all related the sequence of events, including the monsignor's opinion on the likely cause.

Listening closely, the chief remarked that the monsignor might be right that it was nothing more than some student mischief that had narrowly avoided a very bad end.

"But Chief, let me add to what you have heard. I believe I have seen the driver before," said Cloe, and she proceeded to tell him about the incident at the airport and what she thought she had seen at the cemetery.

"Well, that may be a horse of a different color," replied the chief noncommittally, but studying her closely. "We'll keep our eyes open for all possible scenarios."

Cloe suspected that he might not fully believe her story, and now she wondered whether the monsignor had been right that nothing would come of all this. "Well, you have the best description of the vehicle we can provide. If you're finished with us, we had best get back to the hotel and get some rest. We have an important day tomorrow."

"Yes, of course," said the chief. "We'll let you know if anything develops."

On the way out, Father Al fell into step with Cloe. He whispered, "I know what you're thinking, Cloe, but I suspect the monsignor is very concerned about this incident. Coupled with the possibilities associated with the jar, one wonders if this could be a random incident. I believe J.E. may share that concern. Best we all be on the alert. Even now, I suspect the monsignor may well be on his satellite phone with his superiors. Father Antonio Sigliori, who serves as Vicar General, has responsibility for Vatican field operations. I feel certain that the Vatican and the monsignor will respond to this incident with their own resources."

Cloe took this in, nodding quietly, and then gravitated to the heroic actions of her son. Gosh, what a kid. She would call Uncle Sonny tonight, even though it was late, and tell him. Not only had she learned that her father was a bona fide war hero, but she had experienced her son completely disregarding his own safety in order to pull her from grievous injury, if not death, on the bridge. What sort of men were these whose blood flowed in her veins?

As they were clambering out of the car at the hotel, Dean Broussard's cell phone rang.

The dean glanced at the screen, looked at his passengers, and gestured to them to wait. He hit the speaker button on his cell phone.

"Dean, this is Chief Labrouso at Campus Police," the voice said.

"Yes, Chief?"

Cloe and her comrades bent over and listened intently.

"Dean, we think we found the hit-and-run car … Can you and your colleagues meet me at the rear lot of the old Ag Center? Five minutes?"

Five minutes later, the little group stood in a dark parking lot looking at a large black vehicle with substantial damage to the front end. Cloe thought that the car looked almost as formidable and menacing sitting there in the parking lot as it had rushing down the incline toward her.

"That's definitely the car," said J.E. "What do you know about it? Did it crap out on the driver? Did anyone see anything?"

"No," said the chief. "Although the front end is damaged, the car runs fine. It was abandoned."

"Abandoned?" repeated Father Al, sounding mystified. "Why would a student abandon such a vehicle if it's operable?"

"Good question," said the chief. "But it's not a student's vehicle unless the student is also a car thief. This vehicle was reported stolen a few hours ago. It belongs to a dentist in mid-city."

"Chief, what do you make of this?" asked Father Al. "Why would someone steal a car, come to the pep rally, get drunk, and almost run down our friends?"

"It doesn't make a lot of sense," agreed the chief. "We found nothing in the car that would indicate a student and no beer cans or evidence of drink at all. In fact, we found nothing—not even any obvious evidence of fingerprints—although the lab will tell us more after they sweep the car. It looks like whoever used it wore gloves and may have wiped everything down when they abandoned the vehicle.

We don't think whoever used this car was a student or attended the pep rally."

Cloe noticed that J.E. had gone quiet and appeared to be pondering what he was hearing.

"I never thought it was a student in the first place," asserted Cloe, quietly. She was beginning to get an icy feeling in the marrow of her bones as she listened to the chief tell what he knew.

"An accident is no longer our working hypothesis, Dr. Lejeune. As I have said, we may know a lot more once the police lab looks at the car in detail."

"If not an accident, what do you think it was?" asked Father Al.

The chief said softly, "Based on the condition of the car and Dr. Lejeune's possible prior contact with the driver, along with the strange circumstances, we cannot exclude the possibility it may have been an intentional act … a hit."

# CHAPTER 17

As this disturbing possibility sank in, Cloe heard the chief say that he wanted their entire group back at headquarters first thing the next morning, including, he said, the monsignor.

"I don't care if the monsignor has an audience scheduled with the pope himself; he had better be in my office in the morning," the chief emphasized.

"Chief," said Cloe, "we have an enormous amount of important work to accomplish tomorrow. Can we postpone this a day or two?"

"I'm afraid not, Dr. Lejeune. We have our work to do as well, and this investigation trumps whatever you have to do until we have a better handle on what's happening. Between now and tomorrow morning, we will process the car carefully and consult all our databases on possible suspects, motives, and information. Perhaps we'll have something for you when you come in. If you please, may we see you at nine o'clock?"

Cloe considered this polite request. Of course it was not a request. But it had been said with such tact that she marveled at the manners of the officer. This was the way of the folk in Louisiana. "Certainly," she responded. Then she looked to Dean Broussard and said, "Please defer the testing until we get through this matter and are able to rejoin you."

There was little to do now but face the realities of the hour.

\*\*\*

Cloe hung up the phone in her hotel room after talking to Uncle Sonny. How proud he had been after hearing of J.E.'s actions on the bridge. He had wanted to jump in his old truck right away and rush up to Baton Rouge, but she had been able to dissuade him. There was really nothing he could do. She had promised he could come up the next day if necessary. The old man's interest and concern touched her deeply.

Just before they rang off, he had said, "Clotile, the chief here has run the killer's fingerprints through the FBI database and has come up with a tentative identification. He's a professional thief and sometime professional killer. Someone definitely hired him to steal something from Thib or to kill him. There's nothing beyond that."

"But Uncle," she replied, "did dad have any enemies like that?"

"Nobody that I know of," whispered the old man.

"What could it be?" she said to her uncle, knowing she had two mysteries to solve. But everything in her experience told her it had to be connected to the jar.

Before making the call, Cloe had talked for a while with J.E. about the events of the evening. Then J.E. had departed for his room, saying he had some research he wanted to do.

She now felt very alone and lonely. She reflected that these feelings were not necessarily the same thing. Often she had been alone, but rarely had she felt lonely unless her thoughts had turned to her father or mother. Her thoughts now dwelled on Marie Louise and Thib. God, she missed her mother, gone for almost a quarter of a century. Did time really dull the pain of loss? she wondered. Maybe not, at least not between mother and daughter.

And what of her father? He had been dead only a few days but had been lost to her for the same quarter-century. Murdered. And now someone may have attempted to kill her and J.E. She began to cry softly. As exhaustion overtook her, she began to drift off into blessed sleep. The last conscious thought she had was that she would learn the secrets of the jar. She would find out who killed her father—and quickly, now that she knew she and J.E. were in danger. Nothing, absolutely nothing, would stop her.

***

"What the hell is going on here?" asked the chief angrily. He had gathered representatives of the sheriff's department and the Baton Rouge City Police in the conference room at headquarters. This ad hoc task force had been at it since dawn.

"Where the hell is this Monsignor Roques? Last night I specifically asked that you all be present this morning, including the monsignor." It was apparent the chief was not accustomed to being disregarded. The courtesy of the night before was gone.

"We understand," said J.E., "but when we called the monsignor this morning, he didn't answer. We went to his room, but we couldn't find him. He wasn't anywhere on the hotel property. We thought it best to come here and report the situation."

The police officers had had similar results. The hotel desk clerk had confirmed that the monsignor had left the hotel in a great hurry. He had not even taken his luggage.

"What we know is that the monsignor caught a cab to the Baton Rouge airport. For some reason he did not take his own car and driver. We're checking the cab stands there as well as the airlines and the car rental companies. Don't worry, Chief … we'll find him," stated the deputy.

Cloe saw the veins beginning to bulge on the chief's neck, and she nodded at J.E., who was also observing the situation. There were more important things than the whereabouts of the monsignor.

"Chief," asked J.E., "what else have you learned since we were together last night? Is there anything new on the car or the assailants?"

His focus diverted for the moment, the chief said, "We haven't learned much new information, but we've confirmed what we thought last night. We now know there were no prints and that the car was wiped clean where it was left. There is nothing to indicate student involvement, and in fact, a witness walking a dog in the area where the vehicle was abandoned reports he saw two heavyset men exit the car and enter a parked vehicle. They drove slowly off to the south. The witness said he thought nothing of it until he got the e-mail flash this morning—LSU has a local network system to let us notify students and faculty of security alerts and law enforcement investigations."

The sheriff's plainclothes detective said, "We concur with the preliminary conclusion of the campus police. It looks as if this was an intentional act by people who appear to know what they are doing. Dr. Lejeune, these people were possibly after you, and you should act with extreme caution until they are caught."

"Absent further information, at this point the real questions become who and why," said the police department detective. "We know the 'what' of the thing. Someone was trying to harm some member of your group, most likely Dr. Lejeune and her son."

"It's really hard for me to understand someone wanting to harm J.E. or me," said Cloe.

Father Al observed, "We could hardly present a more benign group for such maliciousness. I'm a parish priest in a small parish in Madisonville, and while we do make mistakes, we do not usually develop mortal enemies. Dr. Lejeune is a professor of ancient languages in Seattle, and her son, J.E., is on military leave. Even so, neither I nor the monsignor was the apparent target. Assuming these people knew what they were doing, as you say, Cloe, J.E., or both were the targets."

"Most likely," responded the city police detective. "The car deliberately passed you and the monsignor, apparently focused solely on the Lejeunes. Consequently, we are working on the angle that one or both of them were the potential killer's targets."

"But why?" asked Cloe. "I haven't lived in this state for over two decades and hardly know anyone here. The only reason I'm in Baton Rouge and at LSU at all is the jar."

Events had sped by so swiftly that she had not really had time to connect the dots, but there they were. Someone had gone after Thib and the jar, thinking he had it. Now they were after her and J.E.

"The jar," said Dr. Harrell. "How could that be? Very few people know you are here or know anything about the jar. In fact, virtually everyone who knows anything about the jar either is in this room or is staff that has been with me for years. Even they have little or no idea of the possible significance of the jar."

Cloe, beginning to seriously ache from muscles unused to jumping off bridges, thought about this and said quietly, "There is only one person who knows everything but who is a complete newcomer to us." Incidents were now clicking into a pattern in her mind: the man's mysterious appearance and his encyclopedic knowledge of her and all things surrounding the jar; his strange reluctance to go to police headquarters to tell what he knew; and now his peculiar disappearance.

"The monsignor!" said Dean Broussard excitedly.

"Yes," said J.E., "the monsignor." At that moment J.E.'s cell phone rang, and he glanced at the screen.

The chief replied, "Take it in the hall if you want to step out."

J.E. did so and then reentered the room after just a few moments. "That was a friend in US army intelligence. We went to school together and have stayed in touch. I called him last night. He used his contacts to check out this monsignor. He ran him through the Defense Department, State, and FBI computers. He even checked with the Foreign Service office of the Vatican."

"Good, and what can you tell us of Monsignor Albert Roques?" asked the sheriff's detective.

J.E. looked grim. "There is no Monsignor Albert Roques!"

# CHAPTER 18

The detective from the sheriff's office studied J.E. as if unsure how much he should reveal. Finally he said, "That checks with what we know. This morning we ran the monsignor, as well as each of you, through our databases as well as Interpol, and we came up with zip, nada, nothing on this monsignor. Not a shadow or a ripple. The man does not exist. We were hoping to find out something about him from you today."

The police all turned to Cloe, J.E., and Father Al to assess their reaction to this news. Stony-faced silence followed as they awaited some credible explanation.

"Father Al, how can that be?" asked Cloe. "You said you called in the monsignor when Thib asked you to help protect the jar."

"No, no … what I said was that I called the Church. I simply used the contact information that the monsignor's predecessor had given Father Gillespie. They sent the container to preserve the jar and said someone would contact me. When the monsignor showed up, I assumed that he was from the Church … from the Vatican. But I never asked for identification or anything like that. Perhaps I should have. There must be some logical explanation."

"All right," said Cloe, a bit testily, "it appears you don't know any more about this enigmatic man than we do." Now she was wondering what else they had accepted at face value that they should have questioned.

Father Al chuffed. "Well, you take certain situations on faith to some degree. He had all the accoutrements of the clergy, so I—probably erroneously—accepted him without question. Frankly, I don't have much experience with this sort of thing. It never occurred to me that a person in a cassock claiming to have come from the Vatican to investigate a two-thousand-year-old religious relic might be an imposter. Just saying this now makes me feel old and stupid." The priest stopped, paused, and then slumped back in his chair. "Cloe, I'm so sorry."

The chief said softly, "Dr. Lejeune, you mentioned the jar just before we were diverted by questions as to the monsignor's identity. Why don't you tell us more about it?"

In the space of about fifteen minutes, Cloe, with the assistance of Dean Broussard, filled in the police on what they knew of the jar. Father Al supplied some of the historical background.

"The jar is the only reason I'm here at LSU," concluded Cloe.

"We are aware of your father's death, Dr. Lejeune," said the sheriff's detective. "We have been in touch with the Madisonville police."

"Then you know that the police there think the murderer was a professional thief and killer," replied Cloe, now fully understanding the significance of the fact that the only thing missing from her father's house was the jar, which had not been there when the killer broke in. Could it be? She did not want to believe that her father could have been killed and that she and J.E. were in danger because of the jar. Still, there it was. "Chief, the jar is connected somehow with all this. It has to be."

"So," said the chief, "this is why you said you had such important work to do. This might explain why the assailants were interested in you and J.E. The jar could be the answer to a lot of questions."

"Yes," responded Cloe. "It might even explain why my father was killed. It can't be a coincidence that my father was murdered a few days ago and, last night, an attempt on my life and J.E.'s life was made. If it had been successful, that would have left only Uncle Sonny. I'm beginning to wonder if someone is willing to kill my whole family for this cursed jar. We need to get back in the lab, open the jar, and learn its secrets, if it holds any. If not, it's all moot anyway."

"My guess is that the people in the car last night didn't think the matter moot," said the plainclothes detective. "But we need to have answers to the mystery of the monsignor. Who is he? Where is he? And does he exist at all as Monsignor Roques?"

A booming voice called out from the open doorway. "He most assuredly does exist, and he is just what he has said he is."

All eyes snapped to the door, and there stood the monsignor with two other men. The strangers were broad-shouldered and of medium height and build, totally unremarkable in appearance. The monsignor ordered one to post himself outside the door, and the other took up a position inside the conference room facing the outer door. As usual, the monsignor seemed to seize command as if by birthright.

"Monsignor!" cried Cloe. "What ... ?" Before she could say more, the policemen jumped up and began to move toward the monsignor, with the apparent intent to restrain and possibly arrest him.

"Gentlemen!" shouted the dean. "The monsignor has obviously voluntarily returned here, so I request that you hear him out. Monsignor, please take a seat and kindly explain yourself and your baffling actions."

The policemen muttered and grumbled but settled back down in their seats. Cloe noticed that J.E.'s attention was riveted on the man in the room who had arrived with the monsignor. He was studying him carefully. Even as the man assumed his position, Cloe herself thought that had the dean not intervened, he and the other man might have been prepared to leap forward and do whatever might be necessary to defend the monsignor. An ugly scene had been averted.

The chief said, "Sir, we are waiting, and our patience is very thin."

The monsignor looked around at the forces arrayed against him, but there was no trace of fear or undue concern in his steel-gray eyes. Indeed, he snatched control of the room with an alacrity that Cloe could hardly believe.

"If I may, let me begin my explanation at the point at which you last saw me at the bridge," began the monsignor. "After I left you, I headed back to the hotel. By the time I reached my room, I had gone over everything in my mind several times, and my concern over the situation had grown. What might have initially appeared to be a drunken accident had taken on a more ominous face in my mind. Our circumstances and our mission are, to say the least, highly unusual. I immediately called the Madisonville police and learned what you now know about the thief and your father's murder. And now a potentially lethal accident for you and J.E. after the evident murder of your father a few days earlier—this stretches the fabric of coincidence beyond possibility, so an accident hypothesis is just not credible. I telephoned the Vatican and reported the situation to my superiors, specifically to Father Antonio Sigliori, who is extremely knowledgeable in matters of this nature."

J.E. said crisply, "Whoever you are, you can drop the Vatican thing. They've never heard of you. I confirmed that through military intelligence." J.E. was now standing and facing the monsignor.

Out of the corner of her eye Cloe could see one of the monsignor's men edging toward J.E. But J.E. seemed prepared to press the issue.

"We've had similar negative results through police channels," stated the detective from the sheriff's office. "You can dispense with the pretense and tell us the truth."

The monsignor studied J.E. with kind eyes. "Young sir, ever the diligent soldier … I admire you so much, and I know your mother is so proud. But you must learn this. Not every piece of information is available, and not every secret may be learned, particularly when dealing with a timeless institution such as the Vatican.

"Only four people in the world know of my true identity and of my relationship to the Papacy: His Holiness himself; his private secretary; the Vicar General, Father Anton; and the archbishop of New Orleans. The latter was informed by the pope's secretary since I would be under his jurisdiction and his protection while in Louisiana."

"Monsignor, or whatever your name is, that's an interesting story, but it sounds like more bull, if you will pardon my doubting attitude," said the city cop.

J.E. looked at the monsignor and said, "Why all the cloak and dagger?"

"J.E., what I do could have a profound impact upon the Church. I study bodies of evidence which may prove or disprove scripture sometimes, depending on one's point of view. What's in the jar, in the wrong hands, with a biased interpretation, might provide ammunition to damage or bring down the Church. Whatever the truth, the Church wants the facts carefully gathered and presented for all to see. Thus, I operate somewhat clandestinely until I have all the information."

Cloe continued, "What proof do you have of what you say?" Although she had had her doubts, somehow Cloe wanted to believe this man.

The monsignor reached into the sleeve of his cassock to some hidden pocket and withdrew a handwritten note. The material on which the note was written was either real or effectively replicated vellum. He approached the assembled doubters and handed it not to the police but to Father Al.

Father Al scanned the note quickly and sat back heavily in his chair. He crossed himself, blinked, and handed the note to the chief, who likewise read it.

Father Al said, "I believe this man is who he says he is, and he represents the pope in what he does."

"What is the letter, and what does it say?" asked J.E., still the doubting Thomas.

"It is a personal letter from Benedict himself in his own hand on papal letterhead, with the pope's personal seal affixed, providing credentials for this man," responded Father Al. "There can be little doubt." The old priest mopped his forehead with a handkerchief.

"Father, with all due respect, he may be a con man, and this may be a clever forgery simply furthering his game, whatever it is," stated the chief.

"Unlikely," replied the priest. "Virtually any Catholic cleric would know the pope's hand and his seal and, as important, would recognize the power of his pen. The paper, the seal, the pope's script. These cannot be easily replicated by any man. I believe the monsignor is what and who he says he is."

The monsignor himself spoke next. "Chief, I believe you know the archbishop personally, do you not?" The monsignor had also done his homework.

"Yes, we were in school together years ago and have kept in touch from time to time."

"Good, I insist that you call him immediately."

"Monsignor, or whatever your name is, you are not in a position to insist on anything. I'm in charge here, and the archbishop is much too busy for this type of thing. It would be an impertinent imposition on our friendship," the chief replied. But he was beginning to look at the monsignor with something approaching caution, if not more.

"I assure you the archbishop will welcome the call. On direct orders of His Holiness, if you do not make the call immediately, the archbishop will depart New Orleans and walk through that door in an hour and a half to verify all I have said," retorted the monsignor.

This statement sucked all the air out of the room. The chief picked up his phone and dialed the archbishop's confidential number. Ten minutes later, the archbishop had verified, in every detail, the bona fides of the monsignor. The police had accepted the monsignor's credentials, and the chief had asked him to continue with his account of what had happened after his return to the hotel.

"As I have said, I reported to my superiors, in this case to the private secretary of His Holiness as well as to Father Anton. The Vatican was extremely concerned with the possible implications of the situation and dispatched a papal jet last night to bring help and security to my friends here and for the jar. This is why I went to the airport this morning, to pick up these gentlemen plus their equipment. I needed a van for everything, so I took a cab to the airport and rented a cargo van. It is of utmost importance to the Vatican that our little group be properly protected and that the jar be thoroughly, scientifically investigated so the truth can be known."

"What do you mean, 'security'?" questioned the sheriff's detective.

"I mean just that … the Vatican has provided four Swiss Guards from the pope's private security force to help us. As you may know, the Swiss Guard has served as the pope's personal bodyguards since the year 1506. They are sworn by sacred oath to give their very lives, if necessary, in the service of the Holy See."

Cloe was staggered by this announcement—the Swiss Guard, for crying out loud. First the Vatican sends the monsignor and then the personal letter from the pope and the archbishop. Now the Swiss Guard. What next? For about the tenth time this morning, she wondered what in the world she had gotten involved in.

"Those two guys are Swiss Guards to the pope?" remarked J.E., marveling. "Swiss Guards are some of the most highly trained and dedicated military in the world. They are trained to handle anything. They come under the formal military classification of very bad asses," he concluded wryly.

"Do they come here armed?" asked the chief.

"Certainly," responded the monsignor directly. "The two here and the two who are now guarding the jar are well armed and very able to take care of us and themselves."

"That breaks about a dozen laws in Louisiana," said the chief, "not to mention federal laws. For Christ's sake, this is a school and a zero-tolerance zone for weapons except for duly authorized police."

"We will need their weapons, and they will be placed under arrest," said the city police detective.

Cloe watched the Swiss soldier for reaction, but he stood his post like a rockslide in a pass. Yet events once again seemed headed toward some confrontation.

The monsignor nodded to the guard, who stepped forward, snapped a respectful salute, and laid a passport and a litany of other papers before the chief. It seemed that they had come prepared for just this turn of events.

The monsignor said, "I think you will find that this guard and each of the others is a diplomatic representative to the United States from the Holy See at the Vatican, a sovereign nation, bearing the proper credentials including the right to possess their weapons. As such they are completely beyond your laws, not subject to arrest, and free to help us do what we came here to do—unlock the secrets of the jar."

The monsignor stood and faced the police, who were staring at the papers, powerless to act. "Now," he said firmly, "if we may take our leave, we will proceed to our business."

# CHAPTER 19

At last they were headed back to the lab. The police had had many more questions, which had taken the rest of the morning. In spite of the challenge he had issued to the authorities, the monsignor had consented to stay and assist them in any way he could. He had been extremely patient and had answered every question until finally the police were talked out, if not completely satisfied.

Dean Broussard had suggested that the group grab a quick lunch before the actual work of the day began. Father Al steered them to Tiger Town just north of the campus, an area of student housing and various restaurants, bookstores, and other student-oriented businesses.

With their guards flanking them, the group walked up the incline of what at one time might have been the natural bank of the Mississippi River. The great river was now a considerable distance to the west, hemmed in by man-made levees.

The party passed twin mounds of earth of some significant size sandwiched between the street and several parking lots. Cloe had heard of the famous LSU Indian Mounds but had never actually seen them.

Dean Broussard saw her interest. "Amazing, aren't they? The facts about the mounds are even more astounding. A few years ago we did some coring and carbon-dated the results. The mounds date back more than five thousand years, putting them in the Meso-Indian or Archaic period. They are part of an eight-mound complex built in a sequence throughout Louisiana. All the mounds in the complex were constructed at the same time and have certain common, unique characteristics. They are the oldest such mounds in the Western

Hemisphere and are now protected by law. They've been put on the National Register of Historical Places."

The group passed a cluster of school buildings associated with music and the dramatic arts and connected up with LSU's lane of ill repute, Chimes Street. It was a crusty two-block area of student bars, pool halls, and bohemian-like living quarters that had been around as long as anyone could remember.

Father Al said, "Chimes Street has always appealed to the disengaged, the disaffected, and other such types, from beatniks to hippies to Goths and so on. One of the odd paradoxes is that just a block up, it forms the rear boundary of Fraternity Row."

"How about that," said J.E., "all those different types mingling together in this small area. It must get interesting sometimes."

"Indeed it does," said Dean Broussard, "and when you mix in the athletes such as the football players … well, the chief frequently has his hands full."

They had reached the corner and, led by Father Al, entered a restaurant aptly named the Chimes. It was connected to what was obviously an old movie house, the Varsity Theater. The eatery was packed with students gathering in anticipation of the LSU/Ole Miss football game that evening. The Swiss Guards stationed themselves at strategic but unobtrusive locations so that they could both observe and guard the group.

"Do they eat?" asked Cloe, nodding at the guards and beginning to feel a little better as she sat down amid the crowded, excited throngs of students.

"Of course, but never while on duty," responded the monsignor in all seriousness. His eyes darted from corner to corner as he examined the restaurant with the same precision as the robotic Mike analyzing the jar in the lab. He then took his seat.

"We must all relax. We have our guards, and the police are on alert and have promised to look after us as well," said Cloe more forcefully than she actually felt. "We are completely safe."

"I pray you are correct, Signorina, but better sure than sorry, as I believe your people are fond of saying."

"The expression is actually 'better safe than sorry,' but your turn of the phrase seems more apt for our situation."

"What happened on that bridge could be just the beginning," asserted J.E. suddenly, looking at the monsignor. "We need to know as much as we can so as to be ready for the next time."

"Next time?" asked Cloe sharply. "You don't mean you think these people aren't a thousand miles away from here by now?"

"Mom, the actual people who almost took you and me out are probably not anywhere near here anymore, maybe not even in the country, but that's only because the evil behind them wants it that way."

"Evil?" Cloe was alarmed at this remark. Was there really an "evil," she wondered, or was there sometimes just the absence of good? She was conflicted on this. In a hypothetical situation, was the insane killer "evil"? On the other hand, the worse the deeds, the more insane such a killer could be said to be. Did that make sense? If logic could not get to the end of it … were you left with evil? Her mother had had no doubt about the existence of evil.

"Yes. I don't know who it is or what his or her or their motives are, but I do know a bad thing—evil—when I see it," said J.E. "There is a very bad person behind this."

"Signorina, the young sir is quite correct," observed the monsignor. "Whoever is behind this is motivated by money or ideology or both. It's also my opinion, based on my experience, that ideology often cloaks an unholy greed as motivation for such actions."

"But who could gain from this?" asked Father Al. "And why now, given that the jar has been sitting on Thib's mantelpiece for years? It makes no sense."

"There are so many possibilities that it is hard to create a cogent theory at this point," answered the monsignor. "Perhaps it is a religious group or zealot who believes the contents of the jar will prove or disprove some doctrine. Much harm has been done in the name of religion."

"And much good," Cloe responded with a quickness that surprised her.

"Quite so."

"Or it may be something else entirely … some obscure motive we cannot now comprehend," added Father Al. "It still could be someone in town with an unknown grudge against Thib."

"Then why come after Mom and me?" queried J.E. "I think the one thing we can count on is that what almost happened to us and what happened to Thib are related and involve the jar. Nothing else makes any sense. There's a common goal here, and the people behind it aren't done."

"As to why now, there may be many reasons," said the monsignor. "The jar was in relative obscurity as long as it was in Thib's home. Perhaps it only recently came to the attention of our adversary. Moreover, Madisonville is a very small town, and people notice strangers. But now we are in a big city, and we are on the verge of discovering the secrets of the jar. In the mind of our adversary, this combination may suggest both the need and the opportunity for action."

"You said ideology might be a motive," noted Cloe. "What did you mean by that?" Cloe was coming to grips with the possibility that the incident at the bridge was but one step in someone's plan to get the jar. Even though the authorities were on alert, she and J.E. remained at risk until this person was stopped.

"There are ancient sects that have an interest in the telling of the Jesus story in one way or another and that might view the Judas Gospel, or whatever is in the jar, as a potential threat or even a benefit to their ideology. There are groups that would like to remake the story of Judas in ways they believe would be favorable to their dogma. We can talk of these as we go along with our work."

"What about other recently discovered relics? What about the Coptic version of the Judas Gospel? Did anyone try to steal it?" asked J.E.

"That's being checked both by the local police and by the Vatican. Over the years there have been many attempts to steal valuable relics. People have been killed," responded the monsignor. "Whether our opponent has been involved in any of these incidents remains to be seen."

The group digressed from these serious discussions and ordered house specialties, including an oyster poboy on crusty New Orleans French bread for Father Al and chicken, duck, and andouille gumbo with sticky rice for Cloe. At the end of the meal, the group ordered a large bread pudding with whiskey cream sauce, to be served with six spoons. Even the students at the surrounding tables nodded their approval.

This brought Cloe back to her college days but also, somehow, to her teenage years, having grown up in a similarly food-rich environment. It was, altogether, a wonderfully nostalgic moment, warming her and removing her temporarily from the urgency of their mission and the explicit threat that J.E. and the monsignor had just discussed.

But Cloe's thoughts returned quickly to the matter at hand. "Dean Broussard, we have to get that jar opened. What's our next move?"

"We get back in the lab and get to work," asserted the dean.

She turned sharply toward the monsignor. "Monsignor, you speak of ideology as motivation for what happened to us … what is the interest of the Catholic Church in the jar? What does the Church want?"

He paused, his steel-gray eyes fixing Cloe with the intensity of a tractor beam, and said in a whisper, "The truth. The Church desires only the truth."

# CHAPTER 20

Rather than go back to the photo lab, the party headed for a mechanical lab across campus where the jar and its two Swiss Guards now waited. The lab itself was unremarkable but featured numerous tools, drills, grinders, and equipment. Its major feature was an airtight, metal-lined, window-laden cube that was accessed through a rubber-sealed, vault-like door at its rear, with a system of mechanical arms and appliances in the front. The jar had been secured in the center of this control chamber, and the temperature within the cube had been reduced below room temperature. The humidity had been lowered, but the air pressure remained neutral in the box.

Dr. Harrell had returned to his element and was leading this portion of the examination. He stated, "Our first task is to stabilize the environment in the container around the jar to approximately what we think the environment may be in the jar. Mike has given us the values for temperature, humidity, and pressure based on the ultrasound, infrared, and other spectrographic examinations of yesterday. Even so, it's just an educated guess by Mike as to the conditions inside the jar. However, it's the best we have to work with."

*Was it just yesterday that the first series of tests were run?* Cloe wondered. It seemed like a lot more time had passed given everything that had been compressed into these last few hours. Her overstrained muscles from the fall at the bridge had begun to throb. The stress of an attempt on her life and on J.E.'s, as well as the mystery of the jar, had ramped up her anxiety. And Thib's death was wrapped up in all this. She suddenly felt tired and a little fragile. Nevertheless, she had to find out what was in the jar and solve the mystery. Her promise to Thib came back, and she tapped its energy.

"Dr. Harrell, now that the environments inside and out have been equalized as best we can know, how will we proceed?" Cloe asked. She wanted to play her part, ask the right questions, and make sure risk to the jar was minimized.

"Well, we have determined that the jar has a very stout seal on it. Extracting such a seal could damage the jar or its contents. We would like to determine what's in the jar, if we can, before we take the dangerous step of attempting to remove the seal. Consequently, our strategy will be to bore a small hole in the bottom of the jar and insert a probe that will be lighted and contain a miniature camera. We will go in from the bottom in order to retain the integrity of the sides of the jar, both for structural reasons and because the jar, intact, has value separate and apart from its contents."

"If everyone is ready, we will proceed," said Dean Broussard.

"Let the games begin," said Cloe with a lightness she did not really feel.

Dr. Harrell and Dean Broussard huddled around a technician, who engaged the mechanical arms and picked up a stainless steel drill inside the cube. The drill bit looked to be about an eighth-inch in diameter. Using the mechanical arms, the technician skillfully tilted the jar until it was almost flat on its side and safely locked in place. He then maneuvered the drill and bit to the underside of the jar. The bit was centered, and the action began slowly, with each revolution visible to the naked eye.

Cloe and her comrades moved toward the box and positioned themselves so that each could see as well as possible. The drill bit ground on the bottom of the jar.

Dr. Harrell looked over his shoulder at Cloe and J.E. "This must be done very carefully. We don't know for sure what the pressure is inside the jar. We don't want a sudden puncture that could swiftly—and maybe disastrously—equalize pressures, like the explosive loss of an airplane window or the puncture of the metal skin of a submarine under pressure. In case there is a substantial pressure differential, what we want is to breach the jar slowly so that the effect is like very cautiously opening a soda that has been shaken or easing a cork out of an agitated bottle of champagne. We are looking for the gradual fizz rather than rapid decompression one way or the other."

The noise level grew as the bit unhurriedly revolved and methodically invaded the bottom of the jar. Fine granules of the jar's earthen makeup were gently cast aside by the bit. The tension in the room began to increase, reaching an almost palpable level. Cloe studied the jar for signs of any cracks from the stress of the tool's action. Each revolution of the drill bit seemed to tighten the knot of anxiety that bound the small group of people to the jar in the container. Suddenly the bit sank into the bottom of the jar and caught. The drill gagged, and the electric motor inside struggled to continue the progress into the bottom of the jar.

Cloe's breath caught in her throat, and she could see that the others were similarly stressed. Everyone pressed against the sides of the box. "What's happening?" whispered Cloe.

"The drill bit has caught on something and is freezing up," responded Dr. Harrell. "This is not unusual. These clay jars were constructed in layers, and some layers are denser than others. We will try a little more power to the drill, but not so much as to create a breach, which could cause a failure in the integrity of the jar."

Everyone took a gulp of air and held it as the technician applied additional power to the electric motor that muscled the drill. There was a sharp, almost shrill screech, forcing a cumulative cry from the assembly. Then the bit broke through the heavier layer and continued on smoothly into the bottom of the jar.

"Okay," said Dr. Harrell with a deep exhale.

The progress was slow, agonizingly slow. But progress was indeed made. After eight to ten seemingly interminable minutes, the wall at the bottom of the jar was ever so slowly penetrated with a faint *sisss* sound at the end.

As the drill bit routed out the hole, the scientists could see a neat eighth-of-an-inch portal in the bottom of the jar. Cloe was relieved to see the hole, knowing that this part of the job was probably complete. She stepped away and stretched her back and neck, which had stiffened with tension.

Dr. Harrell spun away from the box and beamed at the group. "We are through and into the interior of the jar. Now we insert the small probe and camera into the bottom of the vessel, and we will see what we will see."

"Dr. H, is there any danger in this phase?" asked J.E.

"Some ... While the light is an LED with a low heat signature, we cannot completely exclude the possibility of combustion within the jar," he responded. "On the other hand, it is unlikely that the materials will be photosensitive."

"Shall we proceed, Dr. Lejeune?" he asked, looking in Cloe's general direction.

"Well, I don't see us turning back at this point." She returned immediately to the table and the box in order to resume her observations.

The technician changed the device from the drill apparatus to a slim probe with a light on the end. As he moved it, the monitor next to the container sprang to life and flashed a picture of the interior of the box and then a close-up of the exterior of the jar. This was followed by an even closer view of the outside of the bottom of the jar.

The entire investigation of the jar was being digitally recorded. In the high-intensity light with the close-up position of the camera, Cloe thought that she saw some very faint texture on the outer surface of the bottom of the jar, but then the probe moved on, and the moment passed. But she noted it for later thought and examination. She recalled that Mike had reported on something on the bottom of the jar but had been unable thus far to determine what it might be.

The probe entered the bottom of the jar and immediately began to encounter some resistance. The little group focused intently on the monitor. There was nothing but blackness in spite of the probe's lighted tip.

"Back out!" cried Dr. Harrell to the technician.

"What happened? Is the jar full of black sludge?" pressed Cloe.

"I don't know ... maybe," said Dr. Harrell with obvious disappointment. "Even so, the jar itself is significant and valuable. But the contents of the jar seem to be black and granular in substance. We have to check this out before proceeding."

The team swiveled and looked at Cloe. She could see the disappointment and dismay in their eyes. She prayed silently that this was just another temporary setback.

Even Father Al was hanging his head despondently."Yes, nothing but black dust. From dust this vessel's contents have come, and to dust so they appear to have been returned," intoned Father Al somewhat philosophically. "We seem to have been undone by the ages."

# CHAPTER 21

A thousand miles to the east, two men sat in the center of an executive jet in what would have to be called the lap of luxury. The plane was set up business-style, with groupings of heavy leather chairs separated by working tables. Both men were of medium height and somewhat heavyset, their solid layers of muscle revealing a lifetime of physical activity. Schooling and experience in many things had prepared them for their dark business. Each spoke English with barely a hint of an accent. Both had a swarthy Middle or Eastern European skin tone, jet black-hair, and—although their faces were carefully shaven—a dark shadow of a beard. They were identically dressed in black cotton slacks, black turtlenecks, and black jackets.

The jet was a Gulfstream V with extended cruising range. The plane was near its certified ceiling of fifty-one thousand feet, high above the Atlantic Ocean, and was headed east into the gathering darkness. If all things worked out, the jet would land at its destination in eight to ten hours, depending on wind and traffic conditions.

"We fucked up," said one of the men. They were seated across from each other.

"Yes," said the other. "Our employer does not take failure lightly." Rem knew that Janik always worried, but this time was different: Rem was worried too.

Janik rested his chin on his open palm, turned toward his partner, and began to drum his fingertips nervously on the handmade wooden table between them. Rem could see he was sweating even though the cabin was chilled.

If only that kid had not intervened at the last moment, they would be flying home like conquering heroes instead of the goats his actions had made of them, thought Rem, who was the leader of the twosome. Even now, Rem could picture the young man's face as he turned for some unknown reason and saw the hurtling car. There was no fear in his face, only estimation and calculation. Rem thought the Lejeune boy had reacted like a soldier—like Rem himself would have reacted.

One of the pilots came back to the passenger area and told Rem and Janik they were on schedule, giving them flight parameters and expected time to destination. The pilot asked, "May I serve you a drink or some food? Our employer has stocked the bar and sent along some very fine Beluga caviar."

Rem ordered a whiskey straight up but declined any food. Janik asked for chilled vodka, also without ice, and agreed to the caviar. A few minutes later, the warm liquid flowed into Rem's system and cheered him to some degree. Janik was also enjoying the food.

*Perhaps it will be all right*, thought Rem. He began to relax a bit and turned to look out the small porthole that passed for a window on the jet. As the darkness wrapped around everything below, he could see almost nothing upon looking down. Up and out, some stars twinkled, and the moon was nearly full. That damn kid. He had snatched the woman, and both had disappeared over the railing of the bridge a split second before impact. Why the employer wanted the woman dead, Rem did not know. Such things were known only to those who needed to know them. That did not include Rem or Janik.

There hadn't been any time for a second try. The two priests were running to the scene even as Janik backed up and sped away. There was nothing they could do after that without killing them all. *Perhaps*, Rem thought bitterly, *that would have been better.*

After the failed action, Rem and Janik had hurried to the parking lot of what appeared to be an old agriculture building—the building was huge, and even from the parking area, Rem could see stalls for animals—to exchange vehicles. They had stolen two vehicles, one from the long-term parking garage at the New Orleans airport and another in Baton Rouge. After quickly wiping down the Baton Rouge car they had used in the now-thwarted murder mission, they abandoned it for the other car, which they had parked in the lot earlier. Then, almost casually, they had departed the scene for the New Orleans airport.

Rem had felt comfortable using the same car to return to the airport. He wagered it hadn't yet been reported stolen in the time that had elapsed. Indeed, they had been able to put the car back exactly where they had found it. This would further cover their tracks since the owner might never know of its nefarious use.

Bringing Rem back to the present, the pilot reentered and asked, "Can I refill those drinks?"

Janik appeared to be dozing, but Rem said yes. He heard his own response sound slurred and slow; the alcohol and exhaustion must be hitting him, he figured.

Rem had finished about half of his second drink when he heard the plane's big Rolls Royce engines begin to spool down. He felt the jet start to descend, but he knew they were nowhere near their next stop. Indeed, they were over open water. He tried to rise but could not. Rem found that he could not use his arms or legs. He gaped dumbly at the half-empty glass on the table beside him.

"Pancuronium bromide," said the pilot as he again entered the cabin. "This drug is used as part of the drug cocktail given to condemned death-row killers as the lethal injection for execution. It completely paralyzes the muscles and will by itself eventually cause death because you won't be able to breathe. But our employer has dictated a different fate for you and your associate."

Rem could move only his eyes. His breathing was shallow and becoming labored. There was no doubt in his mind that he and Janik were about to pay for the failure of the mission. He knew the plane had leveled out, and he saw the pilot move to the cabin door. The pilot struggled with but then opened the door and dogged it back. Cool, damp night air rushed at Rem. The pilot turned and faced them. Rem could see the man was excited by the prospect of what was to happen.

"We had to descend to about eight thousand feet for this part of our in-flight service," said the pilot, amusing himself. "We told the flight controller we were having some oxygen system difficulties and needed to descend so we could turn it off and repair it."

The man dragged Janik from his chair and across the cabin floor. Rem could see no movement or hint of life from his colleague. The pilot muscled Janik's limp body toward the open door and set him up on the doorsill. He leaned over and whispered something in his ear. He held Janik for a second or two in that position and then kicked him out into the open space.

The pilot stood in the doorway for a few seconds, apparently watching Janik fall and, Rem could see, savoring his work. He now turned and came for Rem.

Rem tried mightily to think of some strategy or tactic that he could employ to save his life or, at least, take his killer with him. He had a large-bore handgun in a shoulder holster under his jacket. Rem tried to force his hand to do his bidding and retrieve the weapon. One shot would end this nightmare. But the effect of the powerful drug was all-consuming and unavoidable. He had no resources or options left.

Rem was dragged across the floor just as Janik had been and was poised by the pilot on the edge of the door between two worlds, one of life and the other of ignominious death. Knowing he was on death's doorstep, he experienced an extraordinary sharpening of his senses. He could hear the waves below and smell the salt air. Curiously, he thought he could also smell land, the way a seaman who has been at sea for many days can smell land before he sees it. But this was open water, wasn't it?

The pilot struggled to keep him in position, and Rem knew he was only moments away from death. Well, he had sent a lot of people on this trip of death, and this time, it was his turn.

The pilot leaned over and whispered in Rem's ear, "The employer wishes you to know that he will also take up the matter of your failure with your family."

Then Rem was cascading downward. As he looked up, he saw the cabin door closing, its dirty business done. The jet began to climb toward the sky. He spun, turned, and twisted without any muscular control. His vocal chords would not allow him even the relief of a terminal scream, so he screamed in his head. He thought of what he had unleashed on his poor family and of his evil life, and somewhere, just before impact, Rem repented.

# CHAPTER 22

After the distressing and, perhaps, calamitous examination of the jar, and given the lateness of the hour and the dejected attitude of the group, they elected to call it a day. Cloe and her team retired to the hotel, but all agreed to meet for drinks at the bar of a nearby eatery at seven o'clock. If anybody needed a break and some downtime, it was she and her colleagues. Dr. Harrell said he had one more thing to do to wrap up, but he would meet them later.

J.E. had showered and changed and then joined Cloe in the small living area of her suite. They had a few minutes to kill before taking a cab to the restaurant. As always, they discussed the events of the day.

Cloe had ground her teeth so often during the ill-fated afternoon that her jaw ached. But her faith that she would somehow keep her promise to Thib and find the answers to the jar was unabated.

"You know, Mom, I think we need to reassess our situation," suggested J.E. "We have an ancient jar … we don't yet know exactly how old. It's at the center of everything—Thib's death and the attack on us. Someone wants to kill us and take the jar."

"Agreed, J.E."

"Yes, but why? Also, we don't really know whether the objective is to stop us or to get the jar. There is a difference, but it's hard to see why the goal would be just to stop us. Maybe an ultrareligious sect would want to stop us. They may be afraid of what we might find."

"True. As the monsignor has said, the contents of the jar may prove or disprove some doctrine of various religions or even factions within some religions," said Cloe thoughtfully. "On the other hand, it may be nothing. But such people may not want to take the risk of what we might discover, opting to move preemptively to destroy our work."

"What if the jar holds information that would totally throw Catholicism out the window?" speculated J.E.

Cloe shivered at the thought. "Are you saying we might be in jeopardy from the Church itself? That would put the monsignor on the other side from us. I certainly doubted him at first, but now I'm not so sure. But there could be individuals or groups, inside and outside the Church, which might be threatened by even the idea of such information. These people might act irrationally."

"Maybe that's what we're seeing. But I think a group like that would want to try for getting the jar. Wouldn't they want to know what's in it? I mean, it may help them," said J.E. "So, probably, such an enemy would be okay with destroying the jar and our work in case it might be against them, but if they can do it, they'll want possession of the jar. That's the only explanation that makes sense to me."

J.E. paused for a moment, deep in thought, and then continued. "I have to tell you, I still don't completely trust the monsignor. I think he knows more than he's saying. We need a 'come to Jesus meeting' with him. He's just a little too strange and a little too quick with answers to his weird behavior.

"There's something more than meets the eye happening here. We know there's a bad actor at work, but there's something else too," concluded J.E. "Could it have anything to do with what you said you might have seen on the bottom of the jar?"

"I don't know, J.E. I'm pretty sure there was something there. Mike also noticed something but hasn't yet been able to identify it. It was there for just a flash. Maybe I was wrong. It was very faint, almost a shadow. Still, I thought it was something."

"You know, Mom, I would trust your instincts," said J.E. "We know we are players on this board game. Is the Vatican? Who else … and why?"

***

A little after seven o'clock, the group rendezvoused at the bar. Dean Broussard was there early and had secured the table. The dean had told Cloe that though fans with game tickets would be gone by

113

the time they arrived, there would be a second seating for Tiger fans without tickets.

When Cloe, Father Al, J.E., and the monsignor arrived, the restaurant was teeming with LSU fans anticipating the game with Ole Miss. Again the Swiss Guard deployed strategically to protect them. Television screens had been set up throughout the restaurant. Since this was the game closest to Halloween, many people were in costume. This was also the anniversary of the famous Halloween run of LSU's sole Heisman Trophy winner, Billy Cannon, the great All-American. So the restaurant was even busier and more crowded than usual. Nevertheless, through his influence and contacts the dean had managed to get a table.

"Where's Dr. Harrell?" asked Cloe.

"He was delayed by an additional test," the dean explained. "He may be along later, but he said not to wait."

"Dean, is Dr. Harrell doing a further test on our project, or is it something else?"

"He didn't say, Dr. Lejeune. Hopefully we will hear something later."

They ordered drinks and settled back into a gloomy silence. Though crowded, the bar was very comfortable, with wood-paneled walls and a fireplace lit with gas logs. When the drinks appeared, the dean raised a glass to discoveries yet unmade. Everyone half-heartedly clinked their glasses, but their thoughts inevitably returned to the day's misadventure.

J.E. roused himself and came straight to the point. "Monsignor, I don't believe you've finished your explanation of the Vatican's interest in this old jar. It's time you tell us the whole story."

The monsignor held J.E.'s eyes for a long moment as he sipped his wine. He then gazed, individually, at each of the other members of the group as if he were measuring and reading them very carefully. "There is more to the Judas story," he said finally.

"But you said that most of the Gospels were strangely silent on the death of Judas and that the information that did exist was contradictory," J.E. responded. "We know that he betrayed Jesus in the Garden of Gethsemane with a kiss. He did it for the money. Right?"

"Yes," said Father Al, "that's certainly the accepted story … one might say the orthodox story. However, there are a number of problems with that interpretation. First, Christ himself chose Judas as a disciple along with the Galileans. But Judas was not of a background similar to the others. He was literate and could handle numbers—witness the passage in the Gospel of John where it is revealed that Judas acted as the group's treasurer. He would have collected donations, bought supplies, and provided for the poor. For him to have this role during the public ministry, one could speculate that he must have been trusted by Jesus and the other Apostles at some level."

"So did he later go bad? Or was he always bad and no one knew?" queried J.E. "Surely Jesus knew."

"J.E., you are following the scientific method very well," interjected his mother with a smile.

The monsignor nodded. "Agreed. The Gospels suggest that Jesus clearly knew that the man he had chosen would betray him and that the consequences of the betrayal would be so great that it would have been better if Judas had never been born. The problem really lies in exploring the hypothetical circumstance of what if Judas had never been born. Would Christ have been handed over to the Romans? By whose hand? Would humanity not have been saved from its sin? This is a significant theological question to which there is no credible answer."

"So," summarized J.E., warming to the point, "Christ was the Son of God who came to earth as a man to save humanity from its sin. He chose Judas, even though he knew Judas would betray him, resulting in the fulfillment of the scriptures. Or did he choose Judas *because* he knew Judas would betray him, again delivering on his destiny?"

"It sounds more like Judas and Jesus were partners in seeing that Jesus's purpose was accomplished," observed Cloe. She was following this theological explanation closely. It was fascinating, but where was it going? "Monsignor, this is very interesting, but how does it connect with our project?"

"We have yet to find the connection, if there is one," the monsignor conceded.

"We have to get to the end of the religion class," Cloe said abruptly. "Unless this has something to do with the jar, Thib's death, and all that's happening, I can't see it helping us."

The group was quiet for a minute, and then the monsignor said gently, "Signorina, I know you are anxious, but this information may be critical if there is, in fact, a Gospel—or some writing of or about Judas—in the jar. This may provide the context needed for a translation and, more importantly, the interpretation of whatever is in the jar."

"I can see that," replied Cloe wearily. "You're right, context can mean everything. Please, go on."

"Fine. That's actually the second of the four different theories some scholars have used to explain the actions of Judas," continued the monsignor. "According to this theory, Judas was essential to the end ordained by God and foretold by the scriptures. Therefore, Judas was part of God's plan for the redemption of mankind. If this explanation has any truth to it, then Judas's role has been misunderstood and his end treatment was rather shoddy. But it is hard to know how the story could be other than what we have been told."

"Plainly, Jesus knew what Judas would do," added Father Al. "Yet Jesus made no effort to stop him or to deter him from his course of action."

"There are actually some ancient writings suggesting that Jesus prevailed upon Judas to betray him and, thus, to play his part in the drama," said the monsignor. "We shall get into that when we further discuss the Coptic Gospel of Judas.

"The language in the Gospel of John is very interesting on this point. John reports that at the Last Supper, Jesus was troubled in spirit and told the Apostles that one of them would betray him. He then identified Judas as the traitor by the device of handing him some bread. John says that at the very instant Jesus handed Judas the bread, Satan entered into Judas."

"According to the synoptic Gospels," remarked Father Al, "by that time Judas had already made arrangements with the chief priests and the elders to betray Christ. But the timing in John's Gospel indicates the devil entered into Judas after he had already done the deed. Again the ambiguity of Judas is certainly thought-provoking."

Cloe continued to be intrigued with the Judas exposition and could see how knowing this might shed light on any writings that might be in the jar if they pertained to Judas. There seemed to be no end to the puzzling facts and suppositions concerning the Judas character.

"Moreover, Jesus's last words to Judas in John are incredibly interesting," added the monsignor. "John relates that Jesus said to Judas, 'What you are going to do, do quickly.' Is this resignation? Are these instructions? These words are certainly subject to interpretation depending on the inflection one puts on each of them."

"So, according to this version, Judas was part of the plan, and Jesus's last words to Judas were, in effect, to saddle up and go take care of business," said J.E.

"Well, the young sir has a way with words, but you can see that if the jar contains information that advances or refutes any of these theories, it could be extremely important, to say the least," responded the monsignor. "If the contents of the jar support the notion that Judas was playing a critical role in the redemption story, it would buttress the theological conclusion of some scholars that Judas was simply doing Jesus's bidding and therefore following God's plan."

"Where would that take us, Monsignor?" asked Cloe.

"It would mean there was, in fact, no betrayal and Judas's role has been completely misunderstood."

"If that proved to be true and Judas acted for reasons other than financial gain, someone with an ax to grind against Christianity might argue that if this piece of the Jesus story cannot be trusted, maybe other portions also lack credibility," responded Cloe thoughtfully.

"There are certainly other interpretations and explanations, but that's the way it would be used in the wrong hands," agreed the monsignor.

"My God," whispered Cloe. "What have we gotten ourselves into?"

# CHAPTER 23

Cloe happened to look up just as Dr. Harrell rushed into the dark restaurant and squinted into the dimly lit bar in search of his colleagues. His eyes apparently began to adjust after a moment, and he saw them silhouetted against the flickering firelight. He came straight to the table and, as he passed the bar, called over his shoulder for a very old scotch, neat. Cloe and the others rose to greet him, noting the excitement evident in his manner. His drink came, and he took a long pull on it before turning to the group.

"Charcoal," he said.

"Charcoal!" responded Dean Broussard excitedly. "But of course. Why didn't we think of it?"

"What are you talking about?" asked J.E.

"J.E., one of the basic forms of charcoal is an absorbent," Cloe explained. "It wicks moisture and odors from the environment. It is one of nature's purifying agents. Even some of the ancients were aware of its properties." Cloe could feel her own excitement rise as she began to anticipate what this might mean.

"Yes," responded J.E., "some military filters have charcoal elements. What's this have to do with the jar?"

Having recovered his presence of mind, Dr. Harrell began to explain. "After you left, to wrap up the work properly, we ran a core-boring test on the contents at the bottom of the jar. This was the area where we thought we had hit black sludge. We went back through the layers of material in the bottom of the jar and took a core sample. We then carefully processed it to see what elements it contained."

"What did you find?" asked Father Al, holding his breath.

"We found charcoal!" Dr. Harrell almost shouted as he half-rose from his seat in his excitement. Nearby patrons turned from their tables to see what the commotion was. Dr. Harrell lowered his voice and said, "That and silicone."

"Silicone?" said Dean Broussard, turning now directly to Dr. Harrell. "How were they configured?"

"The very bottom layer in the jar is a two-inch-thick vein of charcoal," responded the doctor. "Above that is a two-inch layer of silicone—sand. It is evident that whoever prepared the jar intended that its contents would be preserved for many years."

"This is astounding," remarked the dean.

"The sand and the charcoal were intended to absorb any moisture or other contaminants that might be in the jar when it was sealed. These would be encapsulated in the bottom layers and away from whatever the jar contains, thus preserving the contents for posterity."

The table was quiet for a time while everyone considered this development and its possible implications.

"In effect, this jar and—I think we can deduce—its mates back in the cave were meant to be a form of ancient time capsule," concluded Cloe. "Whoever put these jars in the cave intended them to be there for a long, long time and to preserve whatever they contained, perhaps for thousands of years."

"Have you learned anything else?" asked J.E. "What about the age of the vessel?"

"Nothing else," said Dr. Harrell. "But given what we now know about the source of the black dust in the jar, this gives us hope that we can continue our investigation and that what's inside the jar may very well be intact."

"Well," said Cloe, "it also indicates that we still have an awfully long way to go. What's next, doctor?"

Dr. Harrell considered for a moment and said, "We have done everything else there is to do to prepare. Now it's time to crack open the seal on the jar and to learn for sure what it contains."

# CHAPTER 24

The man gazed at his opulent surroundings. He smiled slightly in self-satisfaction. Although underground, the bunker in Jerusalem was warm and had every convenience. He sat in a deep-set leather chair with a late-night nibble of fruit and cheese. The wine he had been served was superb. Just as a blind hog will sometimes find an acorn, his servant had stumbled upon a superb vintage. One could almost forget that he was awaiting news of murderous events in the air over the ocean many thousands of miles away, events that he had only recently set in motion.

But murder meant nothing to him. Only the thing he was after held meaning. His progeny were all dead, collateral casualties of a life of violence, avarice, and deceit—all, that is, except Michael, and he hadn't seen him for more than three decades. The man had no friends but many associates who remained loyal to a fault to him and his enterprises, through a combination of exuberant rewards for success and draconian consequences for failure in his service. They were simply servants, pieces on a chessboard, replaceable or expendable as needed.

It had not always been this way, he mused. His thoughts drifted back to his life as a boy, growing up in the country near the border between Armenia and Turkey. A hard, cold life of sheep and subsistence farming had been his family's lot. But he'd had sunny days with his mother and father and sister. He had treasured those times.

Then World War II broke out, and no one was safe in the region. He remembered the day his father sought refuge for the family at the small Catholic Church in the area, when he was a mere adolescent.

"Husband, what did the priest say?" his mother asked when his father returned to their rural farm.

"He said the small church was overwhelmed with parishioners who are trying to get out before the Turkish army comes." His father collapsed at the kitchen table.

Even now in his memory he could hear the enemy's long guns begin their relentless hammering of the region. They were still miles away, but they were coming.

His mother laid hands on his father's shoulders and said, "What are we to do?"

"What is there to do, woman?" his father angrily snapped. "We will pack what we can, and we will go into the woods. Only the church has the contacts to get us out. And it is flooded with hundreds of refugees from the surrounding area. There is no escape there. The priest said as much and gave us a blessing."

"What blessing did he give, husband?"

"He asked that God have mercy on our souls."

That day they packed what they could and headed out with many others into the wooded hills and mountainous terrain that surrounded the region. But a Turkish raiding party found them; they killed his parents and left his sister a babbling idiot after torturing and raping her multiple times. He had not seen her since, and he sincerely hoped she was dead. Whatever thoughts of religion or God the boy had held died that day.

He remembered the corporal in charge of the raiding party who had saved his life, saying, "Take him ... we have many uses for such a young, handsome lad."

He was pressed into the Turkish army as barely a teenager and learned many things that youth should not know. Truly, this was where he grew up. But it was a twisted growing. At night, sometimes, he held his head tightly in his hands for fear that his skull would explode with the depravity of his experiences. But over the years he became reconciled to the violence and brutality. He eventually began to enjoy it. At first it owned him, and then he owned it.

Finally, he escaped to the West and studied at various European universities while running increasingly sophisticated cons to survive.

He was a natural, to use an American term. He was utterly without conscience, and larceny was his game.

As he became more successful, he saw that people envied him and coveted what he had. Even those close to him let him down or betrayed him. He learned that the only things he could trust were his acquisitions, his collection. He became a billionaire in the arms trade in the Middle East during the various Jewish–Arab wars beginning in 1967. A decade and a half later, he used his great wealth to completely vanish. He staged his own death, dividing his wealth into untraceable trusts and accounts that only he could access and then only by computer.

He created a new identity for himself, and he decided that Jerusalem would be his home and the base where he would conduct his activities. His burning passion was to collect those things that he knew he could count on and that would not let him down. He loved ancient relics of all types. He loved nothing else.

***

Now in his early eighties, he thought back over the last few years. He had purchased a small storefront in the Old City through numerous intermediaries. Gradually he and his minions had acquired adjacent property, and his immediate staff had transformed the combined properties unobtrusively into his compound and underground bunker. It had been done incrementally and in such a measured fashion that no attention was drawn to him.

He laughed softly as he thought about the Mossad, the Jewish secret intelligence service. His sources told him that they considered him a harmless purveyor of antiquities. Indeed, they had been to his store many times. The storefront was still there and was filled with very low-grade antiquities, souvenirs, pottery shards, and the like. Each piece had been legitimately purchased and came with a foot-long pedigree. He was above reproach.

Of course, his real collection was underground in the bunker. Each piece there was priceless and had been stolen—in many cases, with great violence. These treasures included lost works of great masters, ancient pieces from tombs of pharaohs not even known to the world, and sacred relics of various religions. Because of his hatred for all things Catholic, he was perversely drawn to anything of, or pertaining to, that religion. His unholy museum had only one patron—the man himself.

He was shaken from his introspection by the entry of his most trusted servant.

"Master, the pilots have returned," the servant reported with a bow.

The man thought about this employee. If he'd had a brother, it would be the servant. They had been together since university. He was also Armenian. He was not just a servant but the man's number one, a party to all his secrets.

"What do they have to say for themselves?"

"They say that their mission was accomplished, and the vermin that failed you now rest at sea."

"What of the jar and the people who have it?"

"Master, the pilots have nothing new to add to the intelligence we have already received," stated the servant. "The woman and her son were unharmed, and although we succeeded in casting division and suspicion between the woman and the priests, they seem to have resolved this. Of course, we know of the personal letter from the pope vouching for the monsignor."

"Yes, some things are beyond even my power." The man seethed with rage at the interference of the Vatican. "We have not succeeded in the physical assault against those who hold what I want, nor have we succeeded in the effort to split them up and turn them against one another. But I assure you, there will be another day, and not only will I get what I want, but the Church will pay for its arrogance."

"Master, now that the effort to move against them is known, perhaps it is best to shift to other, potentially more fruitful opportunities," suggested the faithful servant, seeking to blunt his master's rage but knowing very well the response he would once again receive.

"Neither God nor his angels nor all of his unholy saints can prevent me from eradicating my adversaries and gaining possession of the Judas jar. It is the most important relic to be unearthed in the last two millennia," spat out his master. "This could be the precise thing I have been searching for to bring to ruin the very foundations of the Church itself."

"Still, we are here, and they are there, possibly on the very verge of discovering the secrets of the ancient jar, assuming it holds any."

The man paused, collecting himself, and then said evenly, "You have a wonderful way of recentering me and helping me to refocus on what is important. You are quite right. We must plan carefully to achieve our goals. I will have that jar. I will think about how to get it.

"However," continued the man, licking his lips slightly, "we do have some business to finish with our failed colleagues, Rem and Janik."

"Master, they are dead and under the sea. What more can you want to do with them?" asked the servant, anticipating what the master intended. It had always been so. Failure was not an option.

"My faithful friend, contact our retainers and send them to the families. Have the wife and each of the children of Rem and Janik strangled. Tell them this is the reward given to those who fail me."

# CHAPTER 25

Although it was rare in Louisiana to continue such work on a Sunday, time was of the essence, and at the group's request, Dr. Harrell had agreed to open the lab. The jar once again sat in the control box at the center of the room. Cloe, J.E., and the others donned lab coats and eye gear as Dr. Harrell described the procedure about to take place.

"The mechanical arms will help us loosen and then remove the seal from the jar. We have already taken a sample from the seal. It's an interesting combination of wax and resin from some heretofore-unknown plant of the time from which the jar originated. This was applied around a wooden plug carefully sculptured to the mouth of the jar. The hot wax provided the airtight seal, and the resin gave rigidity and substance to the wax. Altogether it was a formidable combination."

"How will you open the seal?" asked Dean Broussard.

"We will use a laser to heat and cut the edges around the seal. With vessels this old, even the seal itself has value, so we do not want to destroy it."

"Very well, let's proceed," said Cloe. She had not gotten to this point, facing the risks and dangers she had experienced, to turn back now. *Full speed ahead and damn the torpedoes*, Cloe thought.

The technician operating the mechanical arms picked up a device that looked like a fat ink pen attached to a thin electrical cord and positioned it over the jar. Very carefully he took aim, and the end of the pen ignited into a white light. After the tech adjusted the device, the light entered the red end of the spectrum and then became almost invisible. The beam dipped into the wax/resin seal and separated it from the edge of the jar.

125

Suddenly the top of the jar burst into flames. The group gasped collectively, and just as immediately, within a split second of the combustion, some sort of fire retardant spray smothered the fire. All were left staring in shock at the box, which was now filled with smoke and fumes.

"What the hell?" roared Dr. Harrell. Cloe and the others moved closer to the box, trying to see what had happened.

The tech looked up. "Dr. H, the seal of the jar is apparently highly combustible, but the auto–flame extinguisher system has prevented any damage. The laser's not going to work. We will have to use old-fashioned mechanical means to cut the seal."

Everyone calmed down somewhat at the news that no harm had been done.

Cloe said coolly, "By all means, let's move on."

The tech picked up another utensil, somewhat resembling a small jigsaw, and began to work on the top of the seal. The mouth of the jar was wide, maybe six to eight inches across, and the seal was like a plug inserted in the entrance to the jar. There was little resistance to the saw at the edge of the plug, but whenever the saw drifted toward the center, it sounded as if it was catching wood. After a few tense minutes, the tech had circumnavigated the top of the jar. The whole exercise was much like opening a can of peas with a high-tech can opener—except that this can of peas was unique to the world and had an inestimable value.

"Now what?" asked Cloe.

"We pop the cork," said Dr. Harrell. "Actually, we will clamp the top of the seal around its edge and try to remove it from the jar."

The tech selected a pincer-like gadget and carefully fixed it on both edges of the plug that had sealed the jar. It slipped a couple of times, but finally he developed a fast grip. He tried to pull the plug out, but nothing happened. The plug would not give.

Sweat had broken out on Dr. Harrell's forehead. "Be damned careful, David," he said to the tech. "The jar itself may be fragile."

The tech began to work the plug in place to try to loosen it. It moved a bit. Everyone inhaled, and no one seemed to exhale. It moved a little more. The tech's face expressed both intense concentration and signs of increasing confidence. Slowly, he eased the plug from the jar until, finally, it separated completely. The mouth of the jar was open.

All heaved a collective sigh of relief, and Cloe could see the stress lines in the faces of her colleagues beginning to relax.

Dean Broussard said, "The plug seems to be made of some type of wood." It had a tapered, cylindrical appearance and had obviously been prepared to fit precisely into the wide neck of the jar. "Isn't that unusual for vessels of this type?"

"Quite so," said Cloe. "From my experience with ancient documents, many of the people of that time used fabric like a heavy canvas to seal these types of vessels, which might hold wine, oil, or other commodities. They did the same for manuscripts. Whoever prepared this jar went well beyond the norm to preserve it for as long as possible."

The tech had put the wooden plug down and was now preparing to use the illuminated probe and camera to look into the jar. All eyes turned to the monitor as the probe mounted the edge of the jar and entered it.

"My God, that looks like a small book in there!" exclaimed Father Al.

"No, not a book," responded Cloe immediately, "but a bound codex of some sort." Her heart was racing with excitement.

The tech attached the probe to a clip on the mechanical arm and reached into the jar. Fastening the pinchers on the arm to the object, which was about six inches wide and nine inches tall, he slowly began to extricate it from the mouth of the jar. It was about halfway out when Cloe saw the writing on the monitor. She recognized the now-familiar words and quickly translated them in her mind. *There can be no doubt*, she thought to herself.

Amazed and excited, she said, "Gentlemen, I give you what appears to be a fully intact codex containing the Gospel of Judas Iscariot, one that does not seem to be in tatters like the Coptic version."

# CHAPTER 26

Cloe knew that many relics were in the possession of various religious organizations and that scientific research into them was mired in hopeless and obscure bureaucracy. The Shroud of Turin itself had been withheld from proper scientific inquiry for hundreds, if not thousands, of years. That would not happen to the new Judas manuscript. They had decided to refer to it as a manuscript rather than a codex to avoid confusion with the Coptic codex. On direct order of Dr. Harrell, with Cloe concurring, the tech snipped a minute scrap of fabric from the edge of one of the interior pages of the manuscript in order to carbon-date it. Thanks to Mike the supercomputer, this analysis would happen far faster than in prior years. Still, it would take some hours to complete the study and date the manuscript.

Also, Cloe recognized that it was necessary to humidify the document before removing it from its climate-controlled box. Without the humidification process, there was a danger the individual pages of the manuscript would be so dry that they might crumble upon examination. The way it had been packed added to this concern.

This was only the second document by or about Judas that had ever been discovered. And considering that she had never heard of the Coptic version, she had to think it had not been that earth shaking. *What about this one?* Cloe wondered. *Might it be a complete dead end? Or a portal of new knowledge through which I might be drawn?* Energized by the monumental strides they had made this morning, and suddenly acutely aware of all that she did not know about the possible significance of the manuscript, Cloe turned on the monsignor and spoke forcefully.

"Monsignor, it's time that we finish our talk. We've been spoon-fed the background that you wanted us to hear when you wanted us to hear it. Last night's conversation was just enough to keep us intrigued but not enough to let us know what's really going on. We need some answers, and we want them now."

J.E. rounded on the monsignor and said simply, "Yeah, you haven't been completely on the up-and-up with us."

Father Al, Dr. Harrell, and Dean Broussard looked expectantly at the cleric. There was a long pause as the storm clouds among the team members began to gather.

The monsignor accepted this turn of events with equanimity and turned to the dean. "Perhaps you have somewhere where we can chat?"

"Certainly," responded the dean. He exited the mechanical lab and led them, along with their Swiss Guard protectors, to a small conference room just off the corridor. As they were being seated, one of the dean's assistants offered French roast coffee and beignets. Everyone but J.E. accepted the hospitality, and soon they were all somewhat refreshed. It had been an intense and suspenseful morning, and the comfort food helped focus and reenergize them.

"All right, Monsignor, the good, the bad, and the ugly if you please," said J.E., all business.

The monsignor paused as if to catch his breath and organize his thoughts. He looked off into the distance for a bit and then started. "You know I have explained the first two theories that scholars postulate regarding the role of Judas in the Christ story. The first is the conventional view where Judas is the arch villain who betrayed Christ for money—the thirty pieces of silver. The second is the theory that Judas and Jesus were the closest of friends and confidants. After all, as we have previously demonstrated, both were Judeans … the only two in the group."

"That's right. Even though he was often referred to as the 'Nazarene,' Jesus was actually born in Bethlehem in Judea, due to the census," interjected J.E.

"Quite so," said the monsignor. "Another link with Judas. Indeed, this interpretation holds that Christ imparted unto Judas information that he did not tell the other disciples. Under this explanation Judas knew his role, as did Christ, and both performed their parts in the saving of humanity. In effect, the Christ role was played by partners, themselves reflecting the duality of man's nature."

"And if I'm following this correctly, Christ's death and resurrection was the ultimate victory of man over his dark side," chimed in J.E.

"Yes," replied the monsignor, simply.

"I am, and have been, an agnostic pretty much since I came to university," said Dr. Harrell, "but I'm extremely well read, and I have never even heard of this alternative explanation of Judas's role." He seemed confounded by this summary of what he had missed from last night's discussions.

"Dr. Harrell, there is not a great deal written about what I am saying to you today. Much of it was suppressed by the heresy hunters in the early centuries of the Church," responded the monsignor.

"Heresy hunters?" queried J.E.

"Yes, there will be more about them, but I must finish this part of the background. It is only from there that we can begin to fully understand what is happening," said the monsignor. "There are other explanations for Judas's role in the Gospels. The third and least popular is that Judas was, some scholars have suggested, Christ's pawn. He was not a partner but a dupe. He was simply an unwitting accomplice in the condemnation and death of Jesus so that scripture could be fulfilled. All four Gospels literally refute this and suggest other motivations for Judas. Moreover, the moral implications are profound."

"It's the end justifying the means, plain and simple," said Cloe. "That sort of expediency hardly seems to be what Christ came to teach us." Cloe was shocked to hear that responsible theologians could even postulate this as a possible explanation of Judas's role. But she knew scholars put forward many hypotheses in which they did not believe in an effort to be thorough. A theory had to be posited to be rejected.

Father Al looked to the monsignor and said, "Albert, I know you wish to be complete, but such an explanation is very secular in character and nature, and I wonder if all of our lives and efforts have not been in vain if such a thing could be true." The old priest spoke with a grimness that caught everyone's attention. Cloe felt the thin veil of reality tilt a bit as she watched the priest and considered the implications.

"Quite so, Aloysius," responded the monsignor. "The last explanation may be the most secular of all but perhaps not in the way you mean it. It's just this. Judas was a revolutionary. Remember, from our prior discussions, one of the two sources of the etymology of the name 'Iscariot' suggests that Judas was of, or a member of, the 'Sicarii,' which roughly translates as 'assassins.'"

"Yes, they were dedicated to the overthrow of the Roman overlords by any means necessary, including violence. But could Judas possibly have been a member of the Sicarii?" asked Cloe.

"Perhaps, Signorina," replied the monsignor. "Some scholars believe the time of the Sicarii and of Judas could well have overlapped. In some ways, this is the most plausible explanation of all. Judas was not a Galilean, as were all the other members of the Twelve. As an educated person, he may have had strong opinions on the events of the times. Without doubt, he saw something in Jesus. Judas may have come to know Christ as early as Christ's baptism by John the Baptist in the river Jordan. This would make Judas one of Jesus's earliest followers."

Cloe began to think that she was in religion class again, but she had been convinced of the value of this information. She just wished they could get to the end of this, begin work on the manuscript, and find her father's killer.

"We all know the Jews believed that a David-like king would come to establish a kingdom on earth," continued the monsignor. "If what we speculate about Judas is true, he believed Jesus was God sent to save the Jews from the Romans, but not in a spiritual way. He thought the Messiah would raise a great Jewish army, overthrow the Romans, and establish a dominant Jewish state."

"Imagine his frustration," said Father Al reflectively. "He had followed the man for three years, and still the people suffered under the boot of the Romans. Yet he believed Jesus was heaven-sent to bring the people out of their bondage."

"A frustrated true believer, a zealot," agreed the monsignor. "To add to the prior three years' disappointment, Jesus, on Palm Sunday, had ridden triumphantly into Jerusalem during the festival time when thousands of Jews were there. The masses were seething with rebellion against the Romans. Judas must have thought that one little spark would set off the conflagration that he desired to free his people. But Jesus actually had a calming effect on the crowds."

"And then there was that incident in the temple," said Father Al. "Remember, during Holy Week, Jesus went to the great temple in Jerusalem, saw the corruption, and with a whip drove the money changers out, overturning their tables and wreaking general havoc. Hundreds, if not thousands, of Jews were there, and Judas must have desperately hoped that this would ignite the fuse."

"He must have thought, 'Now is the moment,'" remarked Cloe, beginning to understand how the revolutionary Judas might have felt and starting to see with new eyes the importance of what they were doing. She thought briefly about the implications of all this on her career.

"But remember, Jesus had a soothing effect on the crowds, just the opposite of what Judas was seeking," said the monsignor. "No matter how great the provocation, the message of Jesus Christ was still peace and love. It was not violence. One could speculate that Judas may have made up his mind to put events in motion where Christ would have no alternative but to accept his destiny and lead the Jewish people."

"So," J.E. said, "you are saying Judas went to the people who hated Jesus and wanted him dead and arranged their arrest of Jesus. In response to this, he may have thought, the followers of Jesus would have no alternative but to rise up to save him, thus provoking the kingdom on earth."

"Precisely, or at least that's the interpretation," replied the monsignor. "If true, Judas plainly had no clear understanding of the true message of Christ. But there is some Gospel support for this explanation. The Gospel of Matthew states that when Judas learned that Jesus had been condemned, he was filled with remorse and took the money back to the priests and elders with whom he had made the deal to turn Jesus over. He tried to reverse what he had done, telling them that he had betrayed innocent blood. Of course, they did not care as they had what they wanted."

"The language indicates that the thing got out of hand and that Judas did not intend for Jesus to be condemned," added Father Al. "He thought the people would rise up and save Jesus. He repents when it is clear his scheme has gone terribly awry." The old priest slowly shook his head and said, "Could there have been a more desperate soul when he saw what he had wrought?"

For a moment the assembly contemplated the tragic circumstances underlying this explanation. The fate of the savior of mankind possibly had hung on the misunderstanding of his message by one of his disciples. Cloe understood how Christ could have shed tears of blood.

"Well," added Dean Broussard, "there is a prayer that says something to the effect that I pray God to save me from the good intentions of my meddling friends."

"Close enough," said the monsignor with a trace of a smile on his face.

J.E. brushed aside the attempt at levity. "You are saying the most significant event in human history may have resulted from Judas having faulty intel about the true mission of Jesus Christ."

The monsignor gazed into the distance as if his thoughts were far away and replied, "That's certainly the interpretation of some scholars. But that's not at all what the Coptic version of the Gospel of Judas Iscariot translated by scholars in 2006 says."

# CHAPTER 27

One of the young scientists entered the conference room and passed a note to Dr. Harrell. After briefly studying the message, Dr. Harrell announced, "The carbon-dating results, according to Mike, place the age of the papyrus in the new Judas manuscript at the late first century or early to mid-second century AD, give or take."

"Give or take what?" asked J.E. "How statistically significant are those dates? Can we rely on them?"

"Absolutely," said Dr. Harrell, seating himself at the table. "Except, please understand that Mike has simulated a carbon-14 dating process. A true carbon-dating test will take much longer to run—and will be run—but I'm confident such a test will only verify Mike's findings. Mike has taken values from the papyrus and simulated the test much as modern medical science can simulate what would otherwise be very invasive procedures. But the simulated tests have proven to be quite accurate."

"If true, this range of dates would be highly significant," remarked the monsignor, looking directly at Dr. Harrell. "The Coptic version of the Gospel of Judas Iscariot that was made known to the religious and antiquities community around 2006 was carbon-dated to the third to fourth century AD. In the biblical world, the closer the proximity of the writing to the time of Christ, all other things being equal, the more reliable the document may be deemed to be."

"Why is that?" asked Dean Broussard.

Cloe looked at J.E. and saw that although her patience for these seemingly endless tutorials was short, J.E. was nevertheless fascinated.

"It's a simple thing, really," said Father Al. "The closer to the time of Christ that a writing about Christ originated, the more likely that there would have been living people who could have corroborated or refuted what the writing said."

"Just so, Dean," confirmed the monsignor, who rose from his seat and walked to the sideboard to pour more coffee. "People of the time never would have accepted material they knew to be false, particularly on such an important subject. This is one reason why the Acts of the Apostles, the synoptic Gospels, and the Gospel of John have all been accepted by the Church as the most reliable. This is why they form the doctrinal core of the Catholic religion."

"The letters of St. Paul were among the earliest such documents written, beginning in about AD 50–51," stipulated Father Al. "While not all scholars agree on the order in which the Gospels were written, many believe St. Matthew's Gospel was the earliest, written sometime in the '40s to '50s. Consider that Christ was crucified in AD 33 or thereabouts. With the earliest of these materials written a mere decade or so after Christ died, there would have been hundreds, if not thousands, of people still alive who could attest to the veracity of events as described in the works of St. Paul and St. Matthew."

Cloe saw that the monsignor had picked up the coffeepot and was moving around the table, pouring coffee for those who wanted it. She marked that as an attribute of a servant leader and wondered whether she had judged the monsignor too harshly. Time would tell.

The monsignor resumed the narrative. "The Gospels of Mark and Luke were written a bit after Matthew's, and the Gospel of John was written about the early nineties, all still within the first century AD and within sixty or so years of Christ's death.

"The proximity of the events of the day to their chronicling in these Gospels provides the certification of their authenticity. There is also the fact that some of the Apostles had protégés who studied under them. Many of these students were located in far-flung areas of the Roman Empire. Imagine the power and authority a person would have if he could truthfully say he had been tutored directly by one of the Apostles. This is how the early Church grew and prospered. This is one reason why the Church is referred to as 'Apostolic.'"

"This is very exciting … enormously exciting," said Dr. Harrell. "If the manuscript we have removed from the jar dates to a time

135

comparable to the Gospel of St. John, it could be incredibly significant, both from an antiquities standpoint and from a doctrinal standpoint. It could be a huge double whammy in the religious and scientific worlds."

Cloe reflected on the initial insistence of the LSU scholars that this was a purely scientific inquiry and had no religious overtones. Apparently, she thought, listening to Dr. Harrell now, they no longer clung to that view.

"As we said when we started this exercise, this could be the most important relic to be recovered since the birth of Christ," stated the monsignor.

"Except, Monsignor, how could you know to follow this particular lead?" questioned Cloe. "There must be hundreds or thousands of excavations each year in the Middle East—and elsewhere—that produce interesting jars, pottery, markings, writings, and the like. Something has stirred the Vatican's interest in this particular jar. Why is this jar from the humble mantelpiece of an old soldier in south Louisiana so important to the Holy See?"

"A fair question," he responded. "I'm not the only operative that the Vatican has in place to pursue these kinds of discoveries. There are others. And you are correct that we have many leads to pursue. But once we learned where it had been found, the Vatican thought this discovery might have promise. We were aware that certain groups had been active in securing ancient relics in this area. Thus, the jar had a high level of interest for us from early on in our involvement. Also, we became aware of the language on the outside of that jar. Thib also told us about the niche where it was found. If you remember, my predecessor sent Polaroid pictures back to the Vatican years ago. We have been waiting. We have been watching."

"Waiting," said Cloe. "Waiting so long, watching. Is that how it goes? Were you never anxious to find out what the jar contained?"

"Cloe, the Church is not anxious," said the monsignor, looking upon her kindly. "Time and space have no real hold on the universal Church of our Lord Jesus Christ. Men come and go, but the Church is immutable and immortal and continues its service to mankind. Had it been a half a millennium instead of a half-century to get to the truth of the jar and its contents, the Church still would have been there. We are here now, and our waiting is at an end."

# CHAPTER 28

The man thought about his options for securing the jar. He had excellent intelligence and knew what was happening in the Louisiana city called Baton Rouge in almost real time. New agents were also in position. In fact, he had parallel forces in place. Truth be told, he had spies even in the Vatican itself.

He had sent the Gulfstream V to America with several trusted Armenian servants who were now triply ready to serve him. They would cut the hearts out of everyone involved if he instructed them to take the jar by force. The leader of the group had been tasked with recruiting some of the local criminal population to help with certain elements of the operation.

When his untraceable cell phone rang, he answered promptly. "Yes?"

"Master, I have made contact with the appropriate representatives here in New Orleans," said the familiar voice of his field general. "All is in order, and I have secured the services of adequate retainers for our project."

The man knew better than to question the agent on recruitment particulars. He knew his commander would have vetted the personnel far more thoroughly than even he himself could have. He simply said, "Well done." He also knew the soldier's tactical preparation and execution were second to none. Now the question moved to the best strategy to be employed to achieve the objective.

"Do you have instructions for me?" queried the warrior servant.

"I have been contemplating different strategies, but I believe the best thing now is to have patience. With the people in charge still on high alert after the last show, caution is advised. The actors in the play are also watchful."

Despite the safeguards on his phone, the man and his employees remained circumspect in their conversations. With the expectation that the CIA or the Mossad might randomly intercept their cell phone traffic, they avoided key words or phrases that would trigger their infernal computer programs for closer scrutiny.

He continued, "Perhaps it is best to enjoy the play and to see what develops and how it ends. In the meantime, we will know what they learn almost as soon as they discover it. Best to let them do the work and look for our opportunity."

"A wise approach, sir. I shall deploy our resources in a strategic manner, and we shall await your advice." As always, the soldier on the other end of the phone was a faithful servant of few words.

"Very well, my old friend. Please see to it and make sure our people are aware of the reward for success and the price of failure in my service," said the man as he snapped the phone shut.

# CHAPTER 29

Early Sunday afternoon, back in the original photo lab, laid out on the central optical field table, each page of the manuscript was being carefully photographed with film, infrared, and digital cameras in order to make a complete record. Meanwhile, Cloe and the others had donned the usual lab coats, plus face masks meant to shield the manuscript from any bacteria or other contaminants that might be present. Cloe thought that they must look like something from a science fiction movie about one of those deadly plagues infecting the earth.

Dr. Harrell glanced around at the assembly and said, "Cloe, please look at the first few pages of the manuscript and see if you can get anything from them. Mike has read the manuscript, and he's working on a translation, but a real understanding will take a team of scholars and many months or years. Your insights would be very valuable at this point."

Cloe walked forward to the table. Somehow her entire career had come to this moment. Excitement and anxiety coursed through her. She bent over and carefully examined the manuscript. What was the binding? Was it leather or some other animal skin? Yes, the latter for lack of a more precise descriptor.

As Cloe examined the cover, the thought struck her, as it had many times in her investigations of historical documents, that almost everything the ancients did was meant to last millennia. Their cunning in understanding and adapting their meager materials to the task at hand was extraordinary. The manuscript was in surprisingly good external condition considering its age. Cloe had books only a few years old that were in worse shape. Of course, they were of modern materials and construction.

"Has the paper been confirmed as papyrus?" she asked, turning and looking at Dr. Harrell. Mentally, she was clicking through her checklist of relevant points.

"Yes," responded Dr. Harrell immediately. "Mike says it is consistent with the age and time to which it has been dated. That is to say, we still believe the end of the first century is about right but perhaps as late as midway into the second century. The ink analysis shows a carbon-based pigment that was oil- or resin-bound of a general type that had been in use for centuries. It was in common use in the first and second centuries."

"The lettering is certainly ancient Greek," Cloe said, turning back to the papyrus. "But it is written with a flourish and style that suggest an author other than some anonymous monk routinely transcribing ancient literature. My initial thought is that this is the original document rather than a handwritten copy. Of course, this is just an impression, but I would view this point as possibly very important. Much of the writing and certainly all of the copying in that era was delegated to scribes who did this for a living. Their efforts were consistent and predictable. This work was written by someone, I believe, in some position of authority who was fully aware of the importance of what he was doing. I cannot get over the impression of drama and urgency in the script that I'm reading."

"How can you tell that?" asked J.E., looking over his mother's shoulder at the text as if he could make something of it.

"Just intuition, of course. But after looking at many, many ancient manuscripts, one develops a sense about them. Call it an intelligent guess. But Dr. Harrell is quite right. A team of experts will need a great deal of time to go through the manuscript to arrive at anything definitive," Cloe said. "Another thing that is striking is the thinness of the document."

Dr. Harrell nodded. "The manuscript contains about twenty pages, but unfortunately, some of them have been partially or completely corrupted over time," he said, somewhat dejectedly. "This is due not to the paper but rather to the deterioration or smudging of the ink under the conditions in the jar. We know whoever placed the document in the jar went to some lengths to try to preserve it. But the smudging suggests the jar was moved one or more times or otherwise handled in some way. A rough sea voyage could explain such smearing."

"Equally possible," agreed Cloe. "And maybe more plausible is the notion that the manuscript itself was moved, read, or handled to some substantial degree before it was sealed in the jar. This could also account for the smudging."

"There are techniques to isolate the smudging and to clarify the writing, but these will take time and effort," said Dean Broussard. "In due course, we shall see what the entire writing says."

The lab was silent for a long moment as the group absorbed this information and then telescoped out the natural progression of events based on what they now thought. Cloe knew it would be a slog from here. This was the way of scientific discovery—miles and miles of effort possibly leading to one "eureka" moment, or not in many cases. They were on the front end of the bell curve of effort. Time would tell.

"While there's certainly a great deal of work to do, there is one thing we can complete now," said Dr. Harrell.

Cloe's curiosity rose. "What's that?"

"Well, there's little doubt an important discovery has been made. Under such circumstances it is customary to assign a name to the discovery. Sometimes the name is after the place where the discovery was made, such as the Dead Sea Scrolls, or after the person who made the discovery. An example would be the Salk Vaccine after Dr. Jonas Salk, who discovered the vaccine against polio."

"Hmm," said Father Al, chuckling. "We can't very well name it the Mantelpiece Manuscript, but that was certainly where we found it—on the mantelpiece at Thib's house."

"Before that it was discovered by Thib in a cave in North Africa, but we don't know exactly where," added the monsignor.

"There's only one proper name for this manuscript," said the old priest with a smile. "It shall be the Lejeune Manuscript after Thib who found it and now Cloe, given her efforts to unlock its secrets."

There was general agreement on this, and everyone looked at Cloe, who was smiling through the tears in her eyes. She thought her dad would be proud.

"The Lejeune Manuscript it is," she confirmed. "But only after Thibodeaux Lejeune, the discoverer of the jar and its contents."

***

With that decided, Cloe knew there was much to be done. "What remains now is the hard work of translating the text of the Lejeune Manuscript," she said finally. "If we spend only a half day on each of the pages, it will take at least two weeks to draft a working translation. That's if we can translate all the smudged pages. Even that would be extremely tentative due to the distortion of some of the pages. It may take months or years to come to a translation consensus."

Cloe felt her energy level draw down at the prospect of the long effort ahead of them. Well, what had she expected? She had promised Thib she would unlock the secrets of the jar, and she would do whatever it took to do so. Time and tide would tell the tale, or so her mother had often incorrectly said. But it seemed appropriate in this instance.

"Well, that means we have done what can be done, and we have certainly been witnesses to a great event," said Father Al in his usual upbeat manner. "It sounds like it is time for me to return home to Madisonville and to my flock. We all know how the sheep will scatter when the shepherd is away for too long," he concluded with a smile.

"And Dr. Harrell and I have been away from our daily duties as long as is prudent in any event," added Dean Broussard. "However, we will make special arrangements for you, Cloe, if you wish to stay here and work on the translation. The full resources of our labs and of Mike will be available to you. You are really the only one of us qualified to make the translation. The ball is in your court if you want it."

Cloe considered this and her promise to her father when she had read his letter. A leave of absence from her work in Seattle could be arranged without too much fuss. In fact, as she thought about it, the university would probably insist on her remaining on the job in Louisiana. What better use of her time as the vice-chair, and hopefully soon-to-be-chair, of the Department of Ancient Languages of her alma mater than to investigate the authenticity and content of an ancient Greek tome that might be the earliest known edition of the Gospel of Judas Iscariot? Not only would they give her the time off from her duties in Seattle, but they would likely insist that she do this on the university's dime and be prepared to lecture and write about it when she returned.

No matter what she found hereafter in her examination of the jar, the opportunity itself would be a huge boost to her career. Should she find and translate something extraordinary, there might be no limit to the heights she could attain in her discipline. And as she had promised Thib, she would find the answer to the jar. In spite of the attempt on her life and her father's murder, she would find out who wanted it so badly and why.

"Dean Broussard, your accommodation is very much appreciated," she said. "I'll make the necessary arrangements in Seattle, but I'm confident I will be able to see this project to fruition." Cloe was once again energized and anxious to proceed.

The monsignor stepped forward. "I too am willing to work on the project. While the Signorina is very able and versed in ancient languages, including Greek, I believe my knowledge of religious events, customs, and usages will prove valuable in getting to the meaning of the Lejeune Manuscript, or at least those parts that are still readable. Also, I'm the only one of our group who is familiar with the existing Coptic Judas Gospel, the one that dates to the third or fourth century. It is very possible that the Gospel from our jar is an earlier version of that Gospel. A comparison of the two could be extremely significant."

And so it was decided that the monsignor and Cloe would stay and work on the Lejeune Manuscript. J.E. and the Swiss Guards would provide security and logistics.

The group had come together over strange and extremely trying circumstances. As a result, the bond that had formed between them was as strong as the mystery on which they worked was deep. No one wanted to break this link, so they decided that farewell was the correct note of departure. Dean Broussard and Dr. Harrell said they would check in daily. Father Al seemed satisfied with Cloe's promise to keep him apprised of their progress. Nevertheless, he and Cloe both had tears in their eyes early the next morning as he climbed in the monsignor's car for the ride back to Madisonville.

Cloe looked after the car until it was out of sight and wondered when she would next see that kindly, gentle servant of God.

# CHAPTER 30

The phone rang Monday morning, not long after Father Al had departed, in the hotel room where Cloe and J.E. were discussing the Judas Gospel. J.E. picked it up and listened intently to the voice on the other end. Cloe could see his shoulders slump and the steel go out of his young body. After a while, he responded quietly and rang off. He turned, ashen-faced, to Cloe and said, "That was the chief from the campus police. There's been a terrible accident."

"What is it?" she asked softly with a dread and trepidation as deep as any she had ever experienced.

"Father Al is dead," J.E. replied simply. "He was killed in an accident on the way home to Madisonville."

The simplicity and starkness of J.E.'s straightforward revelation was like a cold lightning strike to her heart. Her breath caught, and she could barely take in air. "What? How?" she demanded.

"The details are still sketchy, but it appears both he and the monsignor's driver were killed in an area of the highway under construction between Baton Rouge and Hammond. A third lane is being put in to lessen the congestion," J.E. stated mechanically.

"But he just left, not more than an hour or two ago. How could anything have happened to him? There's a mistake. There are lots of black sedans on the road."

J.E. crossed the room to his mother and wrapped her in his arms. He held her for a good while before answering. "According to the chief, an excavator accidentally swung its scoop into the oncoming traffic lane just as the car with Father Al came through. The blade on the scoop tore through the roof of the car, decapitating both the driver and Father Al." J.E.'s voice cracked and broke at this. He could say no more.

"Horrible! No, no, no!" Cloe felt the very life being sucked out of her as she struggled with the enormity of the news. "He just left!" Her legs gave out, and J.E. lowered her into a nearby chair. "It's some kind of gruesome mistake. It has to be!" Cloe insisted.

"The chief says that the tentative identifications are positive," J.E. replied in a low, sad whisper, somewhat back in control. "Whatever it is, I don't think it is a mistake."

This whole thing had taken another disastrous, deadly turn. "What are we going to do? How can I possibly carry on without Father Al?" Even without him physically in Baton Rouge, Cloe had known that she could count on him and his wise counsel. "I don't know that I have the strength to move forward," she said honestly.

Cloe was as miserable as she had been since getting on that bus as a scared seventeen-year-old runaway so many years ago. Old, hard memories of loss flashed before her.

"The chief will be here in a few minutes," J.E. said. "The monsignor and I have been asked to go to the scene and verify the vehicle. After that, we may have to go to the morgue to identify the bodies. It's basically to confirm what they already think they know."

J.E. was now once again the soldier with a mission to accomplish—a dirty, bad, unpleasant mission, but a job that nevertheless had to be done. Cloe could see that it would get done.

"Oh, J.E., we should never have come to Louisiana. If we had not come here, Father Al would not have been on that highway to die such an ugly, lonely death."

"All death is ugly, and it is the one thing that we do absolutely alone. Father Al was as prepared as any of us and much better than most," he responded. "Father Al believed in our project. No one can explain a senseless accident like this. If it was his time, he might have been run over in front of his church even if we had never come. You just don't know.

"Right now the only thing I do know for sure is that we must stay together." J.E. looked at her with heartfelt conviction as he spoke. "Father Al remains with us in spirit if we believe the project has any merit at all. If we count Bobby Morrow, at least five people, Thib, Father Al, the excavator operator, and the monsignor's driver, are dead directly or indirectly because of the jar and its contents. You and I were very close to being victims as well."

"What's going on here, J.E.? I can't make any sense of it. And you sound like you think the jar has some sort of curse on it. You know I don't believe in such things."

"I'm not sure I believe in curses either. But I'm real sure I don't believe in coincidences. Things happen for a reason, usually because someone wants them to happen. What I know for sure is that Bobby Morrow, Thib, and now Father Al, as well as the others, are all casualties, in a sense, of the jar. You and I were nearly victims in what the chief himself thinks was a hired contract killing. Think about that. Why would someone want to murder us? We hardly even know anyone here. It's the jar, again! It's got to be."

"You're talking like the deaths of Father Al and the driver are connected with the jar. But you said yourself that they were killed in an accident on the highway."

"It's just too many coincidences!" J.E. almost yelled. "I'll tell you one thing, I'm going up to that highway and wherever else it takes to find out what's happening here. If it was an accident, then so be it. If not, I will find out who's behind this, and then God help his sorry self when I get my hands on him."

147

# CHAPTER 31

Two members of the Swiss Guard had been left with Cloe. One was stationed in the lobby, and the other was just outside her door. The campus police and local authorities were on raised-alert status. When she looked out the window, Cloe could see a sheriff's vehicle in the parking lot. J.E., in tactical control by agreement with the monsignor, had insisted that the Swiss form the inner perimeter and would not take no for an answer. No one would violate their bivouac area intent on malice without a hell of a fight.

Dr. Harrell and Dean Broussard had each come by to pay their respects and see what they could do. There was just not much anyone could do. But each visited and waited with her for a while before returning to his duties.

The Swiss Guards were as serious and steely-eyed as ever, and Cloe had to admit that their presence made her feel a little less vulnerable. She supposed the other two were still at the lab guarding the jar and now the Lejeune Manuscript.

She was lost in these thoughts when J.E. returned with the monsignor and the chief. The group headed for the table in the dining room/living room combination in the suite and collapsed there. Cloe could see that J.E. and the monsignor were exhausted physically from the strain and emotionally from the terrible duties they had performed. Father Al, gone—she could scarcely believe it.

"Mom, can you put on some coffee for us? We all have some things to talk about," said her son wearily.

Cloe started water boiling for the coffee and joined them at the table. Soon the familiar aroma of the brew filled the room. Cloe's thoughts had turned inward to such a degree that she at first did not realize the monsignor was speaking to her.

"Signorina, I have to inform you that there is no doubt that our friends were the ones killed on the highway in this heinous manner. We have seen this with our own eyes," he said with great courtesy and sadness. "It is evident that Father Al's car was traveling in the outside ..." He stopped speaking, and Cloe was unsure whether he could continue.

The chief took up the explanation. "There is a continuous line of concrete dividers that separates the traffic lane from the lane under construction. This area was the shoulder of the road before the new construction started. The dividers should have protected the traffic from any hazards of the construction."

"The problem," J.E. said, "is that there are several gaps in the concrete separators for trucks to enter and exit the construction area. Precisely at one of these gaps an excavator had been set up for whatever work it was supposed to do."

The chief resumed the explanation. "As Father Al's vehicle approached, the excavator pirouetted at exactly that time, swinging the blade into the priest's lane of traffic. The blade of the scoop peeled the top of the car back at hood level so quickly that neither man had time to see or react. Both died instantly."

Cloe gasped and could not speak.

"Father Al was found in the backseat, his hand wrapped around his rosary. He must have been praying on the way home," whispered the monsignor.

Cloe saw that the monsignor was grief-stricken to his core. She instantly felt bad for ever having doubted this man. There was certainly no doubt about his love for Father Al.

Hot tears of grief had welled up in Cloe's eyes as she listened to the story of the horrific demise of her friend—the man she now thought of as her priest. She lifted herself heavily from the chair and moved into the kitchen. "I'll bring the coffee," she said simply.

She thought about this man who had been her father's confessor and friend, and she worried that her mission with the jar had at least causally led to his death. In rural Louisiana a priest was irreplaceable, what with fewer younger people entering the vocation and the difficulty of finding priests. Irreplaceable! She felt that she had somehow committed a terrible sin against Father Al's congregation and against her hometown itself.

Cloe's hands shook badly as she poured the coffee, but she heard the chief say, "The cause of death is self-evident, so there will be no need for an autopsy. The bodies will be released in the morning ..."

Cloe could see he wanted to continue, but even this hardened veteran was staggered by the loss of Father Al.

"I will see to the driver," said the monsignor. "He was new to me, but I do know he had a wife and children. A papal jet will be used to take him back to his family. I have already contacted the archbishop about Father Al. His staff has spoken to the deacon and the administrative staff at St. Anselm's Church. They will come up in the morning to escort Father Al back to Madisonville."

"Did Father Al have any family?" asked Cloe.

"Yes," replied the monsignor. "He has a sister who is also a religious, a member of the order of the Franciscan Missionaries of Our Lady. His parents are gone, and of course there are no nieces or nephews. He will be buried in the Madisonville cemetery near where your father and mother rest."

Cloe flashed back to her father's funeral and wondered at the irony of the death of the priest who had just officiated that ceremony. How transformative it had been for her. Now the same scene would be revisited, but this time for the dear old priest.

"We are going back to Madisonville," she said to J.E. "Once again." She recognized the echo of her words after that fateful phone call from Uncle Sonny informing her of her father's death. Although his death and funeral seemed to have happened so long ago, in reality they had occurred less than a week before.

J.E. rose to his full height, walked around the table to his mother, and hugged her tightly. "Mom, we aren't going to Madisonville or to the funeral," he said gently. He looked at her and then at the others.

"But J.E., we must ... Father Al," she replied quickly. "Why would you say such a thing?"

"Because I'm not sure it's safe," he said flatly. "We are caught up in something here that I do not fully understand, and until I do, we are going to maintain a defensible position. A funeral in Madisonville is not defensible. We are not going to take any more casualties if I can help it."

Cloe studied her son carefully. "What are you saying ... casualties? Everything I know says Father Al was killed in an automobile accident."

"Signorina, there are other circumstances of which you are unaware. While attending to Father Al and the driver, we learned some important new details about what happened. One of the things that the chief and the sheriff's department wanted to do after the accident was interrogate the operator of the excavator to get from him an account of the events," said the monsignor.

"Yes, certainly. What did he say?"

"The man could not be located at the scene. It seems he has vanished. When the road foreman was questioned, he said that the usual operator had called in sick and that he had sent for a replacement. The stand-in was piloting the excavator at the time of the incident."

"So perhaps an inexperienced replacement negligently killed our friend? Is that what you think?" responded Cloe.

"The foreman said the credentials for the substitute the union sent over were impeccable. There was no inexperience there. If anything, he was more capable than the usual operator. As is his habit with new or temporary employees on the excavator, the foreman gave the man a field test, and he was impressed by the replacement's dexterity with the monster machine."

"So we've got a skilled substitute operator who can't now be found after this terrible incident," said J.E. "This was enough to send the police to the usual operator's home to see what they could learn. They are, at this very minute, at the home of the original operator. The sheriff's office is also involved. They're running a sketch of the replacement through various databases."

J.E.'s cell phone rang just then, and he stepped aside to take the call. After about two minutes he closed the phone, turned to the group, and said, "That was the detective from the sheriff's department. Mom, you probably remember him from the campus police office the day after we were almost run down. He says they've found no trace of the replacement operator and no hits on his sketch. He has absolutely vanished, as if he was never there."

"What of the normal operator? What did he say when the police tracked him down?" asked Cloe.

"They went to his home to talk to him. They found him dead, his throat cut."

# CHAPTER 32

"The old priest is dead," said the field operative circumspectly into the throwaway cell phone he carried. "He died in a tragic automobile accident witnessed by our colleagues from the city. The driver of the ill-fated vehicle also perished. Seems they ran under a piece of highway equipment on the way from the university back to the priest's church."

"Well," said the man, "it is a dangerous world." The man was nevertheless disturbed that the hired soldiers from New Orleans had jumped the gun on his timetable. Were they in his direct employ, he would teach them discipline and more. Still, he thought, there might be opportunity to be seized.

"Our man has kept us completely up-to-date on the opening of the jar and the discovery of the manuscript, which, incidentally, they have christened the Lejeune Manuscript."

The man sneered at this and said, "Continue."

"We understand that the priest's body will be taken back to his hometown in the next day or two, and undoubtedly, his group of friends will follow for the funeral," responded the soldier. "The only problem in the whole matter is that our city retainers, in their exuberance to accomplish their tasks, may have inadvertently made it somewhat easier for the authorities to learn the cause of the accident. This may occur sooner than desirable."

"Unfortunate," responded the man.

"Quite so, sir. The next opportunity to engage the monsignor and his band will likely come at the funeral."

"Think creatively. I would really like our visit with them to be special and extremely memorable. Let us put forth the full measure of our capabilities on this occasion."

"Sir, you have been heard clearly," the voice on the phone responded. "We will be present and will make sure they receive a more than adequate gauge of our condolences."

***

The man leaned back in the plush leather wing chair in the bunker. A fire in the stone fireplace crackled and popped softly. Classical music played in the background from hidden speakers. His servant knocked softly and entered with a cold supper of smoked salmon, capers, and purple onions served on a bed of fresh spinach anointed with an ethereal oil-and-vinegar dressing. Tonight he had prepared his master's favorite, a dry gin that had been frozen with a bit of water to the point of a syrup-like consistency. As always, it was served straight up in a frozen stem. Life was good, the man thought, completely satisfied with himself.

"Master," asked the trusted servant, "why kill them all? Will that not bring more attention to us? Why not simply take the jar and its contents and be done with these people?"

"The fact is they already know too much about the jar and the writing it contains. Dead, they are silenced, but alive, there will be no end to it. It's a simple calculation."

"But Master, information on the manuscript has been put into the computer."

"Certainly, but this information will be erased from the computer. We will take care of that. That will leave only the jar, the manuscript, and the people who have become knowledgeable about it. We will inexorably isolate and eliminate them so that in the end there will be only the manuscript, which I will have. They will all die!"

# CHAPTER 33

"J.E., I'm really not sure this is necessary or wise," stated Cloe as they climbed into the monsignor's substitute vehicle. J.E. had insisted on a very early start. Father Al's wake was to begin at 8:00 a.m., the funeral at 9:00, in Madisonville, and he wanted to give the correct impression.

The monsignor had wasted no time in replacing the sedan after the terrible accident on the highway. Although Cloe had attempted to dissuade J.E. from his plan concerning the old priest's funeral, he would not be moved. All were dressed as if to attend the service, and to anyone who might be observing, they appeared to be headed to Madisonville for the funeral. A heavy sadness hung over the group. The monsignor and J.E. had spent a great deal of time planning, talking, and speaking with associates at the Vatican and with the local police authorities. Everyone was on highest alert.

"You may be right," said the young soldier, "but if I'm correct, this will tell us a great deal about our enemy. If we are lucky, this may bring them into the open. Perhaps we can end it."

"Agreed," added the monsignor. "It's time we act proactively for our own protection."

All were now huddled in the rear of the big vehicle, like three warriors in a foxhole. They peeked out the windows of the car as furtively as soldiers might peer over the highest edge of their last redoubt. Cloe could not shake the chill from her bones. The dean and the doctor were both occupied with other essential duties back at LSU. The local authorities were keeping an eye out for them, just in case. Two of the Swiss Guards followed Cloe and her group in their own vehicle.

She watched as they began to retrace the route it seemed they had taken so long ago in coming to LSU. The car wound its way around the picturesque lakes until it ascended the interstate highway and headed east. The Swiss trailed them in a separate car to determine whether they were being followed. In due course the trailing car reported by cell phone that the monsignor's car was being tailed as it left Baton Rouge. J.E. had expected this to happen. The main question was whether the stalkers would follow all the way to Madisonville or would, at some point, be satisfied and break off.

J.E. had planned everything carefully, and Cloe had to admit that he'd considered every tactical possibility. She thanked God for her son and his great knowledge and skills.

The heavy black sedan sped east. About twenty miles outside of Baton Rouge, the Swiss called to say that the pursuit car had broken off and exited the highway and now seemed to be returning to Baton Rouge.

J.E. smiled and turned to the monsignor. "As we suspected! Their task wasn't to intercept us or to follow us all the way to Madisonville but to assure themselves and their leaders that we were, indeed, on our way to the funeral. Doubtless, somewhere further down the highway, another group will be stationed to pick up our trail and follow us to the funeral."

"Yes," added the monsignor. "I'm sure there is also a gang of cutthroats in Madisonville just waiting, with a very unpleasant reception planned for us."

"Our friends with the state police and the sheriff's department will be there and will give them all they can handle," said J.E.

"It seems to all be falling into place as we expected," agreed the monsignor.

The sleek road car continued down the interstate for a while so as to verify that their pursuers had, in fact, dropped off. Then it too suddenly exited the highway and headed back to Baton Rouge. By means of several intersecting rural highways, the car continued on until it had virtually circumnavigated the southern area of Baton Rouge connecting with Louisiana Highway 30. From their preparations Cloe knew that this local road connected with the university from the south. They would be at the lab shortly.

# CHAPTER 34

The soldier and four of his men climbed the six steps, entered the building housing the lab, and scanned the area for security and cameras. Nothing, the soldier noted. Just a typical academic building with classrooms and labs. *These complacent Americans*, he thought with a sneer. Their entire country could be taken from under their very noses, and they would not notice. At this early hour, although open in anticipation of the school day, the building was not yet occupied by students or faculty. He could see no one coming or going.

Dressed in black, the intruders carefully crept down the right-hand hallway, each hugging the wall on either side to reduce their target silhouettes. One man was stationed at the neck of the hall and the foyer to cover their retreat. The leader's military background had never failed him or his men; this was second nature. He could not abide even the thought of failure.

"The lab is the fourth door on the right," he whispered.

Approaching the door, he saw that the lab was dark. At the door, the man's agents queued up on either side. Muscles were coiled like steel springs. Weapons appeared like smoke, and the men pumped through the door, clearing left and right, anticipating violence that did not materialize. All was quiet and dark, and it appeared that no one was present.

With the light from the hall at their backs, the commander signaled his men to remain alert. He flipped the light switch, and the room was bathed with that antiseptic light that comes from closely spaced fluorescent fixtures. An atonal hum filled the air. The warrior's finely honed military senses spiked with alarm an instant before he saw at least a dozen heavily armed men initially concealed among the desks and other furnishings. Straight away, he knew he and his men had fallen into a trap.

"Freeze!" yelled policemen dressed in special-forces gear.

"Drop your weapons and face down on the floor!" screamed a plainclothes cop.

Time went into ultraslow motion. With their training his men would do no such things because all were aware of the price of failure. Better to die like rats in a trap than to face their employer's vengeance on them and their families.

Small beads of sweat appeared on the soldier's forehead as he grasped that he would, in a matter of moments, kill or die. He was aware that if he perished at his assigned task, his family would be well cared for and would have no monetary worries. All of this flashed through his conscious mind in a millisecond.

"*Estegh*, on me!" he ordered, and in a flash his men converged on him in a wedge formation with weapons drawn and began an outward tremendous, murderous volley. Their rain of fire was immediately and effectively returned. After that it was chaos, and after that … nothing.

# CHAPTER 35

"As far as we know we got them all," said the SWAT team leader. Cloe and her colleagues were being debriefed in a meeting room next to the photo lab. "The leader of the band and two of his men were killed in the lab firefight. One of them was severely wounded, and he has been taken to the Lady of Lake Regional Medical Center trauma facility. If anyone can save his sorry hide, the Lake can, but it is touch-and-go at this point, and we won't know for a while. For sure we won't get any information out of him for a long time, if ever.

"The kid they left to guard their escape was surrounded on three sides, but he still fought like a cornered bear. He was wounded twice, but he battled on until he was low on ammo," the cop said with something like respect, if not admiration. "When we finally closed on him, he ate his own gun. He would not be captured. The foyer of that class building is pretty well shot up."

A thick silence enveloped them like a curtain as they all contemplated what could make a young person with his whole life ahead of him do such a thing. The word "fanatic" came to Cloe, but that was not quite right because these were paid mercenaries. But something beyond mere money had made them fight to the death the way they had. Was it loyalty or was it fear? To or of whom?

"Well done," said the monsignor, breaking the reflective silence. "What of our casualties?" He sat forward and steepled his fingers as he asked this question.

"One of the Swiss Guards was slightly wounded, but he should recover fully after minor surgery, which is where he is as we speak," said the chief.

"A couple of SWAT team members have impact injuries from bullets hitting their vests," added the SWAT team leader. "But no damage and nothing but precautionary examinations at the hospital. We were well positioned with good intel and good men. We were also very fortunate."

"Altogether a very good outcome, young sir," said the monsignor, directing the compliment to J.E., who was seated directly across the table from him.

"Yes," said Cloe, who was completely astounded by the events and the fact that her young son had helped conceive, plan, and coordinate everything. She and Dr. Harrell were taking in every detail of the report now being given by various law enforcement personnel. Dean Broussard was tied up and couldn't participate.

"How did you know?" asked the chief, turning to face J.E.

Cloe knew the chief and the other officers had been somewhat skeptical of J.E.'s assertion that there would be an effort to take the jar and codex by force. They had thought the trap would come up empty. But in the end, he had convinced them that they could not afford to take the chance something might happen at the lab.

J.E. stood, put his hands on his hips, and looked down in deep concentration. "I didn't know anything for sure, but after some combat you begin to sense a battle plan. I'll just say what I said before. The attack on us at the bridge, the strange circumstances of the abandoned car, the terrible death of Father Al and the monsignor's driver, the inexplicable death of the regular excavator operator, and no trace of anything—all apparently meant to look like unfortunate accidents or random crimes. I just figured that this was all a prologue to what they really wanted, which was the manuscript."

"Even looking at it all from that perspective, nothing quite fit," responded the chief. "But out of the chaos you somehow discerned purpose and order. That's the amazing thing."

Cloe smiled with pride at the acknowledgment of her son's acumen.

"The young sir certainly assessed the tactical situation accurately," said the monsignor, "reasoning that our supposed attendance at Father Al's funeral might provide the opportunity for our adversary to go after the manuscript and the information we have gathered. I will not be surprised if we learn that J.E. was also correct that they made plans for us on the Madisonville end."

"Correct," said the sheriff's detective, who was standing near the door. "In coordination with the state police, we have arrested several well-armed men in Madisonville who were observing the mourners at the priest's funeral. They were not there to express their condolences. We were well assisted by the local authorities, who helped identify people they did not recognize."

"Think of it," said Cloe. "Whoever is behind this was willing to take great risks to steal the manuscript and to kill all of us. It all started with Thib. It's not enough for him to simply possess the Lejeune Manuscript; he must have it and whatever knowledge it contains to the exclusion of all others. To do this, he kills a parish priest and other innocents. What are we dealing with? What kind of monster is after us and what we have, and how did he get on to us?"

Cloe knew there were no answers now to these questions, but they would have to be answered on the way to finding her father's killer. The jar had to be protected and its secrets revealed. "Chief, do we know anything more about these people after all this?" she asked.

"Just before the firefight broke out in the lab, the leader said something that stuck in my mind," said the chief. "You know how situations like that can imprint themselves on your brain. He yelled 'estegh' or something very close to that and then 'on me.' All his men then jumped into some type of triangular formation, and unholy hell broke loose."

"It sounds like a wedge or turtle formation, each of which has been used for thousands of years by soldiers in certain circumstances," replied J.E. "Those formations were particularly popular in certain Near East and Mediterranean areas."

"It was very effective, and if we had not had superior firepower, cover, and the element of surprise, I hate to think what might have happened."

"Chief, you say you think the word was 'estegh'?" asked the monsignor thoughtfully, now leaning back in his chair and lacing his fingers behind his head as if he were straining for a memory.

"That's what I remember."

The monsignor looked off in the distance. After a bit he said, "My immediate thought is that *estegh* is Armenian for 'here.' This makes sense in context because the leader was calling for his men to form up on him. What have we learned of their nationalities and backgrounds?"

The chief said, "Nothing yet. They were absolutely clean. No wallets, no identification of any kind. Fingerprints were taken but no hits yet. The wounded man in the hospital cannot be interrogated in his condition. We don't even know if he will survive. But he has muttered a few words in some foreign tongue."

"So it appears that we have foreigners with military training who may speak Armenian. Basically Armenian mercenaries," speculated Dr. Harrell, who was seated near the chief. "Were those captured thugs in Madisonville the same?"

"No," said the detective, "quite the opposite. They were local talent out of New Orleans who belong to what's left of the crime syndicate there. Once they saw the situation, they had no stomach for a fight. They simply surrendered and have lawyered up. They couldn't be more different."

Cloe said, "Someone with a lot of money and power has the connections to mobilize Armenian hit men as well as thugs from a local crime organization. Whoever it is is absolutely ruthless and bent on having the jar."

"'Bent' is a great description—maybe add 'twisted' and 'sick,'" remarked J.E.

The chief's cell phone rang, and he took the call. He listened closely, spoke briefly, and turned to face the group. "We've got the airplane," he said excitedly, "the one we think the mercenaries came in. It was in a general aviation hangar in New Orleans. However, the pilots are both dead. The copilot shot the pilot when the state police approached and then took that long last flight, biting on a poison capsule, probably cyanide."

Stunned, Cloe exclaimed, "Airplane—what airplane? This is a nightmare ... will it never end?"

"Rather than be captured, one murdered the other and then committed suicide," summarized J.E. "This fits with the almost suicidal fight at the lab. They wouldn't be captured either. My guess is, whoever their boss is, he doesn't like failure, and he swings a big stick. This man is developing a very formidable profile. I'm beginning to doubt that our adversary is a religious group or a group at all for that matter. This has the feel of a lone wolf … a rogue."

"How did you know about the airplane?" asked Cloe.

The chief said, "We've been thinking about that since the incident on the bridge. The questions were simple: how did they get here, and how did they get out? Once we had some idea that a foreign group might be involved, we thought they had probably flown in.

"Commercial air transportation would not do for tactical reasons, so we focused on a private plane," continued the chief. "It had to be a jet because of the need for speed and range. There are only so many runways within a certain distance of Baton Rouge that can accommodate private jet traffic.

"Then it was a process of computer research, phone calls to airports, and finally shoe leather. We had two or three good targets, and we sent tactical squads to each. New Orleans turned out to be the one. We weren't sure, and the pilots might have been able to bluff their way out, but they panicked."

"The same plane probably came in earlier with the crew that attacked us at the bridge," said J.E. He turned to his mother. "Your shark-eyed man was probably in that group. They likely followed us from the New Orleans airport to Madisonville to Baton Rouge, looking for their chance."

"The bottom line," said the detective from the sheriff's office, "is that whoever our adversary is, we have killed almost his entire team here, captured everyone in Madisonville, and recovered his multimillion-dollar jet with the dead pilots. He has taken quite a beating today, one from which most would not quickly, if ever, recover. I think we may have seen the last of our mystery man unless his operative in the hospital survives and knows enough to give us information on him. I'm guessing that he's done."

"Maybe," said J.E., standing and heading toward the door. "Maybe you're right, but I'm not so sure. I had hoped we would smoke out the leader and put an end to this. Now I don't know. Dr. Harrell, I have some work I would like to do, and I wonder if you have a spare terminal so I can use Mike."

"I can arrange that," the scientist said. "Indeed, there is an unused terminal adjacent to the lab where your mother and the monsignor will be working on the manuscript. May I ask what you are looking for?"

"I'm not entirely sure myself, but I have the tail number from the jet. So I may be able to backtrack and find the point of origin. Plus, whoever we're pitted against knows too much about us and about the jar and its contents. I think someone around us is leaking information. If so, I intend to out the rat."

# CHAPTER 36

Although it was good to be back in the lab, Cloe was unsure whether she would ever feel safe again. She would never stop looking over her shoulder and second-guessing everything as long as the people who had killed her father, had tried to kill her and J.E., and now, more than likely, had killed Father Al were out there. The Swiss Guards were both a security blanket and a constant reminder of the danger. Opening the door to her suite, she had seen a police officer, and outside there were sheriff's deputies.

Now she was back in the lab, which itself showed only modest signs of the firefight. Although the anteroom to the lab was heavily shot up, the lab itself was relatively untouched, with only a few stray bullets having penetrated the walls. Still, she felt bunkered up and, worse, was worried the enemy could be at the gate at any time of his choosing.

She had to get a grip and get back to work. This was what she was trained for and was meant to do. Recovering old manuscripts and translating them—in effect, bringing them back to life—was hugely satisfying to her. The Lejeune Manuscript from the jar was a mystery waiting to be solved and communicated to the world. Even in the midst of the violence and ugliness of the attacks on them and the attempt to steal the manuscript, she and the monsignor had decided to go back to work on the translation. The work had to go on. Dean Broussard had been kind enough to visit them to make sure they had everything they needed. Dr. Harrell had left word that he would pop in later in the day.

They were now seated in tall lab chairs at one of the lab tables, taking their morning coffee and discussing how to proceed with the translation. A hush had come over them as Cloe thought about the events of the last few days. Such silence can be a fork in the road leading from one thing to another, as her mother had said, obtusely but often.

"Monsignor, I have some questions about the Coptic Judas Gospel that was translated in 2006," she said, shaking herself out of self-reflection and turning to her colleague.

The monsignor had provided her with a printout of the published translation of that Gospel, which he had downloaded from the Internet, and she had read it several times, trying to get some understanding of it. It definitely was not easy to read or to understand with all of its references to strange deities, upper and lower realms, and truly strange conversations with Jesus.

"Perhaps I can help," said the monsignor.

Cloe commented thoughtfully, "What I really don't understand about the translation I've read is the strangeness of some parts of it. It seems quite at odds with the traditional Gospels.

Here's a concrete example of what I'm talking about." She produced the printout from her bag. "At the end of page 49 and carrying over to page 50 of the Coptic Judas Gospel, in one of his conversations with Judas, Jesus reportedly says, 'And the twelve aeons of the twelve luminaries constitute their Father, with six heavens for each aeon, so that there are 72 heavens for the 72 luminaries, and for each [of them five] firmaments, [for a total of] 360 [firmaments. They] were given authority and a [great] host of angels without number, for glory and adoration, and also virgin spirits, for glory and [adoration] of all the aeons and the heavens and their firmaments.'"

"What can this possibly mean?" continued Cloe. "It's nothing like the Gospels I've read. While the orthodox Gospels do contain a good deal of religious doctrine as well as morality lessons, they are basically fact-grounded chronicles of Christ's life, and they are faithful advocates of the fulfillment of the earlier biblical scriptures."

"Yes, Signorina," said the monsignor, "you are correct. In the orthodox Gospels, Christ is seen and portrayed as a teacher but clearly is something beyond that ... He is the Redeemer. He is the Messianic figure foretold by more than a thousand years of scripture. Some scholars believe the Judas Gospel is written in a sort of code. For instance, in the passage you mention, the twelve aeons may represent the months of a year, making the 360 firmaments the number of days in certain calendars. Some speculate the 72 heavens and luminaries may be the number of known nations at that time."

"But, Monsignor, if we are to believe the Coptic Judas Gospel, Christ is another sort of figure entirely, and the religious underpinning of this version is totally different—all this talk of eons and classes of gods. At least that's what I came away with from my reading … thinking that this was a whole different thing, an outlier, certainly nowhere near the mainstream."

"In my opinion, it's very difficult to make a compelling case that the Judas Gospel coordinates with the orthodox Gospels at all or even in any substantial part. They certainly do not seem compatible. But the research continues. Plus, there are huge gaps yet to be filled from the scraps that have not been placed in the text."

Cloe smiled at the monsignor's amazing talent at understatement in relation to the compatibility point. The Judas Gospel was just plain strange in her mind and nothing like the orthodox Gospels.

"The Coptic Judas Gospel is not lengthy," the monsignor said, "the whole thing covering a period of about eight to ten days before Christ's death … Nor does it purport to be the story of Christ's public ministry as do the other Gospels. According to the numeration convention ascribed to it by the scholars who have studied it, the Judas Gospel is entirely contained in pages 33 through 58 of the Codex Tchacos. The entire work, as we know it, consists of twenty-five handwritten pages. Moreover, it is not written in Greek but in Coptic, which is an ancient Egyptian language."

"Why Coptic? What does that suggest?" asked Cloe.

"Again there is no absolute answer to your questions, but the fact that it was found in Egypt and written in an ancient Egyptian language suggests the author might not have been a Jew or that he may have been persecuted in Israel, causing him to flee to Egypt," replied the monsignor. "It would not be the first time in Jewish history."

"Fascinating, but I'm not sure the Lejeune Manuscript, even if all pages were legible, would total twenty-five pages," said Cloe. "It's probably more like eighteen to twenty pages."

"If that turns out to be true, that could be of extreme importance and may become a focal point of our investigation."

"Why is that, Monsignor?" she asked.

"Because some scholars believe words and perhaps whole sections have been added to make up the 2006 Coptic version of the Judas Gospel."

"Whole sections?" she responded, stunned. "What's that about?"

"You have already put your finger on it. It's very different in perspective and in tone from the orthodox Gospels. The orthodox Gospels are quite consistent with each other in their approach to Jesus and to Christianity. If there was once any core content in the Judas Gospel that comported with the orthodox Gospels, it has been corrupted by the added language, which has a different agenda."

"A different agenda?" mused Cloe. "Fascinating. But one thing for sure is the end is the same. The story of Judas ends the same general way in the Coptic version as it does in the orthodox Gospels."

"True, but were you not amazed by the contradiction?" responded the monsignor.

"Contradiction?" Cloe replied, still somewhat off-balance in response to the idea that words or paragraphs may have been added to the Coptic text by persons unknown.

"Yes, in spite of what we have been told through the orthodox Gospels, we find out in the Coptic Judas Gospel, if it is to be believed, that Judas may in fact have been the disciple closest to Jesus. Indeed, we learn Jesus may have imparted special knowledge to Judas and to Judas alone."

"That comes through clearly," said Cloe. "Indeed, the whole platform for the Gospel is a series of intimate conversations between Jesus and Judas shortly before the Passion."

"Yes, what about the ending?" queried the monsignor. "It belies this closeness—indeed the whole premise of the Gospel—or does it? I guess the answer depends on one's view as to why Judas did what he did. The last few lines are elegant in their simplicity: 'But some of the scribes were there watching carefully in order to arrest him during the prayer. For they were afraid of the people, since he was regarded by all as a prophet. And they approached Judas and said to him, "What are you doing here? You are Jesus's disciple." And he answered them as they wished. And Judas received money and handed him over to them.'"

# CHAPTER 37

Cloe thought about what the monsignor had revealed. It was an enigma within a conundrum. Judas was turning out to be an extremely ambivalent figure who was difficult to put into some convenient, orthodox pigeonhole. Putting aside the strangeness of the Coptic version, the ending had something that implicated motive … Pathos? Resignation?

They had made just a little headway on the Greek manuscript found in Thib's jar. Cloe had been able to get a very rough translation of the first few sentences, which were only a little like the ones in the Coptic version. Thus far, there was nothing about Jesus and Judas being close friends.

"Monsignor, is it possible Judas might have been 'the disciple who Jesus loved'?"

"You are referring primarily to the Gospel of St. John," responded the cleric. "There are several entries referring to the disciple whom Jesus loved or including words to that effect. No, that was not Judas. Most scholars agree that this is probably a reference to St. John himself. For some reason, at times, St. John seemed to favor writing about his role in the anonymous third person. Also, I remind you that this reference is in the orthodox Gospels. It is not out of the Coptic Judas Gospel itself.

"There are several aspects to the 'strangeness' of the Coptic text. It attempts to establish a new relationship between Judas and Jesus," continued the monsignor. "The Coptic Gospel of Judas states that Judas is the only disciple who sees Jesus as he truly is. Judas is worthy, and the others are not—that is the message. Jesus has private conversations with Judas before his death, revealing to Judas his true nature and mission."

"But wasn't he the Son of God?" Cloe was profoundly shocked by the thought of Jesus himself repudiating his heritage as the Son of God on earth. She was beginning to see even more than strangeness in the Coptic version; the word "heresy" came to her mind.

"Remember, that's the orthodox view, but not what he supposedly, privately revealed to Judas, according to the Coptic text. In these conversations with Judas, he reveals a great deal about these upper realms and who will be saved. Mankind is divided into two types, those with knowledge of the truth and those without. The former will be saved, and the latter will not."

"Monsignor, this is so bizarre. I've never heard of anything like this, and as far as I'm concerned, this is totally outside the traditional Gospels. None of this can be true," said Cloe.

The monsignor continued. "There's a good deal more, including a whole hierarchy of angels and deities. Christ supposedly educates Judas on the stars and cosmology. We don't need to go into the details, but this is classic Gnostic doctrine."

"Gnostic doctrine?"

"Yes," said the monsignor. "In the early years after Christ's death and resurrection, there were different schools of thought as to Christ's mission. Two of the strongest were the Gnostic believers and the traditionalists who advocated the direct knowledge of the Apostles— essentially, Gnostic versus Orthodox. As we have said, the orthodox view was that Jesus came from God to redeem mankind from sin. He was the Redeemer.

"Gnostics were not so concerned with sin and redemption but with knowledge. In their view, Christ was first a teacher who brought knowledge. According to their concepts, an enlightened mankind would be saved. You can see how this could have been viewed by the Apostolic church as against its core doctrine—heresy."

"Certainly I've heard of Gnostics," Cloe said, "but my work has been largely secular. I've never had occasion to understand how this might all fit together from a religious standpoint."

"To keep it simple, there were several centuries of debate on the true meaning of Christ's mission on earth, and eventually the orthodox view won out. The temporal proximity of the synoptic Gospels to the time of Christ was a key factor. Further, many people were personally touched by the Apostles and taught by them. Tracing the traditions of the Apostles back to Jesus himself and his teachings was extremely important. The consistency of the Gospels, particularly the synoptics, weighed in on the side of orthodoxy. Nevertheless, the Gnostic tradition has remained out there, although much repressed, particularly by the early Church."

"How do you mean 'repressed'?" the pair suddenly heard J.E. ask.

Cloe turned to see her son standing in the doorway. "J.E. ... did you hear what the monsignor said about the Coptic text?"

"I heard a good bit. Monsignor ... talk about the repression."

"The early Church was in a formative state, and people took sides. The orthodox view came from the Apostles and had the upper hand. Moreover, some members of the Church took it upon themselves to debate the Gnostics orally and in print. In the second century, Gnosticism was branded by certain religious figures as heresy. One famous character in this battle was Irenaeus, a noted heresy hunter, who wrote a prodigious five-volume work in about AD 180 known familiarly as *Against Heresies*. It made the case for the orthodox view and argued against all other views as heresy, particularly that of the Gnostics."

"A heresy hunter," said Cloe. "That sounds so strange and, perhaps, extreme by today's standards of live-and-let-live, no matter what one believes."

"From what you have said, Monsignor, Irenaeus must have considered the Gospel of Judas a great heresy," added J.E.

"Strangely, no ... he does not seem to have considered it so. The young sir has put his finger on an extremely important point. The Coptic Gospel of Judas with the Gnostic thought dates from the late third century to the early fourth century. Irenaeus wrote his anti-heresy tome in about AD 180. Yet he does mention a Gospel of Judas in his work. He does so with a passing one-sentence reference, noting that certain Gnostics had claimed a higher knowledge of the truth by Judas, citing a fabricated work by them known as the Gospel of Judas."

"So we know that Irenaeus was aware of a Judas Gospel even though he wrote his books almost two hundred years before the Coptic Gospel of Judas was written," observed Cloe. "There was obviously an earlier version." Cloe's excitement about the mystery was again on the rise.

"Bingo, Mom," chimed in J.E., sitting down with them. "That has to be what was in Thib's jar! The earlier version of the Judas Gospel. It's the Greek version, the Lejeune version, that carbon-dates to the late first or early second century. It's the version of the Judas Gospel that Irenaeus was familiar with."

Excitedly, Cloe said, "That's got to be correct. Not only that, but it can't contain the same level of Gnostic material as the Coptic version, or Irenaeus would have roundly condemned it."

"Signorina, this all must be correct," replied the monsignor. "Irenaeus did not write five volumes against heresy only to dismiss a classic Gnostic text like the Coptic Gospel of Judas in a single line. By the time the Coptic version was written in the third or fourth century, Irenaeus was long dead. His work on heresy had been in print for nearly two hundred years."

"Yes, he never saw the fourth-century version ... he was looking at the earlier Greek version, the very one we have extricated from my father's jar."

# CHAPTER 38

"Clotile, I need to come up there and help you," Uncle Sonny had said when he phoned Cloe shortly after Father Al's funeral.

"Right now we're good, Uncle," she had replied.

Had it really been only a couple of weeks since she'd left her future in Seattle and reentered her past in Louisiana? Cloe had buried a long-lost father and rediscovered a misplaced uncle. Her eyes teared up a bit as she thought of Uncle Sonny—really her only family except J.E. She had treasured his every entreaty and decided the man had a heart the size of a basketball. Uncle Sonny was now beloved surrogate for both her lost mother and her father. Gosh, she ached for them.

"Uncle, we're doing a lot of research. There's really nothing for you to do. We have our guards, and the police are on high alert. We're completely safe," Cloe had continued.

"Clotile, honey, are you sure?" asked Uncle Sonny. "An awful lot has been going on … what with Thib being shot and the try for you and J.E. Poor Father Al. Are you sure you have all the protection you need?"

"Yes, Uncle," Cloe had said with a certainty she did not feel.

\*\*\*

Now she, J.E., and the monsignor sat at their table in the lab trying to absorb the incredible amount of information they had just discussed.

Cloe was jarred from her thoughts by the sound of her cell phone ringing. *Now what?* she immediately thought. She shivered briefly. Such phone calls had brought nothing but bad news lately. Remembering their recent conversation, though, she thought maybe it was just Uncle Sonny calling again. She flipped the phone open.

"Hello, Dr. Lejeune," said a dry, gravelly voice on the other end.

"Hello," said Cloe. "Who is this?" she asked sharply. Cloe stood and stepped away from the table, covering her free ear to better hear.

"Who I am is not important … it is what I wish that is important," said the voice. There was a faint accent.

Cloe felt her heart flip-flop and begin to race. Her gut clenched instinctively. She had no doubt now about who was on the other end of the line. She didn't know his name, but she knew him. This was the person responsible for a lot of the things happening around her. *How much?* she wondered. His voice and words chilled her to the bone, and J.E. and the monsignor noticed her change in demeanor immediately. They stood intuitively and closed in around her. She had the presence of mind to hit the speakerphone button on her cell phone.

The three listened as the voice said, "You have something I desire."

Not want, but desire, he had said. Was that choice of words significant? Why did it freeze her blood? She could not help but think of the lust that must power this expression. Although she thought first of lust and not greed, greed was certainly there as well. The desires of this person, she knew, must be out there somewhere where lust and greed intersected.

"Yes," she said simply.

"You and your friends have caused me a great deal of bother. While I'm very angry about it," the voice said, completely devoid of any emotion, "I really must compliment you on the resistance your group has put up to my operatives."

"Yes," Cloe repeated, feeling stupid.

"Your pointless resistance has cost me my airplane and several of my agents and is causing my patience to grow short," he said.

She knew not where it came from—perhaps from the seventeen-year-old pregnant vagabond she had been—but she retorted, "And I think you had my father killed because he wouldn't do your bidding and sell you the jar, you lousy bastard."

The voice said immediately, "No one stands between me and what I want."

So there it was, thought Cloe. Rage coursed through her body. "You also killed a priest, for God's sake, not to mention the others who have perished due to your selfish ambitions. And you are no closer to your goal than when you started. You have failed utterly and miserably!" she fairly screamed into the small mike on the cell phone. She had not intended to be so provocative. She saw J.E. smile at her.

The phone was silent for a time. She heard the crackle of cell phone noise. She knew he was still there; she could feel his malevolent presence. She had the sense that he was calming himself, gathering himself.

"You insist on provoking me, Dr. Lejeune," the voice uttered hoarsely. "This is against your interests. Now let me tell you what I desire and what you will do."

J.E. motioned for her to continue to engage the voice. She knew he must have his reasons, and she had certainly learned to trust his judgment. But her skin crawled at the thought of continuing to speak with the man at the other end of the line. She wanted nothing more than to be done with this monster and to go back to the safety of her scholarly pursuits. For Christ's sake, she was a scientist, not a sleuth or double agent. All this was just too much. What could she say to keep him talking?

"Whoever you are … and by the way, are you bold enough to tell me your name?"

"My name matters not," the voice said. "In fact, I have had many names over the years. In some circles, I'm known by what I do. I collect things. What matters critically for you right now is what I want. Now you have certain things that I would have. I suggest that you bring them to me."

Cloe heard a hard "k" sound when he said "collect," such as might be heard in some of the former Soviet satellite countries. She marked this carefully as a clue to the man's origin. Was this his first mistake? "I don't know who you are, and I don't care what you want," Cloe responded, continuing her deception.

Again the line was silent for a time. When the voice came back, the line crackled with urgency. "You will bring me the jar and the manuscript along with all your research. You will delete all files on the computer."

"I don't think I will," said Cloe unwaveringly. "You are nothing ... not even a name. All your games have failed. Your men have been killed and your equipment captured. At this point we're unimpressed by anything but your greed."

She looked up at J.E. and could see the respect and love in his eyes. She clutched J.E.'s hand and squeezed for all she was worth. "You are a toothless, wasted soul ... a person who is to be pitied. I'm sorry for you but not afraid of you," she continued. "Don't contact us again," she concluded with finality and moved to close the top of the phone.

But before she could do so, the man spoke again, and the words chilled her like nothing she could remember. She could finally understand the level of despair, the level of defeat, that the Gospels said had led Judas Iscariot to hang himself in despair at the foul deed he had done.

"Perhaps, before you ring off, you might like to say good-bye to someone," the evil voice came back.

"What ...?"

"Clotile?" The whispering voice was unmistakable. The connection snapped off.

# PART 3

# LYON

And Judas the betrayer … he alone was acquainted with the truth
as no others were, and so accomplished the mystery of the betrayal.
By him all things, both earthly and heavenly, were thrown into
dissolution. And they bring forth a fabricated work to this effect,
which they entitle the Gospel of Judas.

—Irenaeus of Lyon, *Detection and Overthrow of False Knowledge*

# CHAPTER 39

"Oh my God!" cried Cloe into the now-dead cell phone, which fell from her hand. "He has Uncle Sonny! J.E., what are we going to do?" she screamed.

"Let's try to stay calm. I heard the voice. But in the last days and weeks, you've talked a lot more to Uncle Sonny than I have; could it have been someone else?"

"I'm positive. I've spoken to him almost every night since we've been back. That monster has taken Uncle Sonny." Cloe sagged toward J.E., who grabbed her before she could fall and pulled her toward him. For Christ's sake, she thought, Uncle Sonny is ninety years old.

"Mom, I swear to you I'll get Uncle Sonny back safe and sound or die trying," promised J.E. with hot tears of anger and frustration in his eyes. "Making Uncle Sonny a pawn in this thing is so over the top. I give you my word the day will come, and come soon, when this man will pay dearly for grabbing Uncle Sonny."

Cloe saw that J.E. burned with rage and resolve. If the man's intent had been to cow them into giving up and doing his will, he had fatally misunderstood the American value system and pride, particularly that of the Lejeune family. J.E.'s grandfather had fought this type of aggression on at least two continents. J.E. himself had fought it in Iraq.

Cloe could feel the emotions coursing through her son's body as he comforted her. She recognized the anger and the determination—perhaps because these were almost exactly the same reactions she herself was having. She knew that they had to rein in this emotional response and be smart and deliberate in their plans. But they would get Uncle Sonny back in good shape, she had no doubt. If she had to give up the jar and her career, so be it. God help this collector of things when they got to him.

J.E. led his mother back to the lab table and seated her on one of the high-backed stools. Both J.E. and the monsignor also sat down to consider the situation. Though the monsignor had remained quiet up to now, his expression radiated concern and frustration.

"Mom," J.E. said, looking his mother square in the eyes, "Uncle Sonny will be fine, and we will get through this."

"J.E. … how much more of this do we have to endure?" Cloe had her head in her hands as she stared down at the table. "We've lost poor Father Al. My father has been murdered. I can't lose Uncle Sonny too. I just can't."

"Then, Signorina, get to work and decipher the manuscript," said the monsignor quietly, stunning both Cloe and J.E. with his apparent coldness and insensitivity.

"Monsignor …" started J.E., half-standing.

"I know this seems thoughtless, but consider that our adversary wants us unfocused and disoriented," responded the priest, gesturing with open hands. "Our hope is in superior knowledge and tactics. J.E., your mother and I must provide the knowledge, and you must solve the tactical problems. We are reacting. We must think ahead and anticipate this man's next moves. If we cannot clear our heads and do that quickly, your uncle is lost." His hands crashed down on the lab table, and he was silent.

"Monsignor, are you saying that deciphering the manuscript might help us get Uncle Sonny back?" asked Cloe.

"The man knows or thinks he knows something important about the manuscript," responded the monsignor. "Why else would he be so desperate to get it? We must find out what that is. If we can learn why he wants it so badly, this may help us defeat him and get your uncle Sonny back."

"Yes, we need every advantage to beat this man," said Cloe with resolve. She could see the monsignor told the truth and spoke from his heart. Once again the depth of the man came to her, and she knew he alone was thinking clearly.

J.E. pondered this for a minute or two. "Monsignor, you're right. Not only that, but the man will call back. He didn't take Uncle

Sonny without good reason. He won't hurt him yet. There will be a proposal … a bargain of some sort. The question is what will be given and what will be received. We need to be ready for the negotiation."

"I'm not sure we can handle this alone," said Cloe. "We need to call our friends at the campus police or the sheriff's department. In fact, kidnapping is a federal crime. We need the FBI and help with an international reach."

"I may agree with you, but we should wait a few minutes to see if he calls back," replied J.E. "We should learn as much as we can, whether we go to the police and ask them to call in the FBI or not."

"All right, but this man is well informed, has tremendous resources, and is single-minded about his objective. What do we know that can help us?" asked Cloe.

"I have been working with Mike tonight. I managed to trace the tail number on the jet, but it leads to an Isle of Man corporation owned by certain trusts formed in the Cayman Islands. In other words, it's a dead-end trail as to who owns the plane."

"Anything else?" Cloe was impressed by the information, but it gave them nothing more to go on.

"Yes, there is," J.E. said. "This same jet had a problem over the Atlantic a few days ago. Reporting an oxygen-system problem, the plane's crew requested permission to descend to a level where a repair could be made. The course of the airplane caught my eye, and I matched it to a military report of a body being found on a small offshore island. Parts of the body were badly damaged by crabs and other scavengers, but the military pathologists believe that the cause of death was massive internal damage consistent with a fall. The dead man was dressed all in black, and he was armed. Because he landed face down in the sand, scavengers could not get at his face. According to the autopsy report, he had very peculiar eyes, at least what was left of them. The body has been tentatively identified as that of an Armenian mercenary with a long history of criminal activity."

"Once again the Armenian connection," said the monsignor. "Could this be an example of the wages paid to those who fail the man behind all this?"

The ruthlessness of their adversary sank in as all considered the monsignor's words.

"I think you're right … it all fits," said J.E. "And I did find out where the plane ended up. It landed in Jerusalem."

"Jerusalem," whispered the monsignor. "There have been rumors over the years of a person who collects rare objects who is based in Jerusalem. Could it be? It is said that he is dead."

"The other thing I learned in my work is that we do, more than likely, have a rat in our little group," said J.E. "I came in earlier to tell you about this, but you were in the middle of a discussion, and then we were interrupted by the phone call. I looked at everyone's financial situation on the computer. Banking records are nothing for Mike to crack—although I'm sure we will soon have the Secret Service or FBI nosing around to find out what we have been up to."

"What did you find?" asked Cloe.

"Everyone was clean—nothing out of order—until I got into Dean Broussard's bank records. He is heavily in debt and living well beyond his means, and in the last few weeks, he has been receiving wire transfers from an offshore bank in the amount of fifty thousand dollars per week."

"Dean Broussard … my God," said Cloe. "A traitor. We should let the chief know and have him arrested right away—tonight."

"Perhaps, Signorina … but isn't it valuable that we know and that he does not know that we know?" asked the monsignor.

"Monsignor, I'm beginning to like the way you think," responded J.E. "If we are to beat this SOB on the phone and get Uncle Sonny back, we have to be very smart and very careful. To the extent we can feed false information through Dean Broussard, we may confuse the enemy."

"Quite so, young sir … what is your battle plan?"

"The plan is simple. First, Mom deciphers as much of the Lejeune Manuscript as she can so we know whether there's something in there that can help us. We need to know why the man wants it so badly."

"Yes, if we can learn why he wants it, we may be able to anticipate some of his moves," replied the monsignor.

J.E. continued, "We feed false information to Dean Broussard so our enemy does not quite know what we are doing. Monsignor, you and I figure out where Uncle Sonny is, and we go get him. Beyond that we improvise."

"A sound plan," said the monsignor. "The papal jet will be at our service, as will be the Swiss Guards. This is no longer a purely scientific exercise but rather has become a rescue mission. All else beyond getting your uncle back safely is secondary."

"Thank you, Monsignor," said Cloe. "If God gives me the strength and wisdom, I shall find something in the manuscript to help us." Her own feelings surprised her.

"Then, indeed, it is in God's hands," concluded the monsignor.

# CHAPTER 40

Cloe focused on the beginning and the end of the Lejeune Manuscript given that some of the interior of the text was damaged by smearing, and it would take scientists a long time to sort that out. They needed to know how closely this manuscript, particularly at the beginning, tracked the Coptic version.

Three hours later, she called J.E. at the hotel. "I need you and the monsignor to come to the lab," she said. She sat back, rubbed her eyes, and checked once again what she had written. She had come to a point where she had some translated language, but without context she could make no sense of it.

Despite the late hour, J.E. and the monsignor were not asleep when she called; they had been discussing various strategies and alternatives. The monsignor's driver dropped them off at the lab within minutes.

When all were seated in the meeting room next to the lab, Cloe began. "I have been working on the part of the Judas Gospel known as the 'Introduction.' In the Coptic version this part lays out the idea that the Judas Gospel is largely a dialogue between Judas and Jesus in the eight days before Jesus and the Apostles celebrated the Passover. It even suggests that this is a 'secret account' of those events." She looked at each of them and saw that they were with her.

"Yes, some scholars say the language translates as the 'secret declaration,'" replied the monsignor, on the edge of his chair.

"That's not the important part, if I'm correct," said Cloe. "The fact is the Greek version, our version, contains different and, perhaps, additional language not found in the later Coptic text. But I'm having trouble making any sense of it." She shrugged her shoulders as if throwing off some weight.

"What is it, Mom?" asked J.E. He too sensed that they were on the verge of some sort of epiphany.

"Well, our manuscript seems to open with a statement that says something to this effect: 'What is written here is written with the words of a dead man. A man dead in body and condemned in spirit by all. It is all written on the authority of the man of Lugdunum to address the injustice.'

"I'm not sure about a couple of places. The prepositions are difficult. 'Written in' or 'written through the words of a dead man' also would work. What's more, the 'man of Lugdunum' could be the 'one' of or from Lugdunum."

"Hmm," the monsignor said, clearly pondering the information. "Signorina, you realize that no human has seen these words for almost two thousand years. Except for collateral information we have from early writers such as Irenaeus, we know very little ... Irenaeus—that's it!" he almost shouted in triumph. The monsignor stood and began to pace back and forth.

"What, Monsignor?" asked J.E. intensely.

"Irenaeus was the bishop of Lyon, France. He is the very heresy hunter we have talked about before. His book *Against Heresies* was published in AD 180, and it makes reference to the Gospel of Judas— but not with the vehemence of condemnation we would expect if that Gospel had contained the Gnostic concepts that the Coptic text contains. The Coptic text was written about two hundred years after Irenaeus's work, and therefore he could not have known about it. He must have been familiar with the earlier Greek text that we have."

"Okay, but we have discussed this before ... what does that have to do with this new passage that Mom has translated?" queried J.E.

"Just this ... Lugdunum was the name of a place in Gaul when it was part of the Roman Empire," said the monsignor.

"Gaul became France," added Cloe, beginning to understand where the monsignor might be going.

"Yes, and Lugdunum became Lyon ... Lyon, France. Irenaeus was the second bishop of Lyon," replied the monsignor. "His church in Lyon was originally the Church of St. John but later was renamed in his honor the Eglise St-Irénée, or the Church of St. Irenaeus."

There it was, thought Cloe. They just had to understand what it meant.

The room became very quiet and seemed to shrink in size as the players pondered the intuitive jumps they were making. The consequences were almost too enormous to consider. J.E. was the first to break the silence. "Okay, we need a working theory here. We need a hypothesis that we can build on. It's just too much of a coincidence that our heresy hunter, Irenaeus, who wrote about the Gospel of Judas but who could only have known about our Greek version, may be referenced in that very Greek manuscript. This can't be random."

"Can we be sure the 'one from Lugdunum' refers to Irenaeus? Couldn't it have been someone else?" Cloe asked.

"If we look at the context—the 'one' from Lyon, a person in authority under which the Greek text was written—I don't see who else it could have been during this period of time," said the monsignor. "The Romans were largely content to let the locals govern, although under their supervision, and they allowed the indigenous populations to maintain their own religious practices as long as they did not attempt to export them to too great an extent. So I think we can be confident that the 'one' was not a Roman."

"If Irenaeus was the 'one,' that might explain why his criticism of the Greek version of the Judas Gospel was so mild. But if he was responsible for it, why did he criticize it at all?" mused Cloe.

"Mom … you have heard of 'damning by faint praise,'" stated J.E. with a bit of a lilt in his voice. "I think what we are witnessing is the first recorded incident of 'praising by faint damnation.'"

"The young sir is correct as usual," the monsignor said. "Irenaeus could not have completely omitted reference to this Greek text, which, we must assume, was in circulation, without raising issues of his own credibility and perhaps causing people to suspect that he was behind it. The world of people who could read and who had access to books was still not that large."

"All right, our working hypothesis is that the 'one' in the introduction to the Greek version was Irenaeus, the bishop of Lyon," summarized J.E. "If true, this means that the Greek manuscript of the Gospel of Judas, the one from our jar, was written under the authority of a Christian bishop, a known enemy of all heresy. I mean, I'm not much into this stuff, but this amazes even me."

"This is groundbreaking information if we are interpreting the text references correctly and if everything is authentic," agreed the monsignor.

Cloe thought about the rest of the new language in the Introduction. It was somehow all of a whole cloth. "What does it mean to 'address the injustice'? The language says it was all written to address the injustice. What injustice? Could this refer to what happened to Judas?"

"You may have more work to do to answer that question, but the first two new sentences provide some context," said the monsignor, turning to face them. "It says that what is written is written 'with the words of a dead man.' It then refers to this man as 'dead in body and condemned in spirit by all.'"

Cloe quickly added, "Remember, the word 'with' could actually be the word 'in' … 'written in the words of a dead man.' I think 'in' may be more appropriate." She was sweating from the exertion.

"Who was more roundly condemned than Judas, who was certainly dead in body by that time?" asked the monsignor. "Although the Church itself has never judged Judas as condemned, many have, and this has been the source of Jewish persecutions over the centuries. For whatever reason and based on whatever unknown and perhaps unknowable proof, Irenaeus, the bishop of Lyon, may have concluded that there was enough doubt about the orthodox Judas story to let the Judas Gospel be written and published in its original Greek form."

Cloe thought about this—"enough doubt" in the Judas story from the orthodox Bible; this was like doubting the hardness of granite. She wondered, not for the first time, what in the world they had tumbled into.

"A man such as Irenaeus would not have done this out of hand on a whim," replied Cloe. "He must have seen something that changed his mind from the orthodox viewpoint because, according to the monsignor, he was nothing if not orthodoxy itself. He could not have known Judas, and it was only barely possible that he could have known anyone who'd known him. What could have convinced him?"

"Mom ... the answer is right here in the manuscript," said J.E. excitedly, in spite of his fatigue. "What is written here is written 'in the words of a dead man'—that is, in Judas's words. Right?"

"Oh my God," cried Cloe. "You're right ... There was another writing, one written by Judas Iscariot himself from which this Gospel was taken. That's what convinced Irenaeus."

# CHAPTER 41

The new verbiage that Cloe had translated from the Lejeune Manuscript was illuminated on the screen of the lab. The cursor blinked, awaiting instructions. Cloe had sunk back into her chair as they all contemplated the implications. The monsignor stood and walked around the table toward the screen. He studied the new language very carefully. He removed the glasses that he had needed to see the image clearly from a distance and squinted at the writing on the wall.

"What you have deduced is sound," he said, seemingly reluctantly, as he turned to face them. "Irenaeus knew nothing of the later Coptic codex. Certainly, he was the 'one' from Lugdunum, or Lyon. Our earlier Judas manuscript must have been written under his authority to right a wrong that he perceived. We know from all four orthodox Gospels that Judas, in fact, made arrangements for the arrest of Jesus. This cannot be disputed. What Irenaeus learned must have challenged the reported motive of Judas—presumably the general perception of Judas as arch villain and betrayer for money of Jesus Christ. Only something incredibly powerful could have convinced a hardened heresy hunter like Irenaeus that the Judas tale may have had a different storyline."

Cloe rose, walked around the table toward the screen, and said, "But which of the four possible explanations for Judas's apparent betrayal of Christ could Irenaeus have accepted? And why?"

"We don't know that for sure, but the later Coptic version emphasizes the idea that Jesus explained God's design to Judas and enlisted his aid in carrying out the plan for the salvation of mankind," said the monsignor, turning to face her directly. "In other words, in

189

that text Judas was not the betrayer but the facilitator. Perhaps that is the same theme as in our Greek manuscript. You may not uncover the definite answer to that question until later in your translation of this text."

Putting her hand to her chin in contemplation, Cloe said, "But the other writing ... Irenaeus was convinced by something he read, and according to the new translation, it was something written in Judas's words ... in his hand. Even our earlier Greek manuscript was written years after Judas's death. If Irenaeus saw something written by Judas, it was something other than even our text."

The monsignor continued, "We know Judas was different. He was not a fisherman or a Galilean. He was appointed the treasurer of the ministry's finances and therefore must have known his numbers. He could read and write. Is it farfetched to believe that a literate man would have kept notes or some type of journal on the most significant events of his life? Could it be something like that?"

"No, that's not farfetched," said Cloe, turning to him. "It's perfectly rational to believe that he would have. But where have the notes or journal been, and if they ever existed, where are they now?"

"Hard to say," responded the monsignor. "Perhaps in Lyon at the Church of St. Irenaeus."

"A writing by Judas Iscariot," exclaimed J.E., now rising like the others. "And this may, at least in part, form the basis for the Lejeune Manuscript? Do you know what you are saying? Perhaps some diary-like writing chronicling Christ's public ministry—I can barely hold on to the thought."

Cloe's own thoughts were jumbled now by this newfound possibility. Was this to be the culmination of her life's work? Was this what she was meant to do? She wondered whether Thib had ever had an inkling where all this might lead.

"Yes, our manuscript may someday give us some of the very words written by Judas himself," she said, "but it is going to take scholars a good deal of time and effort to reconstruct the corrupted text. In the meantime ... Lyon? You think anything could be left there after all these years?"

"I don't know," said the monsignor. "I only know where the clues point."

"Is this why the man on the phone wants the Lejeune Manuscript so badly?" asked J.E.

Cloe and the monsignor were both silent for a moment as they contemplated this question.

"Cloe, this is very important," said the monsignor urgently. "Have you entered any of your translation work into Mike?"

"No, it's all right here on my laptop," replied Cloe. "Why?"

"Because in that case—that is, if only your laptop contains the clues we have discussed—the man who has your uncle Sonny can't yet know about the possibility of the contemporaneous writing of Judas."

"I see," said J.E. "He may know about the early version of the Judas Gospel we have discovered, but he can't be aware of the 'other writing' referred to by Irenaeus. We still have an advantage."

"Maybe," responded the monsignor. "But he may have the source materials, since Dean Broussard has likely sent him a photographic reproduction of the Lejeune Manuscript. He may be engaged in the very same sort of analysis in which we are engaged."

The shrill sound of Cloe's cell phone jangled everyone from this extraordinary colloquy. Cloe spun and grabbed the phone from the table and flipped the receiver open. "Yes?"

"Dr. Lejeune?" It was the same rasping voice as before. She knew immediately who it was.

"Yes," she said.

"You, the priest, and your son are to meet my agents, and you will bring with you the jar, the manuscript, and all research that you have conducted. You are to erase from the university computer all trace of the research so that you have the only copy. Is that understood?"

Cloe knew that they were now at the point of the bargain or exchange that J.E. had mentioned earlier. The man would tell them what he wanted, and then the game would be on. "Yes," she responded.

There had been no doubt in Cloe's mind that this point would come and that she would comply to save Uncle Sonny. But she noted mentally that "compliance" had many dimensions. It might not end up exactly as their adversary demanded.

"My agents will be at the general aviation depot at the Louis Armstrong International Airport in New Orleans at 11:00 a.m. the day after tomorrow. All of you will be there with what I desire, or your boring old man will die a most terrible death. His shrieks of agony will be heard in the deepest realms of hell. Do I make myself clear? If you alert the authorities, I will know. I have agents in the FBI and in other law enforcement agencies. I will have the manuscript. Is this completely clear?"

"Completely," she said. It was only a word, but that single word had ice and fire in it.

The monsignor and J.E. both focused intently on her. This had not been planned or rehearsed.

"Now, here's what you will do," she continued, gripping the cell phone as if her soft hands were the very Jaws of Life. "First, you will put my uncle on the phone before we talk any further." There was a palpable pause, creating an edgy, thick silence.

After a long gap, she heard her uncle's whispering voice. "Clotile ... Cloe? I'm so sorry. After Father Al's funeral I was at the house, and the next thing I knew, I woke up in an airplane with a bunch of thugs around me."

"Uncle ... are you all right?" asked Cloe quietly. Although her words were soft, her tone was of the cutting edge of the best steel.

"Cloe ... I'm fine, just feeling old and stupid. Don't you worry about me, and don't you do anything they want you to do. Clotile ... for God's sake."

Hot tears welled up in Cloe's eyes as she listened to the noble old man. She could feel the plastic exterior of the phone bend under her stony grasp. With case-hardened resolve she said, "Uncle, put him back on."

After a pause and a click, the voice returned. "Satisfied?" The smugness of that abbreviated question ate at Cloe.

J.E. and the monsignor looked at each other and then at Cloe as she spoke again into the phone, soft as silk.

"Here's what you will do. You will see that no harm comes to my uncle on penalty of death. We will not be in New Orleans the day after tomorrow or on any other day at your beckoning. We will be at the Church of St. John in Lyon, France, at 11:00 a.m., local time, on the day after tomorrow. You will have my uncle in perfect health, and we will have what you want. Do I make myself clear? There will be an exchange. Is that completely clear?"

The voice on the other end of the phone was quiet, but Cloe could feel the hatred. She was almost pushed down by the sheer force of his madness. She staggered into J.E., who grabbed her and provided the needed support.

"Lyon … yes. There is a certain symmetry to that. It appeals to my romantic nature. Eleven a.m. the day after tomorrow."

The phone snapped off, leaving a shocked silence.

# CHAPTER 42

The papal jet was high above the earth, headed east for all it was worth. Cloe sat in front of her laptop with the flash drive inserted. All of their research had been stored on it, and all trace of their work had been erased from Mike, the supercomputer. Although reluctant to take this step, Cloe reasoned that if they hadn't, the traitorous Dean Broussard would have done this himself in any event and would have reported to the man on the phone that they had failed to follow his express instructions.

She, J.E., and the monsignor were near the front of the plane, still trying to make sense of the manuscript. The four members of the Swiss Guard, including the one lightly wounded at the lab, were clustered around a table, aft of where she was, playing some sort of card game. It was the first time she had seen them relax since they had come into her life.

They had said their good-byes to LSU. Although she had hated to lie to Dr. Harrell, it was necessary so as to give Dean Broussard as much disinformation as possible. They had been very coy about their schedule, stating that they would leave considerably later than they actually intended to leave. If Dean Broussard passed this information on to their adversary, as they suspected he would, this would give them the advantage of surprise since they planned to go directly and immediately to Lyon. Any possible advantage might help in their efforts to save Uncle Sonny.

Cloe recalled the brief conference they had had with Dr. Harrell and Dean Broussard to tell them what had occurred and that they had little choice but to attempt the exchange.

"Cloe, you must call the chief immediately. This is a matter for the law enforcement authorities," Dr. Harrell had insisted.

"No police. This is the only way we have a chance to save Uncle Sonny," Cloe had replied adamantly.

"I agree with Cloe, doctor. We must comply with the demands of this demented person, whoever he is," Dean Broussard had said.

The look that had passed between Cloe and J.E. at that moment was like a lightning strike at midnight. The turncoat was ready, eager, to deliver them into the hands of his benefactor.

Since they had decided to use the rat to send false intel back to their adversary, they told their colleagues how afraid they were and of their strategy to comply with every demand of the man who held Uncle Sonny. Cloe had even offered the opinion that due to the circumstances, further research was pointless, so they would remain at the hotel until time for the rendezvous. She hoped that every word would be passed back to the man on the phone.

The friends had then quickly packed overnight bags and rushed to the airport. All they needed were picture IDs since the monsignor had made arrangements for each of them to be appointed as low-level diplomatic representatives of the Vatican. The real strategy was to get to Lyon as quickly as they could to closely examine the Irenaeus element of the mystery and to set some sort of trap for the man who held Uncle Sonny.

Cloe was working on the last few sentences of the text of the Lejeune Manuscript as they flew. They needed to know whether the end was the same as that in the Coptic codex. Though she was near exhaustion, the importance of the mission drove her to press on.

Her thoughts turned for a moment to Thib. She considered how he must have felt all those many years ago that early morning on the runway in Algiers next to Bobby Morrow as they prepared to fly to the jump site. Well, Cloe and her friends were figuratively on their way to their own jump site, a journey that could conceivably end, one way or the other, just like Thib's. She would not know until the end what the end might be. Whatever it turned out to be, she knew she was ready. Something about her upbringing on the river had prepared her for this—her greatest test.

The monsignor slipped out of his seatbelt, stood, and stretched. "Signorina, are you aware that the Church of St. John, now the Church of St. Irenaeus, is being—and, by now, may have been—decommissioned as a church? The building is now of only historical significance."

They'd had little time, due to their quick departure, to talk in detail about that last phone conversation she'd had with her uncle's captor. Cloe knew her mates were curious about why she had decided to arrange the rendezvous in Lyon.

"No, I wasn't aware," she said. "However, that's not relevant. There's a connection between Lyon and the Lejeune Manuscript. Irenaeus is involved somehow. I have not had time to work it all out, but I know intuitively that these things are associated."

"From our discussions, I think you may be correct. How goes your work on the last few lines of the text?"

"Very slowly, Monsignor," she replied, flexing her arms to try to shake the fatigue.

"As you know, the end of the Coptic Judas Gospel is different in detail from the synoptic Gospels in important ways," said the monsignor. "The Judas Gospel says that Jesus was in a structure of some sort and that rather than go into the Garden of Gethsemane for prayer, he went into the 'guest room' for prayer. The text suggests it was at that point that Judas took money and handed Jesus over to 'them,' presumably the priests and elders. That's the end of the Coptic version."

"That's all very strange," noted J.E. "Why would all four orthodox Gospels state the last prayers of Jesus and his arrest took place in the garden, but the Coptic Judas text claim it was in a house or some other structure?"

"That is not known," said the monsignor over the roar of the jet engines as he bent to look at the computer screen. "Some scholars have speculated that the scene in the Garden of Gethsemane may never have happened. Rather, Jesus was taken at the place where he had just celebrated the Passover with the disciples. You will recall from the Gospel of St. John that Judas leaves the supper in progress, with Jesus admonishing him to do that which he will do quickly. It would not be much of a stretch to imagine that the authorities were near, awaiting their chance to grab Jesus. What better place to get him than in a closed structure where escape would be impossible and his disciples would be ineffective in protecting him? However, the scene at the garden has a certain poetry to it and has its own lesson or parable embedded in it."

"Well, there's a different last paragraph, physically located after what would have been the end of the Coptic Gospel," said Cloe, punching the "Enter" button on the computer to activate the PowerPoint display of the new last paragraph. They all turned to gaze at the incomprehensible Greek language on the screen.

"But what does it say?" asked J.E., scratching his head as he gazed at the symbols.

It was only an additional line or two when translated, Cloe thought, but when combined with everything else they had learned, it was a blockbuster. Indeed, civilizations had turned on less. She typed in a few instructions and hit the "Enter" button again, and the English translation displayed on the airplane's wall screen.

They all looked at it expectantly, and the monsignor stepped forward and read it aloud. "Everything I have written has been taken from the hand of the condemned one as presented to the Bishop of Lugdunum and as now resides in the library of St. John."

The silence was profound. There was no sound but the jet engines and, Cloe thought, her pounding heart. As a renowned dead languages scientist, she knew, without doubt, that this was an once-in-a-lifetime discovery.

She said weakly, "The word 'condemned' might also be translated as 'damned,' but I hardly think that matters at this point."

The monsignor flopped back into his seat and was quiet for a long moment. "Signorina, this language confirms our hypothesis that there was a prior writing by Judas. In this context, the only possible interpretation is that the 'condemned' or 'damned' one would be Judas."

"Agreed," responded Cloe. "And 'taken from the hand' certainly suggests a writing by Judas. If true, we would have to assume that Judas kept some sort of journal or what we would call today a diary."

"We cannot know that, Signorina," replied the monsignor. "But it is a theory and one that bears further research. Why would a literate man write only about the last few days? We may never know."

"But what of the rest?" asked J.E.

"Whatever 'it' was, it was presented to the bishop of Lugdunum, whom we now know as the bishop of Lyon and who was none other than Irenaeus. We believe that Irenaeus sanctioned our Greek version of the Judas Gospel to set the record straight. Right?"

"Yes," said Cloe as she focused on the image on the wall. "Monsignor, what is the library of St. John?"

The monsignor appeared to think for a minute. "I had forgotten about this until this very moment, but there is a relationship between St. Irenaeus and St. John the Evangelist. As you know from our discussions, there are several 'Johns' mentioned in the Gospels, and it is sometimes difficult to know who is who. However, it is generally thought that the Gospel of John was written by St. John the Evangelist, who many scholars believe to have been John the Apostle. John had a pupil named Polycarp, later St. Polycarp, who was born in Asia Minor. Polycarp was directly taught by St. John, who obviously knew both Jesus and Judas."

Cloe could see that the monsignor was becoming excited at the connections that were coming out of the manuscript.

"But what's the connection?" asked J.E., impatiently rising and squinting at the Greek translation. "No offense, Monsignor, but who the hell is this Polycarp guy?"

"Well, that's the thing," said the monsignor. "Polycarp was the mentor and teacher of Irenaeus, who also was born in Asia Minor—possibly in what is now Turkey but what then would have been, at the time of Christ, the Kingdom of Armenia."

"The Armenian connection again," retorted J.E. "Why does all this seem to point to Armenia?"

"I'm sure it's just a coincidence that Irenaeus and his mentor were from that area, as is, possibly, our adversary," responded the monsignor.

J.E. turned and said quickly, "You know how I feel about coincidences."

Cloe jumped in. "Okay, we have St. John, who personally knew Judas and Jesus and who taught St. Polycarp. Polycarp and Irenaeus were from the same general area, and Polycarp was teacher and mentor to St. Irenaeus. Our Judas Gospel speaks of the library of St. John, where this work of Judas supposedly lies. Where is the library of St. John?"

"It must lie in or under the Church of St. John, now the Church of St. Irenaeus, which is where we are going. It can be nowhere else," said the monsignor. "The personal journal of Judas Iscariot must lie there."

# CHAPTER 43

"Think of it," said Cloe. "The possibility of a contemporaneous writing of one of the Apostles … even Judas Iscariot. There are absolutely no such writings that have come to light. None. All of the Gospels were written decades after Christ's public ministry. It's not unreasonable to think that someone might have kept a journal. Indeed, it's perhaps less credible to think that no one, of all the people that Christ touched, contemporaneously wrote about him and his mission. What if there really is a journal written by Judas setting forth the details of Christ's journey or even a part of it?"

She sat back in her chair and contemplated the potential of such a writing. Her career was on the line here, but regardless of the enormity of the possible discovery, she had to do what was necessary to save Uncle Sonny. That might mean giving it all up. It was both a terrible choice and no choice at all.

"It would be earthshaking to say the least," responded the monsignor. "We are ahead of schedule, so we can search to see what can be found at the church, if anything."

"Correct, but we have one simple problem," said J.E. forcefully, standing and turning to face Cloe and the monsignor directly. "There is a murderous bastard who will be at the Church of St. John at the appointed time waiting for us, and in spite of all our plans and good intentions to trade the Lejeune Manuscript for Uncle Sonny, I seriously doubt our man will keep his bargain. I fully expect some sort of double-cross on his part. You don't really think that we'll walk into the church and turn over the jar and everything else to him, and he'll say, 'Here's Sonny,' do you? You think we'll all then leave and live happily thereafter?"

"No," said Cloe. "But what are our options? If we don't show, Sonny dies. If we resist, Sonny dies, as well as most or all of us. What can we do?"

J.E. felt a little defeated because there was no good answer. The only thing he could say was something that he couldn't say—which was that Uncle Sonny was a dead man almost any way you looked at it. After all, it was, as the monsignor had said, in God's hands. He was okay with that. But he would do what he could to help God out.

"We will have additional help," interjected the monsignor. "As you know, I have kept up my daily reports to my superiors at the Vatican. Vicar General Antonio Sigliori, known by friends and colleagues as Father Anton, holds a special post in the Vatican with the military ordinariate. Father Anton has control and oversight of the operations side of anything of a martial nature that we do outside of the Vatican. He will be awaiting us in Lyon."

"Monsignor, I thought the Vatican was a religious organization, and the last thing it would have would be a special ops capability with a priest in charge," commented J.E., with a wry smile.

"Remember, J.E. ... while the pope is head of the Catholic Church worldwide, the Vatican is also a sovereign nation. It has no troops and no army, but its agents must go in harm's way from time to time to do the Lord's work. It's best to be prepared."

"Wow," J.E. said.

Cloe wondered whether they would ever plumb the depths of this man and the people behind him.

J.E. then looked at his mother and said, "Mom, we'll go to the church and see what we can find. We really have two goals. One is to save Uncle Sonny, and the other is to see if there is any truth to this 'journal' idea. Here's the thing: understand that the other side is not very likely to keep any agreement they make with us."

"This is no doubt correct," said the monsignor. "But how do we approach this?"

"We expect and plan for treachery," responded the young officer. "We have to carefully examine the area around and including the church. Every contingency must be considered. All our forces must be arrayed as cleverly as possible. If we don't plan and execute properly, Uncle Sonny is dead, and we're all mortally at risk."

Cloe could hardly maintain her sanity, listening to this frank assessment of the potential for violence and death. This was certainly not the ivory towers of academia. She put her hands to her head as if to prevent it from flying apart. "God never gives us a challenge that he does not also give us the strength to meet," she remembered her mother saying. She sat up straight, finding her backbone, and asked, "What is your plan, J.E.?"

# CHAPTER 44

Upon their arrival in Lyon, Cloe and the monsignor used the computer facilities at the general aviation depot to do additional research on the area and on the church and tomb of Irenaeus in particular. As a result of the industrialization of the area around the church and loss of the residential congregation, the church had, indeed, just gone through the ceremony to be decommissioned as a consecrated Catholic house of God. There was only a skeleton crew of staff still present. Sadly, it was now just a tourist attraction.

All three travelers made use of the private terminal's facilities to shower and change to clean clothes and then made arrangements to leave their luggage.

The monsignor introduced them to Father Anton, who had come to the airport prepared. The Swiss Guard doubled in size to eight with the addition of four guards brought by the priest. The guard who had been slightly wounded in the shootout in Louisiana showed little sign of any injury. Weaponry and tactical gear had been brought in on the Vatican jet. J.E. seemed pleased and impressed.

Father Anton was ten to fifteen years J.E.'s senior and had that lean, hard look of military men. His hair was close-cropped but beginning to gray. He listened a great deal and spoke little. What he did say, he said well, and everyone listened carefully. He was clearly used to authority. Cloe felt somewhat relieved, although their core predicament had not changed.

"Monsignor," stated Father Anton, "we have developed some intelligence on our adversary as you requested. We worked on the assumption that we needed to take another look at the alleged death of the billionaire arms merchant who was well known as a ruthless collector of ancient objects.

"Most of our sources confirmed that he had, in fact, died. But with the fall of the Iron Curtain, we have been able to secure previously unknown KGB intelligence reports." One such report flatly states the alleged death was faked. The conclusion of that report was the man, for reasons of his own, had decided to get out of the arms business and disappear."

"Hence this collector may still be alive," mulled Cloe softly.

"Yes, and in his native language, Armenian, the term would be pronounced 'Ko-lek-tor,'" said the monsignor.

"Kolektor … Kolektor." Cloe rolled the hard word off the end of her tongue. "So this may be our adversary."

"It fits," concluded the monsignor. "Anton, was there any other information?"

"Yes, the report contained a partial dossier," replied Father Anton. "It seems this man was born in the mountains on the Turkish/Armenian border. His family was Catholic, and when the war broke out, they sought refuge at the Catholic Church in the region and hoped for expatriation to avoid the Turkish army. For reasons that are not clear from the report, they were denied any assistance. When the Turks arrived, many Armenians were slaughtered, including his family."

"What happened to the boy?" asked J.E.

"According to the KGB report, the boy was pressed into the Turkish army and, in effect, grew up there."

"My God, what a horror," reflected Cloe. "No wonder he has become what he is."

"Mom, no matter the circumstances, we all have choices," stated J.E. "This man had his, and he made his bed. Remember, this murderer may have caused Thib's death and Father Al's death, and he has Uncle Sonny."

Like a cold slap, this brought Cloe back to the center. "What else, Reverend Father?"

"Not too much. Some few sentences on his education in Europe and entry into the arms trade. The report suggests the KGB had thoughts of blackmailing him, but he was considered too dangerous, and his weapons trade was generally wreaking havoc in third world countries, which was part of the Soviet strategy at the time."

"Too dangerous for the KGB … wow," said J.E.

"Oh, a couple of footnotes," Father Anton quickly added. "He is thought to have a home base in Jerusalem, and he has a broad and deep network of thieves, murderers, and operatives who are fanatically loyal to him. These are mostly Armenian."

"Our foe now seems to have a name and an identity," observed J.E.

"Yes, and given his family's rejection by the Church during the war, we might surmise, a new and extremely powerful motive for wanting this particular jar and manuscript," commented Cloe, as she turned to see the reaction of the monsignor to this revelation.

For once the monsignor had nothing to say.

***

Cloe and the monsignor now sat in the back of a taxi. The taxi driver initially had no idea where the Church of St. John was, but when they told him to take them to the Church of St. Irenaeus, he flipped the meter and sped off toward their destination. The day was stark, cold, and dreadfully gray. They traveled for a while on a highway lined with what looked like pear or plum trees, now leafless in the dead of winter. They exited onto the Rue des Macchabées, finally ending up on the Place St-Irénée itself.

The church was more modest and more modern than Cloe had expected, though the monsignor had told her that the present structure was a nineteenth-century version of a much older church. The Church of St. Irenaeus had been destroyed and rebuilt a number of times over the centuries. This latest iteration was only a couple of hundred years old, give or take. Some of its environs were much older.

Cloe rubbed her eyes with fatigue as she stepped out of the taxi. She had managed to catch a couple of hours of sleep on the plane after they made their tentative plans; however, the time difference was working against her. After the rushed packing, getting to the airport, and the long flight, it was now mid-afternoon local time on the day before the day of their crucial appointment. To her, it felt like early morning since that's exactly what it was in Louisiana.

After their conference at the airport, while the monsignor and Cloe returned to the computer terminals to complete one last bit of research, J.E. and the operations group had rented a van and gone ahead to the church to spend some time assessing the tactical situation. J.E. and Father Anton would place the guard members in strategic locations to provide cover in the event of a double cross.

Although the man on the phone might not know of the additional help from the Vatican, he had been absolutely clear that any contact with the authorities would mean instant death for Uncle Sonny. Cloe had no doubt that their opponent would follow through on his threat, and accordingly, they had not alerted the local police. Whatever played out in the next few hours would depend on their wits and the good Lord.

She thought about this and the resurgence of her faith. She was coming to understand that her faith was a little like a very good friend that she had not seen for a while. Having run into that friend unexpectedly, she had taken up pretty much exactly where she had left off.

Her mother's faith had been like a rock. It was hard and fast, and no questions were asked. Cloe felt a little differently. The fabric of her faith was more pliable, but she was coming to understand that it was no less indestructible than her mother's. She could feel the solid shield of that faith encompassing and enveloping her. It had the feel of her mother's arms. She would do what had to be done to get Uncle Sonny back, and she knew that, somehow, God would help her.

Now approaching the old church, Cloe and the monsignor paused at the Mémoire de Lyon plaque that adorned the building. The monsignor read out loud, translating from the French: "This was the primary place of worship of the Lyon martyrs, the first-century Christian martyrs in Gaul. The church and the neighboring calvary which overlook the city date from the nineteenth century. The church replaces one of the oldest churches in France, which was pillaged and rebuilt on several occasions. The admirably restored crypt, surrounding a Paleo-Christian apse, commemorates the martyrs of 177 and the first Lyon bishops: Pothin and particularly Irénée, one of the Fathers of the Church, who is buried in the church."

Cloe said, maybe a little more lightly than she felt, "Well, it looks like we're in the right place. We need to examine the burial area and crypt of Irenaeus in case he's left us some clue as to the whereabouts of the journal."

"Surely, Signorina, there can be nothing left from those days so long ago."

"Maybe," she responded, "but a few days ago we knew nothing of the jar, the manuscript, and its apparent reference to a journal of Judas Iscariot. Sometimes you don't know what you don't know. New information can make references that have been around forever now suddenly highly relevant. There may be some clue. No matter how small or innocent, if there is one, we have to find it."

They climbed the steps and entered the quiet church, slipping away from the noise and commotion of the outside world. Cloe glanced about, noting the traditional pews, the nave, and the altar complex. The altar itself seemed bare after the decommissioning. There was only a single soul in the church, sitting in a pew about a third of the way up the main aisle. The penitent was obviously deep in thought and contemplation.

Cloe and the monsignor walked quietly up the aisle toward the recognizable figure. Cloe leaned over and hugged J.E. as he sat there, thinking or praying—she did not know which. She shuddered to think of the weight on the shoulders of her young son.

"Hey, Mom," said J.E., standing, turning, and hugging her back as if they had not seen each other in a long time.

"Hello, Monsignor." J.E. reached out to shake the monsignor's hand. The monsignor gripped J.E.'s hand firmly, shook it, and gave him a man's hug.

"How are you?" asked Cloe.

"I'm fine," he said tiredly. He had gotten even less rest than Cloe. "We've spent our time carefully checking out everything that we could. But the place is virtually indefensible. It's almost deserted. The only person we've seen is a kindly old priest who is the caretaker of the campus here at the church. Father Anton spoke with him, and it seems most of the church personnel have now been reassigned. Some are in Africa on a Thanksgiving mission and will return in time for the Christmas season. They will be reassigned at some point.

"Unfortunately, the priest has only been at St. Irenaeus for a few weeks, mainly in connection with the decommissioning. He seems to be something of an expert in defrocking churches. He knows relatively little about the church's facilities and the grounds. The only maps he had were some drawings in the various guidebooks. He was not much help to Father Anton.

"The old priest has a small maintenance crew. If they need more help, they borrow from the nearby churches. It goes without saying that there are no further religious services scheduled in the church. We're on our own."

"J.E., where are the Swiss Guards?"

"Father Anton and I have done our best to deploy them around the campus as strategically as possible. But the place is a warren of buildings, walls, and other structures. The church lies in the middle of all this. We would need a hundred men to adequately secure the area. Also, even though we received some additional ordnance, our men have only close-quarters weapons. We don't have long-range sniper rifles or other weaponry that could even the possible odds against us. I'm not sure we could deploy them even if we had them. What we need is a company, and we have less than half a squad."

"J.E., I know you've done your best and that we're as safe as we can be under the circumstances," Cloe said, but a shiver wracked her shoulders as she thought about the man who was coming.

# CHAPTER 45

The church and grounds had been closely examined, and their forces were arrayed as well as possible. The monsignor had briefly conferred with Father Anton and had now returned. They needed to do one more thing.

"Signorina," the monsignor said, "Father Anton earlier queried the old priest about the possible existence of an ancient library, but he says there is none as far as he is aware. Father Anton also checked his Vatican sources. There was once a library of St. John here, but the available records show it was destroyed hundreds of years ago."

"Well, I know it's a lot to expect that there would be anything left here," Cloe said. "But still, the people who held such important documents and information could've left some sign, some clue. In our rush to get here and our study of the manuscript on the way, we haven't had the time to thoroughly research the possibilities. I'm not ready to give up.

"J.E., where's the tomb?" she asked, disappointed but not defeated. She knew he had thoroughly reconnoitered the church and surrounding facilities and would certainly know where the burial site was located.

"The entrance is in a niche at the end of the right transept of the church," he replied.

"Monsignor, let's go look at it," responded Cloe. "J.E., do you want to come with us?"

"No, Mom, I'm going to make another pass and check ingress and egress routes. Also, I'll check on the guards. They'll be here all night to make sure that our adversary doesn't show up early and set up something unpleasant for us."

The monsignor and Cloe left the pew and headed toward the altar. At the old-fashioned altar rail, the monsignor faced what had previously been the tabernacle area and bowed deeply. Cloe paused, genuflected, and crossed herself. It was a moment within a moment. *Some things are always right*, she reflected, even though she, like the monsignor, realized on a rational level that the church had been deconsecrated.

Cloe and the monsignor then proceeded to the right. Toward the end of the transept they saw the niche containing the burial place of St. Irenaeus. The monsignor had told her that, at some point, the Church would remove the remains of St. Irenaeus to another, active church. But, there had not yet been time for that. The niche was deep and smothered in shadows only slightly bested by several wall-mounted sconces holding burning candles. There were also two stanchions, one on either side of the archway leading into the burial tomb itself, that held large lighted candles. Each time a candle flickered, the shadows climbed the walls, only to be beaten back when the wick resumed a steady burn. In spite of her scientific curiosity, Cloe felt a cold chill.

The niche led to a small chamber in which the crypt was located. The church itself had, in effect, been rebuilt around the tomb. More candles illuminated the interior area, staining the high ceiling with God-himself-only-knew how many years of soot. Details on the sarcophagus and on the icons in the room were well worn with time's damage. Features that had once been fine had become gross as the weaker areas wore away or dissolved.

Cloe began to scrutinize the burial chamber. "Monsignor, would you start at the archway and work your way around the room clockwise? I'll do likewise from the other side. We'll save the sarcophagus for last." She wanted to be absolutely methodical in their study of the area.

They circumnavigated the room, touching every icon, indentation, crack, or irregularity. After about an hour they met at the head of the tomb. Their hands were blackened by the smoky soot left by the ages. They looked at each other, but neither had found anything of note. Cloe's spirits began to flag a bit.

"Nothing?" she asked.

"I saw nothing that seemed even slightly out of the ordinary."

They turned to the sarcophagus itself. Again they examined it with the most minute approach, running their fingers over every inch of the surface. The death mask of Irenaeus was the most interesting item in the chamber. As best Cloe could make out from the almost-two-thousand-year-old relic, he was portrayed as a man with a mustache and a beard of somewhat unusual dimension. It had tips on each side with a V-shaped cleft between the two tips. Interestingly, it made a sort of "W" at the bottom of the face.

On a more modern man, the mustache would have been dubbed a drooping, handlebar-style mustache. Irenaeus's hair was receding, but the sides were full. The eyes, though closed, appeared to be large, with the lower face almond-shaped except for the strange beard. The nose was full, the lips a little less so. Cloe continued to be drawn to the odd beard. It seemed outlandish and just not right for the face.

She remembered as a teenager going to the Cabildo in New Orleans and, unexpectedly, coming upon the death mask of Napoleon. She could still recall being riveted. Looking at the mask, she could imagine Napoleon in life, going about his business. Perhaps that's the intended effect. But Napoleon had been completely clean shaven. Something about Irenaeus's death mask ate at her.

"Anything?" asked the monsignor. "I've looked at every inch, and I see nothing that seems questionable."

"I wonder ..." said Cloe. "The beard is odd to me, and it reminds me of something that I can't quite place."

The monsignor walked around the foot of the sarcophagus, leaned forward, and peered intently at the lower portion of the mask.

"Hmm ... it looks like a letter ... the letter 'W,'" he finally said. "I'm not sure that I would even say that except for the fact that a lot of the detail has been worn away. The texture of the beard that was once present is gone, and the 'W' is now unmistakable. Are you saying that this is a message?"

"I don't know ... could it be a message, or an icon in and of itself?" mused Cloe. "And if so, what could it possibly mean? I mean a message in a man's beard, for Christ's sake." Cloe was beginning to wonder if she was reaching for something.

Still, this would be a hidden-in-plain-sight sort of message that most people would not notice or, if they did, that they would not assess as a message. Only people who knew what to look for would identify it as some sort of communication. Cloe knew that secret societies often did such things.

"Well, it can't be a 'W' because that's an English letter, and we can be relatively sure that people of Irenaeus's time had little or no exposure to English. Their languages were Greek, Roman, and perhaps in the Christian world, Aramaic."

"Yes," replied Cloe, pondering. "Hebrew and Aramaic, along with some other ancient languages, were derived from Phoenician script." She paused to think. "Oh my God!" she suddenly exclaimed. "It's not English, certainly. It's not Greek. It's even older. It's the ancient letter 'shin,' which looks somewhat like an English 'W.' It roughly translates to the letter 'S.'"

"What could it mean?" asked the monsignor. "'S' ... I don't get an association with anything we are doing. The names Judas and Jesus both end in 's,' but what is the message in that?"

"Maybe that's not all," Cloe said. "Is there anything else?"

Cloe and the monsignor both turned from their discussion and, once again, pored over not only the death mask but also the entirety of the sarcophagus. After about forty-five minutes they faced each other, shaking off exhaustion.

"I don't have anything further," said the monsignor.

"Me either," said Cloe with a defeated slump of her shoulders. It was now full dark, and the artificial light coming in from the church was rather dim. "Monsignor, I'm not sure we can accomplish anymore here. We need to make a record of the area, and then I suggest we find a hotel and get as much rest as we can for tomorrow."

"Agreed. I'll photograph this room in every aspect. Sometimes in a different light a new detail will manifest itself." He took out a digital camera and spent about thirty minutes recording every element.

"Make sure you get the beard," Cloe said, still focused on what message might have been intended and for whom—if, indeed, there was any message at all. They then headed for the niche that opened into the church.

At that moment, J.E. reentered the building and strode up the center aisle toward them.

"J.E., we're done here," Cloe said. "We haven't really learned anything except that Irenaeus's beard may contain the Aramaic letter 'shin,' meaning 'S.'"

J.E. gawked at her and almost laughed out loud. "Mom, we're all tired, but you're seeing letters in the man's beard. Say it ain't so."

The monsignor smiled at J.E. "It's the only thing we have seen that does not seem to quite fit. Nor can we figure out what it could mean if it means anything. It was not unusual for the ancients to leave clues or messages. But if this is the whole message, there is no correlation in it to anything we know."

"Come on, we're all tired … let's go find a hotel," said Cloe.

"There's one about fifteen minutes from here," said J.E. "Let's take the van. We'll get something to eat. I'm going to sleep for a couple of hours after that and then come back with food for Father Anton and the guards. We'll make sure nothing happens here tonight."

As they walked toward the front of the church, a bent and hooded figure opened the door for them. A cold shadow passed over Cloe's spirit at the sight of the bowed figure. She briefly shivered, and J.E. put his arm around her. But it was the kindly old priest that J.E. had seen on the grounds earlier in the day. They stepped through the door, nodding to him. The elderly priest returned the nod and said in perfect English, "Farewell, my children. I hope to see you here again soon." The massive door clanged shut behind them.

# CHAPTER 46

The small hotel was a welcome sight. When they entered the foyer, Cloe could see that it was furnished more akin to a residence than a hotel. The proprietress met them at the door with a great smile and helped them store their coats. Her English was, at best, broken, but with the monsignor's help, she got her message over: Freshen up and supper was available. Their bags were on the way from the airport.

The food was hot, plentiful, and wonderful. The herbed, roasted fowl with winter vegetables was suburb. Cloe realized that this was the first real meal she'd had in at least a day, probably more. The proprietress, who was also the sommelier, had uncorked a nice chardonnay, and Cloe found it the perfect complement to the fine meal. During the supper, since they had not had the chance to talk at the church, she brought J.E. up-to-date on what they had learned in their research at the airport and on what they had found at in the tomb. He briefed them on his preparations and then retired to get some sleep after asking for sandwiches to be wrapped for his trip back to the church.

Cloe and the monsignor enjoyed a last glass of wine in the parlor of the hotel.

"What do you think will happen tomorrow, Monsignor?" asked Cloe. She was anxious about the day to come, but she welcomed the chance to reunite with Uncle Sonny.

"I don't know," said the monsignor earnestly. "Please … I would take it as a great honor if you would call me Albert. I feel very close to you and J.E. You are now my family, no matter what happens."

She smiled and looked him in the eye and said, "Albert, I'm the one who is honored, and I'll be Cloe to you. And yes, we're family now, no matter what."

"Thank you, Cloe," he said, with perhaps a glint of moisture in his eyes. "The guards and Father Anton will cover our backs as we make the exchange. It has been decided that all three of us must go into the church, or the man will sense a trap. We get in, and we get out with your uncle Sonny. We make no attempt to stop them in their effort to escape. We then go to the nearest police station and tell them our story. Perhaps they can catch our adversaries before they leave the country, which is what I assume he will try to do immediately."

Cloe wanted to talk about the threat to the Church, but she was not sure how to begin. "Albert, there is danger here well beyond Uncle Sonny and us."

"You are referring to the possibility that this man, this Kolektor, wants our jar so badly in part because he may believe the manuscript includes information that could be hurtful to the Catholic Church?" asked the monsignor.

"Yes, the Coptic version of the Judas Gospel contains so much nonsense that it can be easily discredited. But our version, written in Greek as were early forms of the orthodox Gospels, may be very credible and authentic. Suppose it refutes some critical portion of the Gospels such as Judas's role. In the wrong hands it would be used as anti-Catholic propaganda," whispered Cloe.

"Possibly," responded the monsignor. He was silent for a bit and then continued. "Remember, the Church has been attacked many times. The Church not only preaches the Gospels, but we believe in them as the inspired word of God. We do not wish to suppress whatever is in the manuscript. The best thing is for it to be in the hands of scholars who can properly interpret it. The Church will survive … my faith tells me that. Still, it is my duty to keep it from profiteers or provocateurs like our adversary, if I can."

"But Uncle Sonny?" pleaded Cloe.

"Cloe, do not fear," responded the priest, with kindness. "My first duty is to life. Were that not true, the Church would never have survived to this day. We will get your uncle. If the choice is between your uncle's life and the manuscript, life is our choice."

215

"Albert, I want you to understand there is really no choice for me here. What we have and know is potentially one of the greatest discoveries in history, but I'm willing to give it all up for my uncle and not look back. I know we may be walking into a trap, but I've got to take the risk to try to get Uncle Sonny back safely."

"Signorina … Cloe, I may know more about you than you think. The Church itself is about nothing if not about family. The full weight of its resources is behind you, and I promise you that somehow we will prevail over this evil."

She and the monsignor talked on for a bit, but both knew it was necessary to get as much rest as possible under the circumstances. They made plans to meet early the next morning for a last rehearsal of what they hoped would happen at the church.

In her room, Cloe prayed to God that no harm would come to any of them, especially to J.E., who had his whole life before him.

After washing and changing for the night, Cloe sat up in bed with her laptop before her. She began to look at the pictures from the crypt that the monsignor—Albert—had transferred to her computer. Cloe studied the close-ups of the beard. The "W" was clearly there, but was it intended as a message? It was impossible to know for sure. She focused intently on the way the beard forked out into the two legs of the "W."

\*\*\*

The knock at the door came as if from a great distance, but it was extremely persistent. Cloe opened her eyes and saw that it was light and, indeed, not the soft light of very early morning. She jumped and for a moment, not immediately recognizing where she was, nearly panicked at her unfamiliar surroundings.

"Signorina … Cloe," said the monsignor at the door.

"Yes, I'm awake, Albert. I'll be downstairs shortly."

She looked at her watch and saw that she had slept through to a little after seven. She hurried through her morning ritual, dressed, and went downstairs for breakfast, bringing her laptop. Even in her groggy state, she knew she had been on the verge of something last night. She sat with the monsignor but opened the pictures and stared at the "W" in the beard. There was something there, just beyond her reach.

"Albert, my God … if we focus on the center of the 'W,' we actually have another ancient Aramaic letter. It's the Aramaic letter 'yudh,' which is taken to mean variously 'J,' 'I,' or 'E.'"

"Cloe, the combination of the two letters 'yudh' and 'shin' can be translated as 'IS' … possibly, Iscariot. This cannot be a coincidence." The monsignor rose in his excitement and came around to look over her shoulder at the computer.

Cloe pondered the intuitive jump to this conclusion. It made sense. Somebody, perhaps Irenaeus himself, had either inscribed this detail in the death mask or left instructions to do so. Could it be a message that connected the new Judas manuscript references to Irenaeus? In a way, it might have been a nineteen-hundred-year-old confirmation of their conclusion that Irenaeus knew about and probably sanctioned the Greek version of the Gospel of Judas.

The monsignor returned to his seat and said earnestly, "Cloe, if that part is true, the part suggesting a writing by Judas himself may also be true. The possibility adds to this stunning discovery. If the writing still exists, it will set the world on its ear. Even the possibility that it may once have existed and may have been the source document for our manuscript is enormous."

"But does it exist?" she asked, reviewing in her mind everything they had seen. Perhaps there was another clue. She could think of nothing. All they had was the "I" and the "S."

J.E. arrived looking tired and dirty. He flopped down at the table and quickly ordered coffee. After a couple of gulps he leaned forward and said, "Everything that can be done has been done. We swept the grounds many times during the night. We looked for the old priest this morning but couldn't locate him, so we worked on our own. The Swiss have gotten some sleep in shifts. They seem impervious to fatigue."

"J.E. … there's still time for you to take a nap. We're not due for at least a couple of hours."

He looked at her affectionately and said, "I'm going to drink this and go shave and get cleaned up. I don't know whether I can sleep just before the battle, whatever it may end up being. But I'll lie down and try. Just don't let me sleep beyond ten o'clock. The church is only fifteen minutes away, but we want to be a little early to stake out our position."

"Go," Cloe said. She shivered at what might lie ahead. She could almost sense that the man on the phone was near.

\*\*\*

Traffic was light as they drove to the church. When they arrived, J.E. talked with Father Anton and the head of the Swiss Guard and determined that all was just as he had left it. The elderly priest had been seen on the grounds a little earlier but not in the last few minutes. One of the Swiss had observed him entering the old church. Except for Cloe and her cohorts, the rest of the compound seemed deserted.

As they entered the church vestibule, Cloe noted that about fifteen minutes remained before their appointment. They walked up the main aisle and found the church empty except for the old priest and ten hooded acolytes. Apparently the cleric had returned to the church with a group of young priests. With their backs to Cloe, they knelt in the first pew intently engaged in the rosary. She could barely hear the soft voice of the old priest calling out the opening prayers and the murmured responses of what she thought might be young seminarians.

Cloe was comforted by the presence of the old priest and his companions. Who would contemplate violence in such presence? Then the thought struck her that with their enemy, all could be in danger.

J.E., worried about any possible threat, stood intently examining the group of religious. Finally, apparently sensing no threat, he turned to Cloe and said, "We'll sit here and wait. There is only the front door and the door from the side that the priests use. We can see both from here, and the Swiss Guards are covering both."

As they took their seats about halfway up the aisle, Cloe looked at him and the monsignor and whispered, "Do you have any last thoughts or instructions?"

J.E. responded, also very quietly, "Yes. When this person gets here, the Swiss Guards have instructions that if Sonny is not with him he will not be permitted to enter the church, and if he does get in, he will not be permitted to leave with any of us. This is to prevent his duplicity making the situation worse."

J.E. sat on the outside, closest to the aisle, with the monsignor to the inside of the pew and Cloe in between. Cloe saw that the monsignor was carefully studying the group of praying priests.

Cloe turned to J.E. "When I was a teenager, my dad—your grandfather—always said that if someone ever jumps you, you fight at the point of attack," she said in a low voice. She had no idea what the next few minutes would bring but wanted to seize on something of use.

"That's right," said J.E. "You don't put yourself under someone else's power. No good can come from it. If they'll take you, they have bad plans for you, so you fight, scream, and do whatever you can to prevent being taken. We will not put ourselves under the power of this Kolektor. If we do, we're lost."

The bell in the church tower began to toll eleven o'clock. They anxiously listened to it go through its cycle and toll one, two, three … eleven times. Each time the hammer struck the bell, Cloe felt as if a chip had been cut from her soul. J.E. constantly looked back and forth at both entrances as if he expected the devil himself to walk into the church.

But nothing happened; no one appeared. Five minutes went by, and then ten. They sat in silent dread. This was worse than the man showing up on time. The only sounds were of the soft back-and-forth of the priests with their rosaries.

"Don't worry … he's sweating us," said J.E. "This is just a little psychological game to unnerve us and put us off-guard."

"It's working," said Cloe, wringing her hands and looking right and left. All of them were sweating now, even though the church was cool.

Cloe heard the old priest finish the rosary and saw him stand, head covered and down, and cross himself. The acolytes followed suit and began to exit the first pew. When about half of them had entered the aisle, the priest joined the line as they walked, heads covered and bowed in reverence, toward the visitors and the entrance to the church. Cloe thought it was strange that the old priest would join in the middle of the line rather than take the first position or, perhaps, bring up the rear.

She felt the monsignor stir and then reach across her and grab J.E. "They're here," he whispered as the first in line of the acolytes passed by the pew in which they were sitting.

"Where?" quietly responded J.E., looking intently around but still neither hearing nor seeing anything that might signal the Kolektor's entrance. The young seminarians were now almost halfway past their pew and the old priest was coming abreast of them.

"The priests," the monsignor urgently whispered. "The priests. The church has been deconsecrated … they should not be saying the rosary here."

At that point the old priest stopped and turned slightly to face them. He looked at each of them, one by one, but they no longer saw the friendly eyes or kind face of the elderly cleric. Their eyes locked on his, and there was now a hardened, hollow countenance glaring back at them. Finally, his gaze settled on Cloe. The Kolektor, in a flat, dry, gravelly voice that Cloe could never mistake, said, "Good morning, Dr. Lejeune."

# CHAPTER 47

Horror flooded over her in a tsunami-like fashion, wave after wave. Dismay and revulsion ebbed and flowed. The enemy had outsmarted and outflanked them. Now fear reached up from her gut and grabbed her heart.

She watched as the false priests spun toward them and began throwing off their religious camouflage. They pirouetted in an almost choreographed fashion, their movement like some sort of grotesque ballet. Weapons materialized from under the cassocks. The double cross—the man had come with thugs and guns.

Cloe felt rather than saw J.E. jump up and draw his gun. Once again, time slowed to a crawl. The Kolektor stepped back, hands to his chest, as if to ward off an anticipated blow, while J.E.'s arm straightened and swung around toward the Kolektor to train the 40-caliber Glock that he had borrowed from one of the Swiss. Cloe thought, randomly, that for such a peaceable people they had certainly come well armed.

All this took place in that portion of a second where thought does not dwell, but it seemed drawn out, as with characters in a play. J.E.'s weapon stalked the Kolektor slowly, agonizingly slowly, but just as it tracked almost to the Kolektor, the acolyte to J.E.'s left connected the butt of his pistol with the side of J.E.'s head. The impact caused J.E. to fire prematurely, striking the faux priest immediately to the right of the Kolektor.

The report of the large handgun echoed back and forth off the walls of the church until Cloe thought it would never stop. It was not a kill shot; J.E.'s bullet had traveled beyond the vital organs and connected a bit inside the armpit. The thug collapsed to the floor in a pile and lay there writhing and screaming in pain.

Cloe screamed as J.E. went down hard against the back of the pew, blood gushing from the side of his head. His automatic clattered uselessly to the floor of the former holy place now desecrated by violence. The monsignor began to rise from the pew. J.E. was down, and they were now covered by numerous weapons. Cloe could only hope that the Swiss Guard had heard the shots and would be charging in to rescue them.

The Kolektor seemed to have read her thoughts. "There will be no rescue from your friends outside. My men have now locked and barred both doors. We are well aware of where they have been positioned, and you can be sure that in their locations they have heard nothing given the depth of the walls of this old church."

Although barely able to move, Cloe somehow found the strength to lean over to check on J.E. The wound seemed superficial even though it was bleeding profusely. His shirt was covered with blood, but already the abrasion had begun to congeal. He was moving and beginning to come around. He would be all right, she thought. She straightened to face the enemy.

"We had a deal," she said accusingly. "Why have you done this? We've brought the jar, the manuscript, and our research. Where is my uncle?"

"Yes, and you have come with weapons and the soldiers outside to trap me. That was not part of our arrangement. It is you who have failed to keep our agreement. In any event, the bargain was always in your mind," he responded matter-of-factly. "It was merely a device to bring you to a place where I could receive what I desire, including my revenge on you and your meddling associates. However, I'm very glad to hear that you have brought it all."

Cloe realized they were in the middle of the treachery that both J.E. and the monsignor had predicted. The man had not come alone with Uncle Sonny but with many men and weapons. "Where is my uncle?" she screamed.

"Your uncle is quite safe," responded the Kolektor. "In fact, I may yet be persuaded to take you to him as soon as you show me what I want."

The monsignor caught her eye, and she read in his face that it would be error to give the Kolektor what he wanted.

The Kolektor saw the silent communication between them and spoke again in that flat, emotionless manner of his. "Your friend, the priest here, is the most expendable of your group. I do not need him for anything. Provide me with what I want, and I will take you to your uncle and release you all. Fail, and I will kill the priest now. Then you will give me what I desire. Either way … you choose."

Once again it seemed Cloe was faced with lies and impossible choices. Ever since she had embarked on the quest to understand the jar and find her father's murderer, she had been confronted with one after another such decision.

She could see now that once they started down this path, the Kolektor would always have the brutal high ground unless they were able to outflank him at some point. But he had outflanked them already. How? She didn't know. His trump card was Uncle Sonny. She really had little choice but to try to extend the game in hopes of a future opportunity to win. That, she thought, was the way most games were played, even the mortal ones—stay in the game, stay as close as possible, and hope for an opportunity to win at the end. She felt that surge of anger come to her that hardened her mettle and stiffened her resolve.

She turned to her adversary and said, "Very well. The jar and the manuscript are here in the pew with me. You may have them as our part of the bargain."

The Kolektor looked intently at her. "And what of your research and all your conclusions and findings? What of the information gathered at the university in the United States?"

"That is here." Cloe grabbed the flash drive that hung around her neck and held it up for the Kolektor to see. The flash drive glistened in the low candlelight of the church like some postmodern gem. It was fastened around her neck by means of a light chain.

"I will have that as well," responded the Kolektor.

"I think not … at least not until I have the safe return of my uncle," she responded immediately.

The monsignor sensed the stalemate and felt the tension growing in the atmosphere. J.E. began to show some signs of coming around. Something had to give—and soon.

The Kolektor nodded at the faux priest next to him, who moved to take the drive from Cloe.

As he approached, Cloe said, "If you pull this from my neck, as you certainly can, that action will trigger an electromagnetic pulse that will erase, irrevocably, the contents of the drive."

The Kolektor raised a hand, and all stood frozen in place. He considered the situation for a moment. Finally, he said, "I do not believe you. You will give me the drive, or I will have it cut from your dying throat."

Cloe raised the edge of the vest that she was wearing to reveal wires leading from the flash drive to something that looked like a small cell phone clamped to her belt in a cell phone holster.

"You do so entertain me, Dr. Lejeune," responded the man-devil. "I wonder if you are really willing to play this out. I will have the device one way or another. Your life or your death makes no difference to me."

"Perhaps so, Kolektor, but the mechanism in my cell phone holster is rather sophisticated and is rigged to a plate on the back of the flash drive. If the chain holding the drive to my neck is disconnected or broken, the battery will pulse and magnetize the plate, and the resultant electromagnetic radiation will eradicate whatever information is on the drive. Even if you kill me and take the device, a code has to be entered, within a certain period of time, to prevent the destruction of the information. There is only a single opportunity to enter the code. Failure to enter it properly or in the allotted time results in the pulse."

Seeing she had his attention, Cloe continued, "The pertinent question isn't whether you care about my life or any other but your own. We know that you don't. The real inquiry is whether you want the information on the drive or you want to have to do your own research from ground zero. That will put you weeks or months behind. Some things we've learned, you may never find." Cloe took a step closer to the Kolektor and said, "Unless you want to do that, take me to my uncle … now!"

# CHAPTER 48

The Kolektor held most of the cards, including Uncle Sonny. He had the guns, the superior forces, and now the jar and the manuscript. But he did not have what they had discovered. The manuscript was just an old Greek document without Cloe's research. But her research was useless without the written text to verify it. Together they made a whole. She had a piece, and the Kolektor now had another piece. In a way, they needed each other.

Her research, the computer-stored analysis, pictures, X-rays, infrared photos, ultrasounds, calculations, and deductions were every bit on the flash drive. Even the contents of her laptop were there. All this was now hanging around Cloe's neck by a thin chain attached to a dead-man's switch.

The flash drive device was one of the things they had worked on that fateful night before they left LSU for Lyon. Father Anton had made some improvements to it when he examined the contraption at the airport in Lyon. They had all discussed this strategy in detail because of this very possibility. She felt that she had some power, maybe not much, but some.

The Kolektor had been considering the device and now spoke. "Dr. Lejeune, you and your colleagues are endlessly droll with your distractions. But you and I both know that there is some sort of code to disarm the device so you can yourself remove it without losing the information. I will ask you only once … what is it?"

"You're quite right," Cloe replied, not seeing any profit in lying. "The problem is that I don't know the code. No one here knows it. I'm committed to wearing this rig until my uncle and all of us return safely. That's part of the firewall that my son has erected." This too had been carefully thought out by the group.

"I do not believe you," responded the Kolektor, rage and frustration beginning to melt his icy comportment. "You will tell me the code, or I will have the monsignor shot."

Cloe had been superbly insulated from the real world of life and death in her academic world; there, everything was theoretical or abstract. That's the way she really liked it; no one, including her, had to take any responsibility for anything. But now, she mused, this was the real world, and the Kolektor, although a nightmare, was nothing if not real. What could she do? She flashed back to her youth and remembered advice her father had given to her when she was under pressure to deliver a presentation or to perform—to "tap dance," as he had put it. He had always said, "Know what you know" as a way of telling her to stay within herself and on ground with which she was familiar. She thought about that now. What she knew was that if she gave up the drive, they were all dead.

She looked stonily at the Kolektor and said, "You may shoot me or the monsignor, but you will still not have the code. No one here knows it." She watched carefully as the Kolektor processed this information, weighing its credibility. Cloe's heart was pounding so hard she thought the Kolektor must hear it.

The Kolektor gestured to one of his accomplices, who raised his weapon and trained it on the monsignor. Cloe put her head down and waited for the sound of the shot. But it never came. Instead, there came a terrible pounding at the locked front door of the church. It struck Cloe that J.E. must have left some sort of time requirement or signal with the Swiss. Evidently, J.E. had not checked with them within the allotted time, and they were now coming for him.

Straight away, pounding started on the side door as well. The hammering became more urgent, and Cloe looked back toward the front entrance and realized that the Swiss Guard had begun to physically attack the door with a vigor and a vehemence that she could scarcely believe. She recognized the sounds of muted weapons being fired into the door, splintering wood and tearing through its very fabric. It would not be long before they were through the entrance and into the church.

She looked at the Kolektor and saw a brief flash of indecision cross his face. He had underestimated J.E. For a moment she saw his weakness. He saw that she had seen and likely hated her doubly for it. He glanced about as the impossibly loud crescendo at the door somehow increased. "Bring them all," ordered the Kolektor.

Without hesitation he grabbed a weapon from one of his accomplices and fired a single shot into the brain of his wounded man, mercilessly applying the coup de grace. One of the brutes carefully collected the jar and the manuscript. His men then quickly pulled the monsignor from the pew and hustled him up the aisle toward the altar. One large thug picked up J.E. like a sack of rice, threw him over his shoulder, and followed the others. Cloe was the last, and the Kolektor reached out to her as if she were alighting from a carriage. It was a curious gesture of false chivalry and irony.

She brushed past him, almost knocking him aside, and followed J.E. and the monsignor. The Kolektor and the last few of his henchmen chased her up the aisle.

As Cloe moved quickly down, she glanced aloft at the icons of the saints and martyrs lining the church walls. They seemed to look down upon the action in the church with birdlike intensity and disapproval. She passed the life-sized statue of St. Irenaeus and noticed that his beard was full and U-shaped. The death mask flashed in her mind, and she immediately registered the difference. Irenaeus in life was depicted with a normal beard, not the twin-pronged beard of the death mask forming the letters "shin" and "yudh." Cloe filed away this information to consider later—if there would be a later for her.

The Kolektor and his henchmen apparently intended to attempt their escape through the side entrance used by the priests. Cloe drew courage from this, knowing there would be no escape for them. But they went directly to the altar and stopped. Cloe turned and saw that the Swiss had broken through one of the panels on the heavy front door. They would be inside in a matter of seconds. Their comrades at the side door would not be far behind them.

Two of the erstwhile priests stationed themselves at and behind the altar and began firing at the front door. This fusillade slowed the progress of the rescuers, but they continued to work on the door between volleys. The side door, which was not as stout as the front door, began to splinter, and the Kolektor's men turned a volley of bullets on the Swiss there.

Cloe said to the Kolektor, "You're trapped. J.E. has men at both doors. You can't hope to escape."

The Kolektor only chuckled, bent over, and pulled on a hidden lever in the floor behind the altar. A stone trap door came open and fell away, revealing a stairwell. The Kolektor paused at the mouth of the hatchway, turned, and looked at her with triumph in his eyes. "Did you not wonder how we got into the church without the guards seeing us?" he said with a snicker.

Pushing their captives ahead of them, the Kolektor's men pounded down the stairs at a brutal pace. The stairway circled downward for at least twenty feet, ending in a landing that formed the entryway to a long and obviously very old tunnel.

As she hit the bottom of the staircase, Cloe glanced to her left and saw a body in a black cassock sprawled behind some debris. It was undoubtedly the true old caretaker priest. The jar had claimed yet another casualty. She said a silent prayer for his poor soul.

Cloe looked up and glimpsed the Kolektor closing the trap door, leaving his rear guard at the altar to be sacrificed to his unholy enterprise. The shots were now muffled, and she could see that the hatch door had been sealed with another metal bar of enormous size. When she realized the Swiss would never get through the stone and metal to rescue them, her knees weakened, and she almost fell. At that point despair slinked toward her, seeking to steal her courage, to take her heart. Cloe could not remember feeling so desperate.

The Kolektor caught up with her and smiled, the corners of his lips turning slightly downward in disdain. He hurried her along the ancient tunnel, which at first sloped gently downward and then began to climb toward the surface. The clergy of St. Irenaeus's day must have created this underground avenue of escape, Cloe surmised. After all, Christianity was new and not appreciated by all, particularly those in power. She passed what might have been two ancient doors leading off the main corridor. Had the Kolektor's light not flashed briefly on them as she was hustled by, she would not have noticed them. They looked as if they had not been opened for an exceedingly long time. Perhaps there was more to the Church of St. John than they had thus far uncovered, Cloe thought. The tunnel narrowed and then turned sharply left and then right. Swiftly, they were at the end of the tunnel and in a wooded area adjacent to the St. Irenaeus complex. Waiting there were two black vans sufficient to carry them all. The men, their gear, and the hostages were loaded into the vans, and the vans drove calmly away from the Church of St. Irenaeus.

# PART 4

# JERUSALEM

One day Peter stood up to speak to the brothers—there were about
a hundred and twenty persons in the congregation; "Brothers, the
passage of scripture had to be fulfilled in which the Holy Spirit,
speaking through David, foretells the fate of Judas, who offered
himself as a guide to the men who arrested Jesus—after having
been one of our number and actually sharing this ministry of ours.
As you know, he bought a field with the money he was paid for his
crime. He fell headlong and burst open, and all his entrails poured
out. Everybody in Jerusalem heard about it and the field came to be
called the Bloody Acre, in their language Hakeldama."

—Acts of the Apostles 1:15–20, the Jerusalem Bible (1966)

# CHAPTER 49

Once in the van, J.E. and the monsignor were tied hand and foot, and each was gagged. J.E. had begun to moan, and Cloe had done what she could to attend to him. The wound still did not seem anything more than superficial, but it had bled a good deal, and he was still moving in and out of consciousness. She worried that there might be some internal damage. At one point she leaned over him to swab his face with the edge of his shirt, and he suddenly opened one eye and winked at her. He then continued his soft moaning.

They arrived at the general aviation hangar at the Lyon-Bron facility about fifteen minutes later. Right now, Cloe thought, the Kolektor was probably far ahead of any possible pursuit. But never would she underestimate the resourcefulness of Father Anton and the Swiss, so she continued to have hope.

The vans were driven directly onto the tarmac and up to two waiting Cessna Citation X aircraft. Two pilots for each were awaiting them. As the vans rolled up, one pilot entered each jet and began making preparations for immediate departure. The others helped unload and store the gear and saw to the Kolektor's needs. Cloe watched as everything was executed with military precision.

The monsignor and J.E. were carried aboard the first plane and thrown behind the last row of seats. Holding fast to the flash drive, Cloe was escorted aboard the same executive jet and seated immediately across from the Kolektor in the informal seating area. A few of the remaining thugs, likely the Kolektor's personal guard, collapsed into seats on either side while the balance of the Kolektor's minions boarded the other jet.

The copilot of the first plane took his seat on the right-hand side of the cockpit as it began to taxi toward the runway. Cloe looked out the small window and felt a terrible foreboding. They should never have come to Lyon. She and her friends had proved no match for this vicious man who could only be temporarily satiated by possessing relics of astounding significance. But she had had no choice; she had come for Uncle Sonny.

The powerful planes taxied to the end of the tarmac and turned onto the main runway, apparently first and second in line for takeoff. The jet that encapsulated Cloe and her colleagues squatted in that hiatus moment, after its runway approach and before takeoff. Cloe imagined the business in the cockpit as the pilots went through their routines and tested equipment and systems. Soon she heard the mighty jet engines on either side of the fuselage begin to spool up. The brakes were on, and the plane began to vibrate, almost shivering, in its animal-like desire to leap into the atmosphere.

Cloe felt the pilots release the brakes and was pressed hard back into her seat as the jet roared off toward the end of the runway. Long before it got there, the sleek aircraft rotated and shot off the earth as if had been fired from some monstrous medieval catapult of evil design. It assaulted and penetrated the midlevel cloud layer and was soon high above the surface on a horizontal flight to … where? Cloe wondered. Where would this flight end?

The copilot returned to the cabin and served the Kolektor his drink. Cloe noted it was a thick, nearly frozen liquid, perhaps gin or vodka. The copilot also brought their host an appetizer of caviar and various accoutrements. Nothing was offered to her, nor would she have accepted anything, with her son and the monsignor trussed up in the rear of the plane. Still, the Kolektor was seated across from her, and she might learn something.

After he had savored a bit of his drink, he ordered one of his lackeys to bring to him the items he had coerced from Cloe and her friends. The servant laid out a soft black velvet cloth on the table in front of the Kolektor. He fastidiously straightened it and then set the jar and the manuscript on it. The servant had also provided his master with a small leather case, which he opened to reveal various tools for the examination of the relics. The eyes of the Kolektor fairly glowed as he reclined and looked at his prizes. He sat without touching them for a long time. He studied them with an intensity that seemed to look back over the centuries, perhaps to coax from them the very secrets they had held for so long. Though exceedingly strange, it was the only way Cloe could think to describe what she was witnessing.

The Kolektor finally sat forward and began to embrace the jar with his fingertips in an almost erotic manner. He had beautiful hands, she noted. His fingers were long and sleek, just as a pianist's fingers would be. They moved over the surface of the jar as if caressing a long-lost lover. Here and there he stopped to retrace a special point, perhaps to relive a particularly pleasing sensation. He took a small penlight from the case to look inside the jar and used a lighted magnifying glass to minutely inspect the outside. While examining the bottom, he paused and carefully studied a slightly raised portion near the edge. He looked over this area for a long time.

After a while he grumbled to himself, "Hmm ... could those be letters? They could only be Greek or, more likely, ancient Aramaic." He focused on them with a force of will and intensity that Cloe could easily understand. He seemed to burn with concentration.

"Yes, the inverted 'V' and the 'W' like Aramaic or Phoenician letters. 'Yudh' and 'shin,' I believe," he whispered to himself.

Cloe gasped in spite of herself, and the spell was broken. The Kolektor looked up at her as if he had just been made aware of her presence. Hard eyes refocused and zeroed in on her. "This is familiar?" he said. It was not really a question.

"What are you talking about?" she replied desperately, trying to compose herself after this incredible revelation.

How could the same letters that she believed she had found on Irenaeus's death mask also be on the bottom of the jar? Was there a connection? Could the same person or persons have put the letters on the death mask and on the jar? Was this a message about what had happened to the library of St. John? Had some unknown group manipulated all this? Cloe reminded herself that earlier, in the lab, she had thought she'd seen something on the bottom of the jar but had not had the opportunity to pursue it.

"Oh come, Dr. Lejeune. My musings have rendered a stout reaction from you. I can feel it. I can sense your anxiety about my discovery of these possible letters on the bottom of the jar."

"Why should I be anxious?" she responded. "The jar has been analyzed by the world's most powerful computer, and it found no letters on the bottom of the jar. Whatever you think you've found, you are surely mistaken." She was stalling.

"Dr. Lejeune, have you no respect for human observation?" he teased. "I tell you there are two letters on the bottom of this jar, very worn but still there, and I believe them to be the ancient Aramaic equivalents of 'I' and 'S.' Does that mean something to you?"

Cloe thought furiously. The logical explanation was that both the jar and St. Irenaeus were somehow connected with Judas Iscariot. The inscription was the same. Did the "IS" on both refer to Iscariot? It seemed logical, but the implications were enormous. "I have no idea what this could mean, or if it even says what you've concluded," she responded.

He stared at her for a long moment and said, "You are lying, but no matter. We will soon be home, and I'm sure you will tell me everything you know when we get there." The Kolektor went back to studying his prizes. He began in earnest on the manuscript.

Cloe's mind was like a funhouse in an old midway. Everything was exaggerated, and nothing could be trusted. She was scared to death of what awaited her, J.E., and the monsignor, but she was ecstatic over the additional link between the manuscript and jar and Irenaeus. The manuscript referred to Irenaeus, the one from Lugdunum, now Lyon, as the person in authority who had sanctioned it. And both the jar and the death mask of Irenaeus bore the notation "IS," presumably for Iscariot. "They must be connected!" she blurted out in her excitement and emotional turmoil.

The Kolektor's head jerked up, his eyes riveted on Cloe.

# CHAPTER 50

Father Anton was not a man who liked failure, nor did he appreciate, in the abstract, the success of his adversary's tactics. He was, in fact, angry as hell. They had verified that the brigands had made their escape through the underground tunnel into a wooded area north of the church complex. The moment Dr. Lejeune exited the tunnel, Father Anton's electronic equipment had picked up the signal from the minuscule GPS locator he had installed in the flash drive. His team had rushed to the area. Though the kidnapper and his thugs were gone by the time they arrived, they had not missed them by much. Father Anton's men got a GPS direction and distance fix on Dr. Lejeune and the others, but in short order the signal weakened and then ceased.

The tracks and other spoor at the wooded location indicated vehicles had been stashed there for the getaway. Analyzing the data, one of the Swiss surmised that Dr. Lejeune and the flash drive had traveled beyond the short range of the GPS transmitter. The direction in which the vehicles had headed suggested that they were on their way to the nearest airport. Father Anton agreed and issued orders to return to the church and load the van for immediate departure.

\*\*\*

Father Anton reflected that it would be a simple matter to call the French authorities and have the Kolektor and his men intercepted at the airport. However, J.E., the monsignor, and his own superiors had been very clear: he was not to involve the civil authorities. Moreover, his colleagues and friends were now captives. It would be his personal pleasure to take them back and deal with this evil foe.

Father Anton and his men swayed back and forth in the van as it rushed to the airport, seeming to take turns on the two outside wheels on several occasions. As they approached, an executive jet roared overhead. Father Anton looked up and saw it turn to the southeast with its throttles obviously firewalled. Very briefly, as the jet flew overhead, the GPS signal lit up the tracking console. Dr. Lejeune was on that airplane. Almost immediately after the first, a second, seemingly identical jet screamed through the air above them and followed the first plane to the southeast.

# CHAPTER 51

They had flown out of Lyon-Bron Airport hours ago, Cloe thought. The Kolektor had questioned her closely about the "connection" remark, but she had put him off, saying she was merely referring to materials on the flash drive. He clearly did not believe her, but after a while he let her alone and went back to his romantic interlude with the jar and the manuscript. The more he studied them, the more energetic he seemed to become about examining every aspect of them. It was one of the most bizarre things she had ever seen. She could well understand how anyone who got between the Kolektor and what he wanted would fare poorly. The man was covetousness incarnate.

From the signage at the airport where they landed, it was obvious to Cloe that they had flown into Jerusalem. As they sped in a van into the ancient city, Cloe looked at her surroundings through the window. It appeared to be late afternoon. She saw men, women, and a number of couples going here and there. Cloe swallowed a bitter lump in her throat, knowing that she was a captive along with her son and, somewhere, her uncle, while these carefree individuals thought only of each other and perhaps a glass of wine in a curbside café. The weight of the world settled on her at that moment.

Arriving at the evident destination, she saw it consisted of a respectable storefront building housing what was, apparently, a small antiquities shop. So this was the façade for his base of operations. Cloe suspected there was much more both behind and under the shop. A heavy, industrial garage door adjacent to the shop opened electronically, and the van entered an enclosed parking area.

As they got out of the van, the Kolektor's men did not bother to blindfold her or either of the others. Cloe thought this did not bode well for their futures. She would have to take any chance, no matter how slim, to try to escape. Although she was certain she could count on J.E., what about the monsignor in a fight? If she had to bet, she would say he would give as good as he got. That was all she could hope for.

After the bindings were removed from J.E.'s and the monsignor's feet, the three captives were walked into the shop and down several levels into what appeared to be an underground bunker. J.E. staggered and still seemed woozy from his injuries. Cloe couldn't tell whether this was a clever charade or J.E. was more seriously hurt than she had previously thought. Hands still bound, J.E. and the monsignor were led off to what Cloe gathered would be a secure cell in the Kolektor's underground retreat. The Kolektor smiled coldly at Cloe and retired to his private quarters to rest.

Cloe's watch and other belongings had been taken from her on the plane, but she believed it was probably approaching early evening, some six or seven hours after the terrible rendezvous. Almost crushed by fatigue, she wondered whether she would be thrown into a cell too. It didn't matter since she thought she could sleep on a cold concrete floor if given the opportunity.

But a servant, a man referred to as Dadash by the Kolektor, took her—actually, half-carried her—to another area of the bunker. Eventually, Dadash showed her what was obviously a bedroom wing in the Kolektor's fortress. He locked her in one of the rooms, but not before providing a light meal and drink. He also saw to it that there were bedclothes for her and told her, not unkindly, that she better get some sleep before the Kolektor awoke.

She looked around, taking in the bedroom. It was large, spacious, and well appointed with antiques and what appeared to be authentic and valuable Persian rugs. Well, she thought, the man was, after all, a collector. In the en suite bathroom, she washed up a bit, but she neither ate nor drank anything for fear the Kolektor might try to drug her or poison the food or drink to get the flash drive away while she was unconscious or worse. Though she needed rest, she struggled to stay awake to safeguard the drive. The hours crawled by. Finally there was a knock on her door, which startled her; in spite of her resolve, she knew she had dozed a bit.

"Dr. Lejeune," Dadash called, "my master desires your presence."

Cloe was groggy, confused, and exhausted, but she still had her hand clamped tightly to the flash drive. "Where …? What time is it?" She turned in the bed out of habit, looking for a night table with a clock on it.

"It is just before midnight. Please freshen yourself. Clean clothes have been laid out for you. You have five minutes."

"But Dadash, it's midnight," Cloe said. "Why are you calling me now?"

"The master sends for you. He keeps his own hours. Now he wishes to carry on his discussions with you."

Cloe saw that the meeting was inevitable, so she went back into the bath and washed her face as she considered what was to come. After a sponge bath, she felt rejuvenated. She drank some water from the tap on the assumption that the Kolektor could not drug the whole water system. She was as ready as she could be.

Cloe put on the fresh clothes that had been offered and found, not surprisingly, that they fit well enough. The Kolektor had certainly convinced her of his thoroughness. She considered briefly whether that could be used against him in some way. She needed time. She did not know what could be done for J.E. and the monsignor, nor did she know whether Father Anton would be able to follow and find them. She wondered whether J.E. had been able to come up with some plan to set them free. With J.E. and the monsignor locked in a cell in the Kolektor's bunker, perhaps shackled, and guarded by who knew how many thugs, Cloe was not optimistic. What she did know was that the Kolektor would, one way or another, eventually get the information he wanted out of her. Then he would have no use for any of them.

# CHAPTER 52

"Jerusalem?" Father Anton boomed into his satellite phone as he sat in the cabin of the papal jet, which was airborne and headed southeast. His inquiries to the aviation staff at Lyon-Bron Airport plus the hit on the GPS had convinced him that the two executive jets he had seen taking off were indeed those of his foe. But as is the case with private planes at many general aviation terminals, no flight plan had been filed.

The Vatican jet had been ready and warming when Father Anton and his team arrived. Once again the gear and the soldiers had been transferred from one conveyance to another, and they were in the air in a heartbeat.

Father Anton prayed that they could shorten the margin of time the enemy had gained for himself and his men. He now was in contact with his operations center at the Vatican. It had access to the world's most sophisticated computers and, at some level, to most of the world's intelligence organizations. Father Emilio was the senior monk in charge of the intelligence operations center.

"That's affirmative, Reverend Father—Jerusalem," said the monk. "By means of radar and satellites, we have tracked the planes to Jerusalem. Both are now on the ground at the general aviation depot."

Father Anton envisioned Father Emilio and his cohorts toiling over computer terminals in the ops center deep below the Vatican. They were an order of specially trained, highly computer-literate monks. It was ironic, Father Anton reflected: at one time in history these very monks might have been forbidden outside access, and each might have spent his life transcribing, by hand, ancient texts—possibly, in that day, some of the very pages included in the manuscript that the Kolektor had sought and now possessed.

"At least we know they landed in Jerusalem, but did they continue on to another city, into a rural area, or indeed, into another country?" queried Father Anton. He knew that if someone wanted to hide and had the right resources, the trans-Israel territories were a warren of places where people who did not want to be found could remain secreted away. The kidnapper and his hostages could be anywhere in the area.

"Father Emilio, we desperately need some direction, even an educated guess," continued the priest. "There is no predicting what this madman will do to his prisoners. Our friends are in a very bad way if we cannot find them … and quickly."

"Yes, our working hypothesis is that this man is the same person as the notorious arms merchant referred to in the KGB report," replied the monk. "We believe the man faked his own death as a sort of exit strategy from the violence of the arms business. He had made his money and wanted out."

"Yes, yes, but where does that take us?" asked the cleric in frustration.

"It allows us to further backtrack the man's known history— cities and places he frequented, known associates, tendencies and propensities … things of this nature," replied the monk. "Putting together his profile will help us narrow the target area."

"Father Emilio, I appreciate your good and careful work, but I need answers now!" stressed Father Anton.

The satellite phone was silent for a moment and then crackled back with urgency. "Here's my belief, my hunch, as the Americans would say," said the monk from a long distance away. "The man *is* the former arms dealer. He was also known for his relish of ancient things. He is the one known as the Kolektor. He's in Jerusalem."

"How do you know?" asked Father Anton, now testing the information.

"When he was in the arms trade, he was known to frequent Jerusalem. Some thought he had a place there. Jerusalem is the crossroads for traffic in ancient relics. Most serious dealers are there, along with the usual crooks and frauds. From his profile, that's where I would say he is.

"That, and if he were going somewhere else in the region, there are much better airports to use. The Jerusalem airport is small by modern standards, and the area is mountainous."

"That's pretty thin," said Father Anton.

"You wanted an answer," responded the monk. "That's the best one I have."

"I need an address," the field operative said. "My GPS device is only good if I'm in its immediate vicinity."

"My people are working on that. We are going through lists of antiquities dealers, looking for clues," continued the monk. "By the time you land, you will have, if not an address, our best list of possible addresses."

"There must be hundreds of such traders. How will you know?"

"We are assuming he has done and will do nothing to call attention to himself. His record with the authorities will be spotless. You would be surprised how many dealers that eliminates. Most of the best dealers are in the Old City, in the City of David, or in and around the Mount of Olives. We focus there and leave it in God's hands," said the monk.

***

Father Anton looked around and saw the Swiss breaking down and cleaning their weapons. He was proud to lead such men. He knew he was committing his men based on weak intel and guesswork, but he had little choice. If God smiled on them, they would liberate their comrades. Even though they would do their utmost, as the monk had said, the thing was in God's hands. He picked up the intercom and instructed the pilots to put the throttles to maximum power. On to Jerusalem … there was no time to lose.

# CHAPTER 53

The Kolektor sat in his study before the ornate table he used as a desk. Placed on it were both the jar and the manuscript. There was also a larger case with more tools. He was very comfortable here as he ruminated over his new treasures.

Once again he had laid out each on a velvet cloth, much as one would do to carefully view a precious diamond in a jewelry store. Desktop lamps focused soft but intense light on the objects. Later the Kolektor would view the Judas Gospel by candlelight, the very light by which it had been written. He shivered a bit in his excitement at the prospect.

But now, the Kolektor had a variety of magnifying glasses, close reading goggles, and other viewing instruments. The Kolektor knew what he was doing and was making a very thorough study of the ancient relics. And why not? This had been his life since leaving the arms trade. For many years he had seen and possessed the best of the best of old things. He had consulted with the most knowledgeable people, and today, after many years, he was probably one of the world's foremost experts on certain types of antiquities, including ancient codices such as that in front of him now. Pity, he thought, that no one would ever know of or celebrate his expertise.

No matter. He also knew that this particular manuscript might contain that for which he had searched from the beginning, information refuting some key portion of the orthodox Gospels and potentially undermining doctrine of the accursed Catholic Church. This was his grail.

He glanced up as Dadash escorted Cloe into the room and said, "Good evening, Dr. Lejeune. Be seated, if you please."

Now back in the Kolektor's presence, Cloe sat and waited. For a long moment after she entered, he continued examining the jar, holding it carefully on its side. Finally, with seeming reluctance, he looked up and focused his gaze on her.

"I hope you have gotten a little rest. Certainly the events of the day must have been taxing on you," he said mildly.

The man had a subtle way of rubbing it in, she thought. She merely sat quietly, awaiting his first move.

"Not feeling chatty, I see. Well, Dr. Lejeune, I'm convinced that the jar bears the very faint Aramaic or, perhaps, Phoenician letters of 'yudh' and 'shin,' which translates to 'IS.' The order could be wrong, and it could be reversed to read 'SI.' What do you make of that?"

Cloe had not considered the possibility that she might have read the letters in the wrong order. What could "SI" mean?

"Ah, I see I have introduced something new to you. Perhaps it is something you have not considered."

Cloe was irritated that he had read her thoughts so easily, and she resolved to maintain her poker face. "Kolektor, I'm perfectly willing to have a scientific discussion with you regarding these relics, but I'll do and say nothing until I have seen and spoken with my son, my uncle, and the monsignor."

"You will do and say just as I tell you to do and say," he replied placidly, once again distractedly scanning the bottom of the jar.

"You'll do as you wish," she replied, grasping the flash drive tightly to her chest. "We're completely within your power. You may, of course, torture me and force information from me." Cloe wondered if this was her fate.

"Oh come now, Dr. Lejeune ... let's not be so dramatic. I have no intention of torturing you, although I certainly have the means to do so. Perhaps you would like to see my collection of ancient torture devices. The Iron Maiden is particularly interesting. Indeed, now that we have all the time in the world, it might be entertaining to show you my entire collection," he said. "What I do intend to do is to bring your son in and to put a bullet in his brain if you do not answer my questions fully and truthfully."

Fear spiked through Cloe like a frozen lance, piercing her heart and threatening to extinguish her spirit. The Kolektor had tapped into her greatest fear. She knew that she had to remain in control of herself.

With enormous effort she steeled herself, marshaled her courage, and replied, "Kolektor, you may do that—but if you do, I'll know that we're all lost, and I shall rip the flash drive from my neck. This will create the magnetic pulse and destroy the information on the drive. It will take you weeks, if not months, to recreate what we have learned even if you have the special equipment available to do so. Some things we've learned may never be revealed to you."

The Kolektor raised his eyes from the jar, set it down, and studied her closely. His eyes seemed to bore into her mind, testing her credibility and resolve. Cloe felt she would wilt under the gaze, but she stared back with every resource she had.

"Yes, I believe you would," the Kolektor finally said. "Even though such an act would result in a very bad end for you and your friends."

Relief flooded over Cloe. She felt tired and ragged from the lack of sleep but knew the Kolektor had blinked, even if only slightly. She saw a quick flash of respect cross his eyes.

"Dadash," he said sharply. "See that Dr. Lejeune visits her friends and then bring her back here."

"Immediately, Master."

Dadash moved to her side with a quickness that surprised her and took her arm. A moment later they were leaving the study. Cloe looked behind her and saw that the Kolektor had gone back to his examination. As the door closed, he did not even look up, so focused on the jar that he was unaware she had left.

Maintaining a tight hold on her arm, Dadash led her through a series of rooms and hallways and eventually down to a lower level. Cloe studied everything she saw in hopes that one or more of these items might provide a marker for her to navigate through the bunker. Everywhere there were treasures of great age, from delicate pottery to the wicked engines of torture of which the Kolektor had spoken. There was an endless series of manuscripts containing God only knew what ancient wisdom or drivel, she thought. She even recognized a couple of paintings by old masters that had been reported stolen. Altogether, from what she could see, the collection was stunning. Under other circumstances, it would be the achievement of a lifetime for someone like her to examine and catalog at least the ancient manuscript portion of this collection.

Finally, they approached a locked and guarded steel door. The guard stepped aside, and she looked through the glass portal into the room. The room was very brightly lit from many angles, to the point that there were absolutely no shadows. It crossed her mind that this itself was viewed as a form of torture by some. She wondered whether J.E. and the monsignor had been subjected to this excessive light from the time they had been brought in. If so, they must be doubly exhausted. Then her gaze fell on ninety-year-old Uncle Sonny.

"Open the door," she said peremptorily.

The guard glanced at Dadash, who merely nodded. "You have two minutes."

She entered, and the door swung shut behind her. It took a second or two for her to get used to the brightness of the light. J.E. and the monsignor appeared lethargic and moved very slowly. They were shackled. For a moment they did not seem aware that she was with them. J.E. was the first to react, stumbling up from one of the cots in the small, windowless room and trying, despite his chains, to sweep his mother off her feet with a grand hug. Cloe saw that he didn't have the strength, but the hug was welcome. She greeted the monsignor and turned to Uncle Sonny, who had been there the longest and who was having a lot of difficulty getting to his feet.

Rage boiled up inside Cloe as she looked at his white skin and unhealthy pallor. In that moment she hated the beast upstairs with a terrible fury. As she gently helped her aged uncle to his feet, he seemed to begin to perk up just in response to Cloe's presence. She saw that his spirit was still backlit with Lejeune feistiness.

"Uncle, are you all right?" she asked.

The tough old bird looked her in the eye, smiled his great smile, and said, "Clotile, it will take more than that lunatic peckerwood upstairs to see the end of me. I *will* say I'm tired of these infernal lights, which are on night and day."

Cloe chuckled in spite of herself and the situation. J.E. smiled, and Cloe could see Dadash peering through the glass portal, carefully scrutinizing their every movement. This sobered her a bit because he surely knew as well as anyone what their fate would be.

Assured that her uncle was as well as could be expected, she quickly brought J.E. and the monsignor up-to-date on her conversation with the Kolektor. She assumed that they were being watched and that what they were saying was being heard, so she chose her words carefully. The others caught the gist. Although it was difficult, she tried to remain upbeat to raise their spirits as much as the circumstances would permit. She could see the monsignor and J.E. rallying and beginning to reenergize.

Dadash was now opening the door, telling her the two minutes were up. She said her good-byes and hugged J.E. again. As she did, she whispered, "I'm feeding the Kolektor information to delay his plans for us."

He responded in her ear, "We can't get out. Stall for time ... help is coming."

# CHAPTER 54

The papal jet had landed without incident and had been able to avoid customs and other red tape by main force of its diplomatic credentials. While the jet taxied to the general aviation terminal, the Swiss made preparations to disembark. Two vans and trusted drivers familiar with Jerusalem's Old City and the other target areas had been provided. As the Swiss loaded their gear into the vans, Father Anton surveyed the list of addresses sent to his cell phone by the monks at the ops center. These were their best guesses as to where the Kolektor might be located—addresses of various antiquities dealers who fit the search profile.

Father Anton had requisitioned an additional GPS sensor so that the vans could operate separately. It would be so much easier and faster, he reflected, if they could use a couple of helicopters to fly low over Jerusalem in search of the GPS signal. However, he knew questions would quickly be asked, and they had no explanation for the Israeli authorities as to what they were doing. Certainly, without convincing answers, they would soon be facing the Mossad, the crack Israeli intelligence force, who would want to know everything. So they had to improvise with the vans.

Father Emilio had reported that, as the monsignor had surmised, this Kolektor had a blood grudge against the Church—something to do with the loss of his family in World War II. The monsignor had said that it was imperative that the jar and manuscript not fall into his hands. Yet that was exactly what had happened, and now it was Father Anton's sacred duty to find his colleagues and recover the relics before any real harm could be done.

Still, there were twenty-seven addresses on the list, spread out over the four quarters of the Old City and adjacent areas. It would take several hours to cover them all unless they got lucky and had an early hit on the GPS sensor. That this was all guesswork and that he really did not know whether the Kolektor was even in Jerusalem at all gnawed at Father Anton.

Logic dictated that they first consider the Armenian Quarter. Everything that they knew of the Kolektor's background screamed "Armenian." They headed there now, as Father Anton prayed hard that one of the four addresses in the Armenian Quarter would light up the GPS sensor and lead them to the Kolektor and his captives before it was too late.

# CHAPTER 55

As Cloe was escorted back to the Kolektor's study, she inspected everything she could see on the way, in hopes the information would prove useful. Self-help and self-reliance had always been her way.

Once she was again seated in the Kolektor's study, Cloe prepared herself for their discussion. Her foe had eaten and had begun to refresh himself with his trademark beverage of what she now believed to be frozen gin, if her nose was any judge. Her stomach turned over, and she remembered that she had not eaten anything in a good while. She might be on the edge of her own oblivion, but no one, she thought, had told her stomach. This brought a shadow of a smile to her face.

She saw the Kolektor note her expression, but he resisted asking anything that would move them away from the story. "Dr. Lejeune, please begin your narrative," said the Kolektor.

"What I'm going to do is tell you what I know in chronological order so it will make some sense," she responded, hoping in this way to buy some crucial time.

She described the lengthy process of opening the jar at LSU. She talked about the photography, the pressure and temperature issues, and the processes used to address these matters. The Kolektor was very interested in the packing of the jar with charcoal and silicone and asked many questions.

"I have not seen this type of material in other antiquities I have acquired," he noted. "The effect must have been a longevity not possible with other arrangements."

"Yes, that's what we think as well."

She had not gotten far when he stopped her and asked about the origin of the jar. She then backtracked and related the information she had about the Battle of El Guettar and how the jar had come to be located, leaving out personal details about the letter, her father, and Bobby Morrow. Even so, the Kolektor was generally aware that her father had found the jar during the battle. Somehow, he had learned where it had been all these years and how she had come to possess it—probably through the good offices of his many informants such as Dean Broussard, she thought.

"Where was the jar when my servant came for it?" he asked.

If she had been unsure before, she knew now she was looking at her father's murderer. "It had been taken to the local Catholic Church at my father's request. He had become alarmed when someone, I assume on your behalf, tried to buy it," she responded evenly.

"The Church, the Church, always the damnable Catholic Church … in my way," he raged, going off so rapidly that Cloe was taken aback.

Calming himself somewhat, he looked at her with great intensity and said, "What you have delivered to me, I believe, will enable me to take my revenge on the Church. The Judas Gospel may throw Church doctrine over. If so, I shall be there when it topples."

Both were silent for a while, but then the Kolektor pressed for details of the military expedition, locations, and anything that might mark the site of the jar's discovery. He asked many questions, and it was plain that he was fascinated by the prospect of a cave with scores or even hundreds of such jars.

He also wanted to know about the monsignor and the Vatican's interest. She answered these questions with as little detail as she could, hoping that such information would not focus him on the possibility that Vatican rescuers were, she was sure, even now searching frantically for them. On and on this went.

She continued in this vein for at least three hours. Now it was quite late—or early, she thought, depending on one's point of view. Her neck hurt, and she was desperately tired. She stretched and turned in her chair, seeking some relief from the stiffness. As exhausted as she was, she had to marvel at the Kolektor. He didn't seem fatigued at all. Indeed, he appeared to feed off the information. He asked innumerable questions and never seemed completely satisfied. By this point, she had told him almost everything.

She even revealed her suspicions to him about the possibility of a journal. He peppered her with numerous questions about this, but of course, Cloe herself had only questions. The only thing left to explain was what they had learned in Lyon about the letters constituting a possible connection between Judas Iscariot and St. Irenaeus. This might tie everything together. Even now, though, she was unsure about the letters. Were they "IS" as she and the monsignor had thought, referring to Judas, or "SI"—referring to what? She didn't know. What she did know was that she was just about out of ammunition, and she needed to make something happen.

"A journal written possibly in Judas's own hand," he said, shaking his head in amazement. "The world has always wondered why there were no firsthand, contemporaneous accounts of the public ministry. Now there may be one. Such a journal would have far more weight than the Gospels, which were all written decades after Christ's death. The journal would be the most proximate record. It could completely rewrite all Christianity."

"Caution, Kolektor," she responded. "We have no such journal; we have only clues. It may not exist, or if it does, it may not have been written by Judas. It could have been another Apostle. It may also confirm everything written in the Gospels."

"Or completely deny it," he snapped. Again there was a pause as each considered the implications.

"Kolektor, before we go on, I want my people out of that cell and brought up here with me," said Cloe, stopping the discussions. "I'm very worried about my aged uncle's health. We're almost finished, but there is some detail that they could add to the narrative. Since we're close to the end of our research and findings, I also want your assurance that we will be set free when we finish. You will have everything."

"Some additional narrative from them?" he mused. "Why should I believe that? Perhaps you think if they were here, you could overpower me and retake the jar and the manuscript."

"I have kept my word. Have you heard anything from me that you don't believe to be true?" she asked.

"Perhaps we can make arrangements for them to come up here and be refreshed. Dadash ... see to it."

"Yes, Master," the servant said, departing the room immediately.

She was now alone with the Kolektor. She knew that he felt no fear of her whatsoever and that he was amazingly spry for a man of his age. The events at the church had certainly proven that. Still, she was half his age and in good shape. If she could seize something to use as a weapon, she might succeed in hurting him badly or even killing him. She glanced around in search of an item to use on him. No sooner had the thought come to Cloe than the Kolektor produced a small automatic pistol and aimed it squarely at her. His motion of flipping the weapon from its hiding place and aiming it on her was snakelike in speed and stealth. She froze as he looked directly into her eyes from behind the gun barrel.

Cloe's heart almost stopped when she realized that she was looking back at—there was literally nothing there. The man who loved things had no humanity left whatsoever. There was absolutely no spark of mercy or compassion. In an instant she could see that he was a mere shell of a person, one who could act and change expressions like the lizard he now had grown in her mind to resemble. But he felt nothing, no matter what face he put on. His mask now had not only slipped but fallen completely off as he faced her with the gun.

"My dear," he said, without any malice whatsoever, in that dry, gravelly voice of his, "I have been working on the solution to the failsafe device for the drive around your neck, and here you have offered me the perfect opportunity to test it."

At that moment Cloe knew that her idea for trying to overcome him would be rewarded with a bullet. The Kolektor's eyes were black and soulless as he pulled the trigger on the small weapon. Cloe saw the small puff of smoke and felt the impact to her chest at the same instant. She never heard the sound of the automatic. The bullet took her full above her right breast, and the impact knocked her head over heels; both she and the barrel-style chair in which she was sitting somersaulted backward until they came to a dead stop against the wall. She knew nothing but blackness.

\*\*\*

Later, from a distance away, she heard J.E. calling her. Because she knew she had to get to him, she began to struggle and to fight. But the battle was with and within her. She couldn't make her body obey. Was she trapped or, maybe, tied up in an exceedingly dark room?

Eventually, she began to see a faint light at the edges and at the same time began to experience pain. As the light grew, the pain became excruciating. Finally, her eyelids fluttered partially open. After the blackness the light was blinding. She still could not move, so she was forced to lie there while her eyes slowly adjusted to the light.

As she slowly took in the scene around her, Cloe caught sight of her blouse covered in blood on the right side. Then she began to remember what the Kolektor had done. In passing, she thought that at least the blood did not seem to be pumping, which she took to be a good sign. She could hear J.E. calling her from across the room. She turned her head toward the sound. J.E., the monsignor, and Uncle Sonny all sat in chairs near the Kolektor's desk. Why, she wondered, didn't J.E. come to her?

"As you can see, Dr. Lejeune, I have brought your cohorts as you requested. I'm afraid they are in better shape than you are," the Kolektor said. "You seem to be all out of cards. Do you have anything left for me?"

Reactively, she reached for the flash drive around her neck and found that it was gone. She looked around wildly but could not see it. Had she lost it when she fell?

"Is this what you are looking for, Dr. Lejeune?" asked the Kolektor, holding up the drive and the cell phone holder with a smugness that made her angry despite her extreme pain. "The dilemma was how to get it off of you without your breaking the chain or triggering the electromagnetic pulse. The fail-safe equipment relies on breaking the circuit. So I thought, why not simply shoot you and remove it, whole, from your neck? Problem solved! While you were unconscious, my servants merely slipped it off your neck, along with the cell phone gadget from your holster. Then my computer expert disarmed your backup code protocol. It was actually rather simple. We will later examine the drive at our leisure."

"You bastard," she blurted out, before going limp with pain and fatigue.

"Perhaps, but I now have your research, the jar, the manuscript, and a rather complete explanation of everything from you," said the Kolektor as he hung the flash drive apparatus around his neck and put the cell phone activator on his belt. "It seems I no longer have any need for you and your pesky friends."

# CHAPTER 56

The Armenian Quarter had proven unproductive in terms of picking up the signal from Dr. Lejeune's GPS. Father Anton and his men had combed the streets carefully and checked all four addresses but had found nothing.

No one knew whether the Kolektor was Muslim, Christian, or Jewish. However, the cleric knew that the predominant religions in Armenia, depending on the region, were Christianity and Islam. Realizing the Kolektor was very devious, Father Anton had considered that the man might have decided to hide in an area to which no one could connect him. Therefore, he had decided against searching the Muslim Quarter or Christian Quarter next. Instead, surmising that the Kolektor, if he were in the Old City, would be in the least likely section, he had proceeded directly to the Jewish Quarter.

But Father Anton and his troops had combed the Jewish section as well as the Muslim and Christian sections, all to no avail. There was simply no signal. They had raced up and down each street in the Old City without any result. Either the captives were not here, or perhaps they were underground at a level where there was no signal. He feared he would not reach them in time. It also occurred to Father Anton that the GPS device might have been found out and destroyed. He dared not accept the latter possibility. In that case, there would be no way of finding their colleagues, and he shuddered to think of their fate. He and his men were becoming more anxious now about the need to find them because they knew time was fast running out. He had to find them and deny the Kolektor the manuscript. He signaled his drivers to broaden the search and head for the City of David, just outside the Old City.

# CHAPTER 57

Dadash had thrust a towel into her blouse to help stanch the bleeding, but it was plain that the Kolektor had no long-term plans for her—or for her companions. Whatever his short-term plans, though, he wanted her alive for them. Cloe could barely keep her eyes open through the pain. She knew that they were close to whatever final design this madman had for them. Since she seemed to be the only one not bound, she had to conserve her energy and be as ready as she could be if some opportunity for escape came.

Cloe gritted her teeth and through half-closed eyes looked around. As she had suspected, J.E., Uncle Sonny, and the monsignor were all bound, but with medieval-looking chains and cuffs. The restraints were old but heavy, well kept, and formidable, she had no doubt. There would be no escape from those bindings. She looked at J.E., and his eyes pleaded his need to come to her rescue.

"Our time together is at an end, Dr. Lejeune," said the Kolektor. "Now we shall go to a place not too far from here, where I will be able to repay you and your friends for all the difficulties that you have caused me."

At least they were not to be murdered here, so there was still time left. They would have to be transferred to a vehicle and taken somewhere else. Hope again began to arise in her. Cloe sighed and said in a voice that seemed to come from a long way away, "I've given you everything that you asked for. Honor demands that you keep your word and set us free."

She would try anything and everything, including appealing to whatever little sense of honor and fair play he might have left. She had almost no hope here, but she would try, perhaps only to delay the inevitable.

"Honor? The only honor is in the thing ... in having the thing that I desire. All else is beside the point."

Cloe could see J.E. struggling with his chains and his captors. There were at least two thugs for each of them. She was overwhelmed by the odds against them, and with that thought in mind and her body desperately needing rest, Cloe passed out.

***

She did not know how much time had passed, only that they were no longer in the bunker or in the Kolektor's shop at all. She was on the floor of what she took to be a van or panel truck. Although she was not bound, apparently because of her wound, she had so little strength that she might as well have been. She could barely open her eyes, much less move or in any way protect herself or her son and friends. Her attention was drawn to the wound in her chest, and it appeared that the bleeding had stopped. Cloe could feel caked blood on her face and neck from the tumble she had taken. But she didn't think any bones were broken. After examining the wounded area, she turned her head slightly and saw J.E., Uncle Sonny, and the monsignor. All were tightly bound and lying near her on the floor of the vehicle. The Kolektor was in the passenger seat, and two of his men were in the rear with guns drawn.

In what direction they were headed or how far they had traveled, she could not determine. She only knew they were on their way to somewhere from which it was unlikely they would return. Strangely, she was not afraid. She was sad more than anything else. Sad and angry. She missed her long-dead mother. She certainly had unfinished business with her and a great many things that she had wanted to say to her if she could ever return to the grave site in Madisonville. She had unfinished business with Thib too. Now it seemed her life was filled with unfinished business.

The sadness became almost unbearable when she thought of J.E. and Uncle Sonny. She had gotten them involved in all this. She had suspected they were in over their heads from the very beginning. Still, she had plowed on, excited by their discoveries. What had she been thinking? Her career, her blasted career, had blinded her—that and the passion to find her father's murderer. She should have gotten everyone out when the attempt was made on her and J.E.'s lives at the bridge. In a strange way, that incident had only convinced her of the validity of her research efforts. She had become insensitive to the dangers. True, great breakthroughs had been made, but at what cost? Yet, when she asked herself what she would do differently if she could go back in time, only more questions came.

And what of J.E.? He had his whole life ahead of him. But regrets were worse than useless. She would find a way for him to have his future. Adrenaline fired by anger coursed through her veins, restoring a bit of her strength. She had slept deeply after passing out in the bunker. She now realized that she did feel a little rested. She did not know what would happen, but she would not abandon hope. She was the only one who was not bound. She would nurse her anger and her strength and look for her opportunity.

# CHAPTER 58

"We have a contact," said the Swiss soldier monitoring the GPS sensor.

"Are you sure? Where is it?" queried Father Anton.

They had been searching for hours in the vans. He and his men were exhausted. They had had little rest the night before the fiasco at the church and none at all since, except what little they had been able to grab on the plane or in the vans themselves.

"Yes, the frequency we use in these devices is unique, so there can be no mistake when we do pick up a signal. There is no error. It is our signal, but it is very weak. The source is either shielded inside a solid building or underground, or alternatively, it is a far distance away."

"Which is it?" questioned Father Anton impatiently. "This might be our only chance." He rose and half-walked, half-crawled back to the monitor and looked over the soldier's shoulder.

"Based on the signature characteristics of the reading I'm getting, I believe it is a good distance away, at or just beyond the range of the device," replied the soldier.

Father Anton looked at the monitor and mentally concurred with the analysis. He knew that they were on the far side of the City of David, having just completed their sweep of that area.

"Can you overlay the vicinity map on the GPS sensor screen?" he asked.

"Yes, sir," the soldier replied, and with a few taps of the keyboard, the map came up, showing their position as well as the position of the very faint contact that was the device built into Dr. Lejeune's flash drive.

Father Anton studied the map and the probable location of his colleagues. He could see that the dot signifying Dr. Lejeune's location seemed to be on the edge of the Hinnom Valley. But what was there? He thought about his biblical history and Jerusalem's topography for a moment, and then it all clicked into place.

"Oh my God," he exclaimed, turning white. "Hurry, we've got to get to that location, ASAP!"

Even as the words were still coming out of his mouth, the driver spun the vehicle around and raced off toward the innocuous red dot on the screen.

"But sir … what's there? What is it?" pressed the soldier.

Father Anton could say only one word. "Hakeldama!"

# CHAPTER 59

Cloe had dozed off and on in the truck, but she was awake now and recognized that she and the others had been brought to some dark, eerie vale somewhere near Jerusalem. They had left the vehicles and traveled along a wooded path. Now they were in a sort of clearing. She knew that this was the end of the line. Whatever the Kolektor intended to do to them, this was where he intended to do it. The Kolektor's men wore headlights much like miner's lamps and were carrying hand lanterns, so Cloe could see a little of the surroundings. The terrain walking in had been very rough, but the floor of the clearing was smooth and surrounded by gnarled old trees.

She had been carried to the clearing over the shoulder of one of the Kolektor's thugs and roughly deposited on the ground. J.E., Uncle Sonny, and the monsignor had been half-walked and half-yanked with her. As they now came abreast of her, she met J.E.'s eyes and saw him give her an almost imperceptible nod. Whatever J.E. had in mind was about to unfold. What could he possibly do against these odds? She didn't know, but she caught the monsignor's eye and signaled him to be ready.

Cloe saw the monsignor look around, assessing the situation. As she examined the Kolektor and his men, she could see they were distracted with the entry into the clearing and with organizing themselves. *Now!* she thought.

As she watched, J.E. suddenly—and completely without warning—exploded into action, attacking his guard using as vicious weapons the very cuffs and chains with which he had been bound. Cloe could scarcely believe that such violence resided within her son. She heard the guard mutter something, but he went down dazed, with

263

J.E. on top of him. She glanced at the monsignor, who was also trying to join the fight, but she saw that he was instantly covered with drawn guns by two of the Kolektor's men.

Cloe heard Uncle Sonny hollering in the background as she grabbed a nearby stone, staggered up, and swung it at the nearest guard. He dodged easily and backhanded her across her face. She went down hard on her face, gasping for breath, and then rolled to her side, facing J.E. and the battle.

She screamed as J.E. rolled off his guard, looking for the next brute, because by then several of the other hoodlums had converged on J.E., and she saw one hit her son from behind with a pipe or a sap. J.E. fell awkwardly and now was out cold, or worse. The thugs dragged him to the center of the clearing. He was laid beside her, but she could see that he was breathing.

As the commotion ended, she could see the Kolektor chuckling at the impotence of their efforts. Cloe prayed for J.E. as she took stock of her surroundings. The walls of the rising summits on either side closed in around the little clearing. A more foreboding or creepy venue, she could not imagine.

Giving voice to her question, the monsignor asked, "Where are we, Signor Kolektor? What are your intentions?" In spite of everything, the monsignor's voice was clear and strong.

The Kolektor responded in his own usual voice, dry and raspy. "We are on the edge of the Hinnom Valley. Does that mean anything to you, priest?"

"Hakeldama!" the monsignor whispered. Cloe recognized the word but grasped for its meaning.

"Yes … Hakeldama, Akeldama, or Aceldama, depending on which ancient text you consult. It's all the same. The Field of Blood, or the Bloody Acre. Priest … do you remember your scripture?"

"I remember very well. My life has been spent studying and following scripture," responded the Lord's servant. Cloe knew this was a different kind of fight, and the monsignor would give as good as he got.

"Well then, perhaps you can appreciate the irony of our presence and your fate here," replied the Kolektor. The beast was coming closer to revealing his plans for them. Cloe knew he was enjoying this enormously.

"What do you think you know of this place?" asked the monsignor. He had smashed the Kolektor's serve back at him. "I think your true knowledge of this place and its significance is like your appreciation of all your ancient relics … superficial. For you it's only the rarity of the thing, and not the true significance of the relic and its historical and religious context, that drives and inspires you. A man such as you can never appreciate the amazing place that is Hakeldama."

Cloe was transfixed by the war of words playing out between these two adversaries. Although she did not know where it would lead, she knew it would win them time. Where the hell was Father Anton?

"I remember the Acts of the Apostles, which is part of the orthodox Bible," said the Kolektor, "and particularly, chapter 1, line 18, where Peter tells of the fate of the traitor, Judas Iscariot. Do you know it, priest?"

"Certainly," replied the monsignor evenly. "In Acts, Luke reports a presentation by St. Peter in which he states that Judas himself bought a field with the money that he was paid for his crime of betrayal. The amount of time that it would take to engage in such a purchase transaction implies that Judas may have lived on after the death of Jesus Christ. But no one knows for sure.

"According to the text, Judas fell headlong and burst open, presumably leading to his death. St. Peter notes that everyone in Jerusalem heard about this, and the field came to be called the 'bloody acre,' or in their language, 'Hakeldama.' St. Peter in Acts asserts that Judas died on this very field … Hakeldama. Thus, this area is stained with the blood of the arch traitor, Judas Iscariot."

"Just so, priest," said the Kolektor after a pause. "We are here tonight near that very site. And it will soon be stained with your blood. It is my desire that you and your friends meet your fate here on the field of Hakeldama. There is a certain irony in that which appeals to me. Here on the very field where Judas may have died, you will die having brought me the jar and the manuscript which I believe will enable me to find the journal of Judas. In my hands this will spell the downfall of the almighty Catholic Church. What do you think of this quirk of fate, priest?"

"Kolektor, you tempt God with your arrogance," asserted the monsignor boldly.

Cloe heard these words and smiled, in spite of her injuries, at the pluck of her friend Albert. They were not done yet, she thought; while there was a breath in her body, there would be hope.

"Come now, priest, you cannot hope to turn aside my intentions with some superstitious rubbish. There is no God, and there is no time or place but here and now. There is no hereafter. It's amazing how knowing that frees a person. If there were truly a God, he would come to your rescue. He would not have let you fall into my hands and would not have sanctioned the loss of these precious relics to me." The Kolektor was virtually spewing his words now as he proclaimed his unholy creed.

"You may have convinced yourself, but you will never convince me," responded the monsignor. "As evil men before you, you mistake the absence of some dramatic action by God, such as a lightning strike to your breast, as sanction for your evil. You could not be more incorrect. It is up to good to triumph over evil. Our God gives each of us the power to overcome evil. You yourself at one time had the power to triumph over your own evil tendencies. But despair is now written upon you, and it is as plain as that of Judas's two thousand years ago. You have not been sanctioned; you have merely yet to meet your fate of eternal damnation for turning against God. As my colleague Uncle Sonny opined while we were your captives, your turn in the barrel is coming, and I want to be there for it."

Cloe smiled upon hearing Uncle Sonny snicker at the priest's accurate portrayal of his sentiments. She looked to J.E. and saw that he was woozy but was coming around.

The Kolektor had had his fill of the truth and turned forcibly to his men, gesturing fiercely at them. "Take them!" he screamed.

The henchmen grabbed Cloe, J.E., Uncle Sonny, and the monsignor and tied them to the trunks of the ancient trees lining the little clearing. The walls of the valley sloped up on either side as mute witnesses to the coming abomination.

"Start with the young man," snarled the Kolektor, regaining control of himself.

Even though he was already tied to the tree, two of the Kolektor's men lifted J.E. slightly from his feet while a third brought a large case, like a tool kit, to the Kolektor. The Kolektor opened it and removed a pistol-like object from it—except, Cloe thought, she had never seen a pistol so large. Immediately, all three men began to struggle violently against their bonds; they seemed to know what the device was and what the Kolektor intended.

"What is it?" she screamed, sensing their anxiety. "Are you going to shoot us?"

"Do you think I have gone to all this trouble and distance merely to shoot you?" the Kolektor replied, giggling insanely. "No, I'm going to crucify you, but with a modern twist."

He raised the weapon, and she could now see that it was a large nail gun. Razor-sharp tips of oversized nails glistened in the magazine of the industrial-sized tool. He walked over to the tree on which J.E. was hanging, and as his men held J.E.'s arms forcibly out, the Kolektor raised the nail gun and shot a nail into the tree just above J.E.'s right wrist, slamming the steel pinion about two thirds into the tree. The nail gun made a thundering *thwack*. Cloe cringed and prayed for help.

*Thwack, thwack* came the terrible sound as the Kolektor demonstrated the efficiency of the instrument on the tree all around J.E.'s body. The Kolektor was toying with them, enjoying his handiwork immensely. The cretin was virtually drunk with his power over them, his sense of irony, and now, his time of revenge.

The Kolektor's laugh rose to an enormous cackle of triumph. "Where is your God now, priest?" he barked contemptuously. "Where is your savior?"

"He is here … He is with us always," replied the monsignor steadfastly. "If we die in his name, we join him, but on your death you pass into the darkness for all eternity. Your arrogance is a great blasphemy. Kolektor, repent … this is your last chance!"

# CHAPTER 60

"Reverend Father, we are about two minutes from the field known as Hakeldama."

Father Anton thought about this and issued his orders. He expected that the Kolektor might have left a rear guard at the area where he would have parked his vehicles. If so, there would be a firefight before they reached their objective, and they would lose the element of surprise. The Kolektor would know they were coming.

The caravan paused at the entrance to the circular drive that passed close to the Field of Blood, and they saw the panel truck and the other vehicle that the Kolektor and his men had used. Their long-distance night-vision goggles revealed at least two armed guards moving behind the vehicles and surely intending to use them for cover. The priest knew that a fight was inevitable. He could not choose the place, but he could select the tactics. He would make the Kolektor's men pay dearly. Father Anton had business in the Bloody Acre.

The warrior priest knew that time was the enemy. Although he would have preferred to carefully flank his opponents and trap them in a long-distance field of cross fire, he did not have this luxury. His only option was a full frontal assault with overwhelming force. The question was how long it would take before they could get into the interior of the field.

"All right," he said. "We will rush to the far side of the Kolektor's two vehicles. Radio our comrades in the other van to cut in on the near side of the vehicles. In this way we will flank them as well as we can. They will have to divide their fire. We will then engage the defenders and cut them down. Time is of the essence. We must take care of them immediately and be on to our friends in the field of Hakeldama."

"Understood, sir."

The orders went out as Father Anton had decreed. The men were locked and loaded. Only God himself could help the poor souls the Kolektor had left to guard his rear.

Tires squealed, and the vehicles charged ahead, with Father Anton's van passing the Kolektor's trucks and turning in rapidly. His men jumped out, and the rat-a-tat of automatic weapons rang out with the accompanying pings and dings of bullets hitting the metallic walls of the vehicles. The Kolektor's men might have held their own, considering that they were well armed and hunkered down behind good cover. But just at that point, the other Swiss van swung in to their rear and began firing. Now the guards had two separate target groups and were therefore caught in cross fields of fire as Father Anton had planned. The firefight was fierce, and it was apparent that the Kolektor's men would die at their posts rather than fail. Still, the men fought on. No matter how evil, every man will strive to survive. The fight was not as brief as Father Anton had wished, but it ended with both members of the Kolektor's rear guard dead.

"Our casualties?" demanded Father Anton of his aide.

"One man slightly wounded, sir, but none out of action," he replied. "We have cleared the vehicles, and we are ready to proceed."

"Very well," said the priest. "Into Hakeldama!"

# CHAPTER 61

Cloe heard the small arms and automatic weapons fire and guessed that their rescuers were here and were engaging whoever the Kolektor had left to guard his rear. Her mind screamed to them to hurry as the Kolektor relentlessly hammered at her son and the monsignor as a prelude to nailing them to the trees. As close as they were, she feared they would not arrive in time.

*Thwack, thwack.* The unremitting sound continued. She so wanted to cover her ears from that dreadful noise but could not. Thus far the Kolektor had teased at the men to prolong their agony. Now he too heard the firefight from the parking area. He knew time was limited, so he turned to his real business.

He looked at Cloe, smiled, and said, "Whoever they are, they will not get here in time. My men will die at their posts before letting your rescuers through. I have also set additional men with weapons and explosives along the trail in case my men in the parking area are overrun. Your rescuers have failed and will die in my ambush. We will be long gone before anyone finds you, dead, hanging on these trees."

Cloe was close to despair, knowing finally that although rescue was close, it would not come in time. There would be terrible loss of life as the would-be rescuers rushed to help her and her friends, and they would all die anyway. Father Anton and the Swiss would be massacred on the trail. She screamed a terrible oath at her tormentor. "May God curse your awful soul!"

The Kolektor merely turned briefly and smiled his dreadful smile at her before going back to his bloody work.

Cloe heard J.E. grunt as a nail slammed into his hand or his arm. Even now, he was so brave. She looked at him achingly and tried to extricate herself from the rope binding her to the tree. She instantly knew that if Father Anton got through at all, he would arrive only to take them down after it was over.

Suddenly there was only silence in the clearing. She could still hear the battle raging at the edge of the entrance to the Bloody Field, but the nail gun had gone quiet. With difficulty she turned her head and saw that a dozen or more figures had entered the little clearing where the Kolektor was doing his hellish work. The Kolektor and his six remaining men were completely surrounded by these strange figures, who moved without a sound.

The new players on this stage were dressed in black fatigues, with Bedouin-style headdresses and scarves over the lower halves of their faces. These strangers were clearly not part of Father Anton's Swiss Guard, and they were certainly not expected by the Kolektor. Although there was a military aspect to them, they did not appear to be armed. There was a certain something about them that Cloe could not quite put a finger on but that seemed strange and out of place. Cloe wondered if she was imagining things. Who were these people, and what were they doing here? Cloe almost did not care because whoever they were, they had stopped the Kolektor before he could do further damage. Poor J.E. had been hit by at least one nail.

Each group was assessing the other, she saw. That there would be a fight, she had no doubt. These poor weaponless people would be cut down by the Kolektor's mercenaries. No sooner had the thought crossed her mind than one of the Kolektor's men began to move his weapon into firing position. He raised it to train it on one of the newcomers.

The Kolektor's man was cat-quick, but before Cloe could even blink and before the weapons of the Kolektor's men could be effectively aimed at the interlopers, the strange figures stepped forward with blazing speed and produced short knives. With these they dispatched the Kolektor's men with a cruel efficiency and in an eerie silence. Only one of the Kolektor's men got off a shot, and this was as a reflex to his grisly death by means of a dagger to his throat. All of the Kolektor's men lay dead or dying in the clearing, the miner's headlights giving off freakish strobes with the death throes of their owners.

Cloe could hardly believe what she had seen. She stared hard at the black-clad figures. Although they were certainly trained in a military manner, Cloe thought they had a distinctly feminine profile. Was she seeing things?

The Kolektor himself was unharmed but now surrounded by the death-dealing dagger people. "Who are you? What do you want?" he cried, now alone without his protection.

Cloe could see his confidence draining as he found himself isolated and powerless. How many people had he put in such a position?

Several of the black-garbed figures now moved to Cloe and her friends and gently released them from the trees. They laid J.E. out on the ground and began to tend to his wound. Uncle Sonny had not been subject to the nail gun, but he was in a bad way. After they checked his pulse, they gave him what looked like a liquid potion of some sort that almost immediately began to calm him down. Cloe felt that she would pass out again, but two of the figures sat her down and began to administer first aid to her too. Could it be that they were safe? She could hardly believe it.

One of the strange operatives stepped forward toward the Kolektor and said in a voice that Cloe could not quite classify, "We are the Sicarii, and we have come for you, Kolektor."

# CHAPTER 62

The Sicarii, Cloe thought in wonder. They were the group of first-century assassins with whom some scholars thought Judas might have been affiliated. Many maintained that his last name, "Iscariot," was derived from the term "Sicarii," which literally meant "dagger people." These people had certainly proved their prowess with their knives tonight. But the Sicarii had been devoted to the violent overthrow of the Romans. If they were the Sicarii, what were they doing here? Moreover, it was generally accepted that they had all been massacred by the Romans at Masada toward the end of the first century. Those not killed in battle had committed suicide rather than be captured. Nothing she was hearing here fit.

Cloe reflected on the letters from the death mask of Irenaeus. She'd thought they were "I" and "S"—"IS"—for Iscariot. But her conversations with the Kolektor had left her unsure. He had suggested the order might be reversed. But what "SI" could mean had stumped Cloe until this moment. The Sicarii, she thought. She was so tired and beaten down that she could not process the idea right now. She would have to think about it.

The leader turned to the monsignor and said, "Would you like to go to your friends in the parking area and lead them back to us? My people might be mistaken by your colleagues for the enemy. We have dispatched the additional soldiers and weapons the Kolektor stationed for an ambush along the trail. The way is safe now."

The monsignor looked closely at the leader's eyes, which were all he could see under the headdress, and he blinked. He took a step back and shook his head, almost stumbling. Then Albert looked at Cloe and smiled. Because he saw that what could be done for them was being done, he turned and took off in the direction of the parking area and the remaining intermittent gunfire.

Cloe was teetering on the edge of consciousness. She murmured, "The Sicarii were all destroyed at Masada."

The leader turned and looked at Cloe. "True, all of the men and many of the women and children of the Sicarii were annihilated at Masada, but seven survived, and we continued. We will talk of that when you are stronger."

The leader turned back to the Kolektor, who was now on his knees, cowering in the middle of the clearing.

"Kolektor, we have long known of your activities, and although reprehensible, you had not passed into our realm. Now you have, and we have little choice but to put a stop to your vicious behavior. Your crimes have condemned you. Judgment has been passed upon you. There is no appeal."

One of the strange figures reached over and lifted the Kolektor as one would lift a child. The Sicarius put the small blade to the Kolektor's throat and awaited orders from the leader. The Kolektor began to mew and cry like the coward he had always been. The knife inched closer to his jugular. All it would take was a slight flick of the wrist.

But the Sicarii leader shouted, "Hold!"

Everyone froze, eyes fixed on the scene developing in the center of the clearing. Cloe raised her head as high as she could, which took an enormous effort. She was extremely weak from blood loss and the stress of the hellish events they had just experienced. Still, she would see the end of the man who had tormented them for so long and who had caused so much death and destruction. She would see the end of the man who had killed her father.

"No," said the leader. "A quick death by blade is too good for this man. He shall reap what he has sowed this night. There is a symmetry to the justice of the Sicarii that will be meted out to him. See to it."

Three of the Sicarii quickly came forward. Two of them grabbed the Kolektor, and the other picked up the nail gun. The Kolektor began to scream. Long, keening screams came from deep within his black gut. He was carried to a large tree, and while the two held him up, the third made short work of nailing his hands, arms, and feet to the tree. The Kolektor bled profusely from the large nail holes.

***

The monsignor rushed into the clearing with Father Anton and the Swiss. The scene was unbelievable. The Kolektor was pinned to a large tree with nails protruding from his body. If he was not dead, he soon would be. Nobody moved to bring him down. Beyond that, the clearing contained only the dead thugs, J.E., and Uncle Sonny. The Sicarii had vanished with Cloe.

# CHAPTER 63

Cloe awoke in a hospital room. She turned her head slightly, and pain racked her right side. She could see that she was hooked up to various drip bags, and there was a morphine pump for pain. Slowly, things began to come back to her. She opened her eyes more widely and started to look around.

"Signorina," said the familiar voice of the monsignor. "I am so happy to see you back."

She turned further to see him and immediately noticed that he had tears in his eyes, and he clearly was exhausted with worry. She wondered what had happened since the night of Hakeldama.

"J.E.?" asked Cloe. There was nothing of greater concern to her than her son.

"J.E. is in a hospital in Jerusalem," he responded. "He is very sore and has had to have some reconstructive surgery on his right wrist, but he will be fine in good time. He has asked for you day and night and will be here as soon as he is able."

"Water, please," she asked.

The monsignor filled a glass with water, dropped in a straw, and held the straw to Cloe's dry lips. She drank deeply until the monsignor said, "Let's pause for a bit. You don't want to overdo it."

"What of Uncle Sonny?" Cloe did not know how much of this type of excitement Uncle Sonny could undergo without his health being badly affected.

"Uncle Sonny is fine for a man of his years. In fact, he left yesterday for his home. He flew out by commercial jet. Although he wanted to stay, we persuaded him it was best for him to go. He made sure that you and J.E. were on the mend before he would consider it.

He was here in your room for two days and then alternated between here and J.E.'s bedside. But in the end, he recognized that when you and J.E. got better, he did not want you worrying about him. He loves you and J.E. very much. Cloe, you are very fortunate with the family you have."

Cloe thought of her mother and father and thanked God for Uncle Sonny. She promised herself that she would go back to Madisonville and get to know Uncle Sonny again. Indeed, she thought she would get to know Madisonville, Louisiana, and the people again. She had traveled too far from her roots. Cloe would seek them out and embrace them. She lay for a moment, letting these feelings wash over her. It felt good.

"How long have I been here?" she asked.

"Four days. Late on the day after the events in the Hinnom Valley, we received anonymous word as to where you could be found. It was a simple, untraceable cell phone message."

"Where am I?"

"In a private sanitarium outside of Jerusalem. You are being well cared for, and your medical treatment has been prepaid in cash by unknown donors. You were lucky with your wound. While it was very serious, it would have been fatal had the Kolektor nicked a vein, artery, or vital organ. As it was, he did not—whether intentionally or not. But the hours without medical attention and the blood loss almost proved fatal. If you had had lesser care and attention, you might not be here."

"Who brought me here?"

"J.E. and I believe the Sicarii brought you here and made the arrangements, either directly or through intermediaries. But we don't know for sure. We may never know."

"What of the Kolektor and his organization?" she asked.

"The Kolektor is dead. His organization is broken. The Israelis have become involved due to the violence at the Bloody Acre. They raided the Kolektor's bunker and have been amazed at the findings. You have nothing to fear from the Kolektor. He and all his minions are either dead or on the run. Without the Kolektor himself, there is no possibility that they could regroup. Even his number one, Dadash, is on the run."

"Can we be sure, Albert?" she asked.

He only smiled at her in response, and she felt comforted in spite of her injuries.

"Are we in trouble with the Israelis?" she asked.

"No, we have made some limited explanations, but they are mainly interested in the trove of artifacts they found in the Kolektor's bunker. The art and antiquities are almost unimaginable in terms of value and significance. In fact, they are aware of your background, and there has been talk of inviting you to catalog the manuscripts. You will have to give a statement, but then we will be permitted to leave. They know nothing of the jar and the manuscript."

"Have we lost our work?"

"No, the Israelis did not find those pieces. The Sicarii must have sent a second party to recover what they consider their property from the Kolektor's bunker."

Cloe turned away and thought about all that had happened. Her long talk with the Sicarii upon their departure from the clearing was coming back to her, but she was very tired. She began to drift off and felt the monsignor tucking the bedclothes around her. She felt warm and protected.

Cloe opened her eyes after not so long and immediately saw the monsignor still there. Half-awake and before she could drift off again, she said, "Albert ... go get a nap, a shave, and a shower, and we will talk. I have much to say about the Sicarii."

***

Once again, Cloe felt as if she were under water but beginning to surface. All had been blackness, but she could see light, and she began to swim toward it. She had no idea how much time had passed, but she knew that she felt a little better and that she was hungry. Her eyes fluttered and opened. The light hurt, but it was a good hurt after so much bad hurt. She heard voices and looked around. J.E. was beside the bed, holding her hand with his own good hand. The monsignor was in the background, looking refreshed and cleanly shaved.

"J.E.," she said.

"Hi, Mom," he said, smiling that great, bright Lejeune smile at her.

At that sight, she knew everything somehow would be all right. But she could see that J.E. was bandaged across his right arm, wrist, and hand. "J.E., how?"

"Mom, I'm fine," he replied. "I've felt worse after some days in basic training. The docs say that in a couple of weeks I'll have nothing but some sexy scars. But I've been really worried about you."

"I think I'm okay," she responded. "I'm actually hungry."

They asked for food, and the nurse brought the predictable Jell-O and iced tea. Cloe thought that nothing in her life had tasted so good before. After she was somewhat refreshed, she began to talk. They let her go and asked few questions. They seemed to know she had to get it out in her own way.

"The Sicarii that we met at Hakeldama are the descendants of the Sicarii from biblical times. They are now all women, each generation passing on their traditions to their daughters. The men were destroyed at Masada. Husbands, fathers, and sons were all killed. Many wives, daughters, and mothers were also massacred, but seven souls survived and carried on. These few continued, but their mission changed after that devastating defeat. They learned that a small band, through violent means, could not bring about the demise of the Roman Empire.

"The survivors realized that the Christian movement would spell the end of the pagan Roman Empire in time. Consequently, they began to build alliances with Christian leaders. The Sicarii collected ancient texts and began to care for them and to encourage Christian writings. This naturally brought them to the attention of Irenaeus and his cohorts, who covertly cultivated them as allies. It had to be covert at that time because the role of women in the Church was being deemphasized.

"Decade after decade, century after century, they encouraged Christian zealots and gave them aid and comfort. Finally, their goal was accomplished, in the third or fourth century. I can't remember the exact timing, but Emperor Constantine declared himself a Christian, and the pagan leviathan that had been the Roman Empire was done. It would take a while after that, but the seeds were sown."

"So what have they been doing for the last fifteen or sixteen hundred years?" J.E. asked. As always, Cloe thought, her son went straight to the heart of it.

"They have guarded the knowledge of those early Christian years. Manuscripts and codices were preserved and stored in many places, including at the Library of St. John. Scholars were given clandestine access to some of their treasures, but this required movement of them from time to time. Finally, everything was consolidated in the cave in Tunisia.

"During the war years, they had covert sentries in place around the cave. The treasure trove into which Thib fell those many years ago was their sacred trust. Indeed, there is an 'SI' tattooed on the bottom of each jar in the cave. But Thib's accident changed everything. The Sicarii identified Thib from their observations of him after the Battle of El Guettar was over. From a distance, they watched what happened to the jar, eventually following it to Madisonville. They had little concern as long as it sat on Thib's mantelpiece. But when we took it to LSU, they knew it was only a matter of time before the truth would come out."

"But what truth, Cloe?" asked the monsignor.

"Look at the whole thing, Albert," she replied. "The truth was that they had guarded Holy Scripture and had worked with Irenaeus against heresy. The truth was that they had convinced him to sponsor the true Gospel of Judas Iscariot, which was published in Greek in the late first or early to mid-second century. The truth was that the explanation of the role of Judas in the orthodox Gospels is at best incomplete. While we may never be able to know Judas's true motive, the Sicarii have decided it is time that this come into the public realm for examination and debate."

The monsignor nodded in understanding. "Maybe Judas was a revolutionary who made a terrible mistake. Maybe he was a willing participant in the plan for the salvation of mankind. Possibly he was a dupe or an avaricious turncoat who betrayed the Son of Man," he summarized.

"Precisely," responded Cloe. "Due to Thib's accidental discovery, the Sicarii believe there is no choice but to get all the information in the jar out and let scholars analyze the whole thing—let the chips fall where they may. The big question is whether we will ever see the possible contemporaneous journal of Judas Iscariot. That would be something."

"Mom, I don't know for sure what they were thinking," J.E. said, "but while you were unconscious, the Sicarii left you here with the jar, the manuscript, and the loaded flash drive. We have it all."

"Sure, J.E., but I'm not sure if any of that moves us further toward finding the Judas journal—if, indeed, there is one. And what of the cave filled with jars like the one we have? What we have is wonderful, but it all could have been so much more. It's a shame."

"Yes, Mom, but the Sicarii left something else. They left a second jar."

# EPILOGUE

Cloe had been back home for about two weeks. She paused at the thought of the word "home." She reflected on it, and yes, she knew she was home. The Bobby Morrow scholarship fund at St. Anselm was now fully endowed as her father had wanted. Cloe had repurchased the Water Street house from the church, and now it was home again. Prior to all this, she had spent several more days in the private hospital before they pronounced her fit enough to travel, and then the monsignor had flown her and J.E. back to Madisonville in a papal jet.

She and J.E. had healed well enough. He showed almost no effects of his wound. Cloe's right arm was in a sling in an effort to keep the right side of her body as static as possible.

The monsignor had continued on to Baton Rouge with Thib's jar, the Lejeune Manuscript, and the second jar that the Sicarii had left for Cloe. The Sicarii had chosen her to learn and reveal whatever secrets the jar contained. At LSU the monsignor had conversed extensively with Dr. Harrell. The good doctor was shocked at all that had occurred to them, but no more so than about the arrest of Dean Broussard. The authorities had determined that Broussard was complicit in the attack on J.E. and Cloe at the bridge as well as in the kidnapping of Uncle Sonny. Disgraced for money, he had now been arrested on charges of attempted murder and kidnapping.

Dr. Harrell and his team had gone through the same rigorous process in opening the second jar as they had with the first. They had extracted the contents and carefully photographed them. Unfortunately, the second jar did not contain a neatly packaged codex like the first. Rather, it held pieces and scraps of a manuscript. Some were whole pages, and some were stamp-sized scraps and everything in between. Whoever had written the manuscript had written on whatever was available.

The experts at LSU estimated the age of the papyrus at over nineteen hundred years and predicted that once properly assembled the various pieces would be the equivalent of about 230 handwritten pages. Cloe could barely fathom the possibility of that much new biblical literature on the life of Jesus Christ.

The monsignor had called the night before and said that he would be in Madisonville that morning with a flash drive containing reproductions of all the pieces. He and Cloe were now sitting on the porch of Thib's house. After they poured their cups of the strong French roast coffee she'd brought outside, he quietly handed the flash drive to her. She plugged it into her laptop and watched as the fragments began to appear. She saw immediately that the manuscript was written in Aramaic. Someone had, at some point, tried to burn all or part of it.

She knew that she was being asked not only to work on the translation but also to figure out the placement of the fragments. It was rather like an ancient jigsaw puzzle. Although it would take time, she was certain she would solve the mystery. Cloe reflected on how the jar Thib found had led to this. As Thib had believed, his jar was special, and Cloe had honored her promise to find out why. She had found Thib's killer, and he had met his justice. The combined efforts of her colleagues and Father Anton had prevented great damage to the Church. And now all would be presented in a thorough, scholarly way rather than perverted by the Kolektor for his revenge.

She clicked on one of the pages, which seemed to have some sort of title or legend on it. She focused on the ancient words and haltingly began to translate.

"Today, I was with the Baptist at the river; a man named Jesus from Nazareth came …"

# AFTERWORD

Every work of fiction intersects at some level with fact. Although I had concluded that, because of the dates, an earlier version of the Gospel of Judas must have at one time existed, I acknowledge and appreciate the confirmation of this I received when I finally read the fine work *The Gospel of Judas*, 2nd ed. (Washington, DC: National Geographic, 2008). Quotes in this book from the Gospel of Judas come from this work. My thanks to all the editors and contributors who did the groundbreaking work on the Coptic version of the Judas Gospel.

CPSIA information can be obtained at www.ICGtesting.com
Printed in the USA
LVOW041215120912

298407LV00002B/41/P